PINE MARTEN

PINE MARTEN

WALLACE J. SWENSON

FIVE STAR

A part of Gale, Cengage Learning

GALE
CENGAGE Learning®

Farmington Hills, Mich • San Francisco • New York • Waterville, Maine
Meriden, Conn • Mason, Ohio • Chicago

LIBRARY OF CONGRESS CATALOGING-IN-PUBLICATION DATA

Swenson, Wallace J.
    Pine Marten / Wallace J. Swenson. — First edition.
      pages ; cm
    ISBN 978-1-4328-3121-9 (hardcover) — ISBN 1-4328-3121-6 (hardcover) — ISBN 978-1-4328-3117-2 (ebook) — ISBN 1-4328-3117-8 (ebook)
      1. Fathers and sons—Fiction. 2. Life change events—Fiction. 3. West (U.S.)—Social life and customs—19th century—Fiction. I. Title.
    PS3619.W4557P56 2015
    813'.6—dc23   2015022035

First Edition. First Printing: November 2015
Find us on Facebook– https://www.facebook.com/FiveStarCengage
Visit our website– http://www.gale.cengage.com/fivestar/
Contact Five Star™ Publishing at FiveStar@cengage.com

Printed in the United States of America
1 2 3 4 5 6 7 19 18 17 16 15

PINE MARTEN

CHAPTER 1

The deep shadows of a thick forest formed the young boy's realm where he spent his days scrounging for food and listening, his nights surviving. To see him, you'd know he wasn't an Indian, but only because his dark brown hair wasn't black. Naked, his immature body bore many open sores and livid scratches. One place in particular vexed him: twin puncture wounds on his right arm where something with sharp fangs had resisted his efforts to kill it; steel against claw, his desperate need for food against an animal's powerful will to live.

When not out foraging, he hid in a wide shallow cave. One wall and part of the floor were strangely warm, the naked granite radiating heat from within. The boy neither questioned nor fully appreciated the source of the heat; he simply sensed that without the shelter, death would come to him with the cold and dark. The hole in the unyielding rock had been his sanctuary since one terrible night when survival meant running. Into the darkness he'd fled, screaming, as his tormented brain purged itself of the horrible scene that had played out in the stuttering light of an oil lamp. He'd plunged blindly into the forest without sense of direction or time to arrive here. He knew not when.

Fretful, he stirred in the cave's darkness, gripped his knife tighter, and shrank deeper into the stained and tattered cloth covering forest debris that was his bed. Even in the pitch black he was afraid to open his eyes, because he knew another pair could be waiting for him, looking back, unblinking: blank, dead, accusing eyes. Only daylight could set him free, and darkness would hold sway for many more hours.

He knew when something stole silently across the face of the night, searching, and fear shocked him when he imagined it finding his hiding place. And now the threat waited outside. The trembling boy had never seen what lurked just beyond the narrow opening, but many times before he had sensed the prowler, and he knew to be deathly afraid of the stalker that came in the dark.

Closer now. Any second, the rattle of labored breath would come, and then the smell—rotten ripe, rancid—would foul the still air. A whimper formed in the boy's throat and as it tore free, its sound drove the terror deeper into his heart. The power of the menace outside seemed to steal the air from the cave, and once more the trembling soul trapped inside lost sight of the last feeble ember of hope, to sink through the final shade of black and into the emptiness of total defeat.

It was nearly noon when Salem Greene set the head of his ax on the toe of his brogan and glanced at the late-August sun. Not a tall man, Lem's lack of stature made the width of his enormous shoulders even more impressive. Stretched taut across his back, his tan flannel shirt laid open at the neck, its sleeves rolled up to his elbows. He leaned on the ax handle, and even though idle under the tanned skin, the muscles in his forearms moved fluidly as though eager to get back to work. His free arm swiped across his sweat-beaded brow, and he gazed at the seventy-foot pine he was working on. A feeling of discomfort chilled his damp torso as the tree hissed in the light breeze: "Seeeeeeee. Youuuuuuu." He glanced over his shoulder and searched the forest's dappled depths for—what? The shadows mocked him as they always did, and he turned back to his work. After setting his feet, he effortlessly raised the gleaming tool over his shoulder and swung.

The pale yellow wedges flew from the deepening cut as Lem settled into the rhythm learned from years of cutting trees. This one, and many like it, would be reduced to four-foot lengths to be hauled to the edge of the Missouri River and stacked. The ricks would sit there until a passing steamboat captain saw his signal flag and pulled to the bank. There, the boat's crew would take the fuel aboard for the ship's boilers, leave payment, and lower the flag.

With a shuddering creak, the tall tree lost its hold on the earth and angled to the ground, stripping neighbors of branches, shaking the forest floor as it died. Lem swiped at the sweat on his brow as he moved alongside the trunk to the first branch. There, with powerful precise blows, he lopped off anything smaller than a couple of inches thick. An hour later, the once stately tree, stripped of its emerald cloak, lay naked and vulnerable. Lem set his ax in the top of the stump, and spent the rest of the day with a single bucksaw, cutting the trunk and thicker limbs into pieces.

When the light started to fail, he gathered his tools and set off for his dwelling, his steps hurried by the impending gloom. A few minutes later, a small, one-room log cabin, little more than a hut, came into view, and he started to relax. He went to the tree at the corner of his place, and stuck his heavy ax in the trunk, the movement natural, almost unconscious. With one more glance over his shoulder, he went inside.

In the dim light, Lem struck a match and lit two candles, putting one on the shelf above the hearth, the other on the small table located under the window in the front of the single room. The flickering yellow reflected off the polished silver of a tiny bell that sat alone in the center of the rough plank top. He dug around in the warm ashes of the morning's fire until he found two potatoes which he put on a pewter plate. After sloshing a tin cup full of water from a nearly empty bucket, he set the plate and the cup on the table. A large ham, roughly butchered, hung from the ceiling, and yielded a thick slice to his long knife. He added it to the potatoes, and with a furtive glance at the darkening window, sat down to eat.

After supper, he swung the window shutter down into place, and with his fist drove four wooden wedges onto slots alongside it. He tugged hard at the bottom and let out a satisfied grunt. He didn't know which he disliked most, the false sanctuary of night, or the full exposure of day. The oppressive thoughts were always with him, hanging over his head like a mystic maul, poised and ready—almost eager, it seemed—to exact some retribution for his horrible sins. Lem glanced at the stout plank door and solid oak bar that locked everything out—and him in. He smiled ruefully—the walls that made him safe also made him a prisoner. With a puff, he blew out the candle above the fireplace, then picked up the one from the table and went over to the slop bucket in the corner. Afterwards, he sat on his bed and pulled off his heavy shoes. With a resigned sigh, he lay back, took a final look around the small room and pinched out the candle. Darkness settled over him.

The dull aches of an overworked body kept him shifting from one side to the other as he fruitlessly tried to keep his mind quiet: the story waited just behind his eyes. Maybe tonight he wouldn't have to see all of it. Maybe tonight he would escape before the full weight of the tale drenched him in sweat and made his heart flop wildly in his chest. Maybe, he thought, but not likely.

Lem's eyes shut as he gave himself up to his conscience's revenge, and once again sleep took him on the nightly journey he dreaded.

CHAPTER 2

Ax in hand, Lem smiled as he strode into the clearing, and his son disappeared through the two-room cabin's wide open door. Even with the temperature late-April cool, his wife insisted on keeping it that way for the light. He hadn't liked it much when she'd first done it, but after several weeks of his grumping and her ignoring it, he'd silently made the concession.

"Home, build solid . . . and safe," he thought as he walked across the open to a tree he'd left standing by the northeast corner of the cabin. Approaching it, he swung the ax in a short arc and stuck it head-high in the trunk, secure for the night. He looked back toward a wide river some two hundred yards away.

"Hi, Pa." The friendly voice belonged to the man's twelve-year-old son. He stood in the cabin door, his alert eyes on the ax.

"Evenin', Martin." Lem walked over and put his huge hand on the youngster's shoulder. "You been working on that wood pile like we talked about?"

"Yup." The boy still looked up at the ax. "Be better if I had yours."

"You leave the big one alone, understand?" As soon as the words passed his lips, Lem knew he'd been too harsh.

The boy's gaze instantly dropped to his feet, and he clasped his hands over his belly.

"You got to get as big as the ax first," Lem added gently. "And you will, I can see it. But for now," he nodded at the tree, "we make our living with that ax, and you have to do the best you can with the hatchet."

The boy looked up with a rueful smile. "Yeah, I understand. I'll wait."

"Good. Now, I want you to go in the house, and if she's not using it, get Ma's butcher knife. Time you learned how to put an edge back on."

"Sure, Pa." The boy scampered into the cabin and returned a minute later with the blade. "Ma says supper's ready when you want it."

"We won't be long." Lem reached up on a shelf by the door, found a long, pink-streaked gray stone and held it out to his son. "Take good care of this," he said brusquely. "Never leave it on the ground, and make sure ya never drop it."

"Okay, Pa."

Lem sat on a long bench. "Get me a dipper of water there." He pointed at a wooden bucket sitting on a low table beside a washbasin. The boy did as he was told, and hurried back. "Keep the stone wet, otherwise you can ruin it." Lem trickled water the length of the ten-inch stone, and then laid it on his leg. "Turn the edge toward you, and draw it across the stone like you was cuttin' shavings off it." He drew the knife-edge along the whetstone, the steel close to the handle at first, then drawing away to the tip as the blade moved the full length of the sharpening tool. "Do that six or seven times, then turn the blade over and do the same to the other side. Ya watching?"

"Yes, Pa. Like cuttin' slivers off. And don't drop it."

"And one other thing . . . see how the back of the blade stays the same distance away from the stone every time I stroke it?" Lem tilted the back of the knife up and down. "Ya have to keep that space the same, else you'll never get it sharp." He made another pass with the blade. "Think you could do that?"

"I think so, Pa. Want me to try?"

their heads, and Lem prayed.

"We thank you, God, for the bounty of this land and ask that you bless it. Thank you for our health and your hand when the devil gets in the way. We ask that you deliver to us the animals we need, and shield us from those that would do us harm. And Lord, guard my womenfolk from the heathens while I'm away. Amen."

Lem cut the meat into pieces and his heart swelled with pride as the children eagerly filled their plates and started to eat. Mercy, delicate and proper, ate slowly, while Martin attacked his food like he was starving. Lem's eyes met those of his wife and they traded love across the table. Contentment settled on him and he speared a large chunk of venison, his mouth watering. Tomorrow, he would go to town.

Lem woke up with a start, looked at the shuttered window, the barred door, and reality returned: cold and hard as the morning. Dim light shone through the many cracks, and he heaved a sigh as he swung his legs over the edge of the bed and sat up. It was always clear whether his dreams had revealed the complete story or not; his dry clothes told him all he needed to know.

Standing up, he shuffled across the dirt floor to the door, lifted the bar, and set it against the wall. Pulling the door open, he stepped into the cool morning air to find shallow fog shrouding the small clearing, the bushes along the edge ghostly humps of gray-green. He surveyed the surrounding forest for a few seconds, and then went back inside to put his shoes on.

Shortly, he went back out with his slop bucket in one hand, water bucket in the other, and headed toward the misty forest. Just inside the trees, he dumped the foul one in a shallow trench, set it by the trail and continued on about seventy-five yards south to the stream he used. The two seeps that fed it came from under a rock outcrop. When he'd first seen it, he was hard-pressed to believe his luck: the water on one side of the rock face was warm, while the other side was as cold as you'd expect a spring to be, and sweet. He filled his bucket from the pool behind a dam someone had built, and then started back.

Twenty feet along the trail a sudden chill danced over his body, and he turned so quickly he spilled half the water. A figure, obscured by the mist, stood by a tree. Lem, the hair on his neck bristling, stared wide-eyed as the form seemed to sink into the damp ground. He shook his head vigorously, and then, for a few seconds, concentrated on the spot before frantically searching elsewhere for what he'd seen. His gaze flicked from the low bushes to the tall trees, then along his back trail to the rocks, and saw nothing. Gradually his breathing slowed, as did his heart, and he glanced at his half-empty bucket. "Leave me in peace!" he shouted. "Leave me alone." The misty green around him silently swallowed his protest, and with another glance at his bucket, he turned and hurried back to his cabin, grabbing the slop bucket as he passed.

Alternating mouthfuls of ham and cornmeal mush, he gobbled his breakfast. His skin still crawled as he sipped from his tin cup and tried to imagine what stalked him. Several times since he'd come to the hut, he'd charged with his ax into the undergrowth, his fear that he'd find something as strong as his fear that he would not. Swallowing the last of his meal, he gathered his gear and stalked out of the cabin.

A few minutes later he entered a wide meadow and his hobbled mule greeted him raucously, hopping awkwardly toward him. Once he had a pair, but now he needed only one. He'd chosen this animal because it was so friendly. "Good morning, Mr. Mule," Lem said when the animal stopped in front of him and extended its muzzle. "Got nothing good, old friend." He rubbed the soft upper lip, and then slipped the halter over the long ears. "We got lots of work to do today." He buckled the straps, and then, with the lead firmly in hand, he stooped to undo the leather figure eight that bound the mule's front ankles. "Let's get going," he muttered, and together they headed into the forest for the timber he'd cut the previous week.

For the rest of the day, Lem and the mule dragged the short logs from the forest to the riverbank. Hot and tedious though the work was, he felt thankful he could work in the sunlight where he felt safer. Back and forth he led the mule until he laid one last piece of wood in place. With a sigh, he slumped to the ground with his back against a tree that braced one end of the three-cord stack of wood. He surveyed five others just like it, built over the past month. Into an oilskin pouch he put a paper list he'd dug out of his shirt pocket. With a length of string he then tied the bag and a piece of white cloth to a short flagpole. The list contained a few things he'd need to get through the winter, and he relied on a steamer to see the stacked wood and stop.

The sun, sinking behind him, cast a peculiar light across the slow-moving river, the surface taking on an oily sheen, looking solid enough to walk on. He'd seen the occasional scow drift past, and once watched a steamer pounding laboriously upriver, black smoke and sparks belching from twin stacks, stern wheel thrashing the water to foam. It might have been the skipper who'd bought his last load; he'd never know. The transactions were made anonymously, on trust.

He flexed his back muscles hard against the rough wood, and stood. Selecting one of the more slender logs, he expertly split one end partway up, wedged the short flagpole in the gap, and removed his ax. The white flag hung limply in the still air. "Guess we'll have to trust in a little breeze when we need it, eh, Mr. Mule?" The sturdy beast raised its head, cocked both ears for a moment, and then lowered it again. "I'm tired too," Lem murmured. "Let's go home."

His cabin stood half a mile from the river, about as far as the riverside variety of trees went, and far enough away to screen any smoky message his fireplace might send into the air. He moved into the forest of cottonwood and sycamore, the mule following placidly at the end of his eight-foot lead. The path wound through some open sections, but for the most part the trees closed in on him, the thick canopy shutting out the sun. Searching the pools of shadowy darkness on either side of the trail, his eyes soon became as weary as his nerves. He was about halfway to the cabin when the mule snorted, and a second later Lem heard a noise to his left. He stopped, his heart thumping wildly. Frozen in place, muscles pulled tight and ready, he strained to hear what had alarmed his mule. Then, his breath was torn from him when he felt a hand on his back. His sense of time and space vanished.

He'd wanted this, waited for it, which was why he didn't carry his rifle. God had taken everything he had except his life, and now it was up to God to take that too, whenever He wanted it. That was what he'd decided in the darkness of his cabin, brooding in the long night hours, safe behind his heavy wooden door and shutters. But now, the powerful will to live would not be denied. Heart pounding in his ears, he spun around to see, barely an arm's length away, the placid brown eyes of his mule looking back at him.

"Thunderation, Mule, you'd like to give me a fit!" Lem's legs threatened to fail him, and his heart still beat wildly. "But you heard it too . . . don't stand there and say ya didn't." Twin ears bent toward him. "Well, ya did. I can tell by the way you're lookin'." Lem scowled at the animal. "And quit sneaking up on me like that. I wanted ya that close, I'd take a short hold on this lead." One of the mule's ears rotated backward for a second, then joined its mate at attention again. "C'mon, then." Lem walked to the end of the rope and gave it a tug.

The rush of panic had left his legs weak, but his eyes and ears even more alert. He hurried the mule as fast as he could, the light failing rapidly, and had nearly reached the cabin when the animal snorted again and balked. Once more, the flush of fear gripped Lem as he peered through the thick trees toward his cabin. "What'd ya hear, Mule?" he whispered. The animal's ears, twitching slightly side to side, were trained on the trail ahead. Lem stood silent for a few seconds, and then encouraged the mule forward. He'd taken only a few steps when the mule jerked back on the lead, and this time Lem saw the reason.

Dark against the forest shadows, a short, stocky man stood in the middle of the trail, his long rifle held harmlessly across his chest. Lem released his pent-up breath. "Dammit, friend, can't ya make a little noise or something, instead of standing there like some devil's fetch?"

"Whatcha want . . . a lullaby?" the man said in a strange accent, and then his swarthy face broke into a toothy grin. The gun remained angled in his crossed arms, the muzzle threatening only the treetops.

"C'mon, Mule." Lem started along the trail again.

"Mite skittish," the man said. "The mule I mean," he added when Lem scowled.

Lem walked up to the stranger. "Don't see many folks out here."

"Good reason for that." The smile flashed alive again. "They ain't many. M' name's Dufrey Comeaux." He lowered the muzzle of the rifle, slung it under his left arm, and extended his hand. "I see you're living in Mariner's old cabin."

"I didn't know it belonged to anyone. Looked abandoned."

"Percy won't mind. He went to a better place."

Lem took the offered hand. "Dead?"

"Hope so. I buried 'im."

Lem couldn't suppress a smile as he studied the stranger. Apparently, the man had been here before and if he meant any harm, he'd have had his way already. Better to have him close than to wonder where he was. "Well, come on to the cabin, then. You're welcome to supper and a place to bed down. My name's Salem Greene. I'm called Lem."

Dufrey nodded, then picked up the pack at his feet and slung it over one shoulder. "Hopin' you was gonna invite me. Hate sleepin' outside."

Together they walked the short distance to the clearing where Lem pointed to a bench set against the front wall of the cabin. "Take yourself a seat while I go tend to the mule." Without looking further at his visitor, he turned and walked into the forest.

Minutes later, Lem arrived back at his cabin to find his guest sitting on the bench. A floppy felt hat covered most of Dufrey's face, and his legs were stretched out in front of him, crossed at the ankles. Dressed entirely in soft-looking leather including supple boots that rose nearly to his knees, he pushed his hat back as Lem approached. The man's inquisitive brown eyes, set deep under bushy brows, followed him. Lem nodded as he stuck his ax in the tree. "Live around here?"

"Been upriver a piece makin' Indian talk fer the army, and doin' some huntin' fer 'em."

"I didn't know the army was around." Lem took a seat beside him on the bench.

"Walk in a straight line long enough and you'll run into the US Army." Dufrey chuckled. "Usually find 'em in the shade, restin'."

"Hunt what? I've been here for months and haven't seen more than a few rabbits."

"Ya ain't lookin'. Three deer walked right past me while I listened to you snortin' up the trail . . . a doe and two fawns."

"You should've shot one." Lem got off the bench and started for the door. "Hope you don't mind fried corn mush and ham."

"Don' mean to stir in yer skillet, but I kin make that mush talk back at ya."

"How so?"

"Got some things in my kit that'd make oak bark taste good . . . least to a Cajun."

"I was wonderin' about your lingo."

The leather-garbed man smiled. "Sometime I don' understand my own self."

"You're welcome to do with it what ya can . . . I hate cookin'. Come on in." Lem pushed the door open and went inside.

The boy stirred from his fetal curl and fully opened his eyes as soon as the morning sun lit the cave. Once fully awake, he moved to the cave's entrance where he paused. The raucous sound of crows arguing in the distance came to him first; then, the music of smaller birds, much closer . . . and nothing else. This didn't surprise him, his demon visited only in the night.

He slipped through the narrow opening and hurried away from the cave as fast as a slightly lame right leg would allow. Thirst was uppermost in his mind, and not far away a small stream trickled from under a rock overhang into a natural pool. A delicate crust of crystalline white adorned the edge of a natural basin nearest the rock. Many creatures knew of the pool, and he approached stealthily, listening and watching. On the far side a barely visible path led out of the bushes, he'd seen other forest dwellers use it. The boy froze in mid-step as a small rabbit moved warily toward the water. He licked his lips at the sight and stood stock-still until the animal reached the edge of the water and started to drink. Slowly, the boy dropped to his belly to watch. After a short time the rabbit rose from its crouch, shook its head, and quickly departed along the trail. When the animal had disappeared, the boy hurried to the pool, lay down on his belly, and drank deeply of the sweet, tepid water. His thirst satisfied, he moved a short distance up the trail the rabbit had used and slipped off of it into the undergrowth. Sitting, he scooped debris over his legs and hips, then lay down and covered the rest of his body with still more. Eyes trained on the uphill path, he slowed his breathing and waited, his knife ready.

All day the boy lay hidden and had nearly given up when he detected movement a few feet up the trail. An animal, lively black eyes glinting above a shiny nose, tested the air, nostrils twitching. For a full minute the creature peeked out from the bush before it stepped onto the path. With broad, rounded ears set forward on a fox-like skull, it was about two feet long with short legs that carried it low to the ground. Soft-looking fur shading from a light tan on its head to a black-tipped tail covered the sleek body. The boy recognized the pine marten, and thought about the puncture wounds on his forearm. This time he knew to get a good grip on the animal's neck, even if the slender body seemed the easier place to grab.

The weasel crept forward, head turning side to side, nose to the ground. Seemingly more confident as it neared the water, its head came up as it passed abreast of him. The boy's hand shot out of the leaves as fast as a snake strike and seized the animal by the throat. Just as fast, the weasel's back feet raked claws the length of the boy's forearm. Gritting his teeth against the pain, the boy rolled and grabbed the hindquarters of the writhing critter, pressing it to the ground. With a high-pitched squeal, it twisted its head, short, sharp teeth exposed in its gaping mouth. The boy slipped his thumb under the beast's chin and snapped his wrist forward; he heard a soft pop, and the weasel went limp. Heart pounding, the boy stood and looked down at his prize; for the first time in many days he'd eat meat.

With a furtive look around, he picked up his knife and started back to the cave, lengthening shadows hurrying his steps. Once he had his sanctuary in sight, he stopped and knelt. Deftly, he cut the weasel's head and feet off, then stripped the soft fur from the carcass, turning the skin inside out as he did so. A powerful stink made him turn his head for a moment, the odor so strong it made his eyes water. Careful not to cut a gut, he opened the belly of the animal from the bottom of its ribcage to its tail, and gently removed the innards, including the offending scent glands. He hurried the rest of the way to the cave, the naked flopping body of the butchered creature in hand and ducked into the safety of the rock.

Though stringy and tough, the coppery taste of the bloody meat, and the warmth in his hands made him close his eyes with pleasure as he ate. By the time he'd chewed the last bits of meat off the backbone, the light at the mouth of the cave had faded to a dim hint. He threw the ravaged carcass into the blackness at the rear of the cave and stood, his lips sticky and the back of his throat tight. After studying the cave's entrance for a moment, he stooped and hurried outside. It was lighter than he'd expected, and he breathed a sigh of relief as he took off at a half run toward the water, favoring his right leg.

The air felt warm on his naked body, but he sensed that this would not last. He dimly remembered cold—numb fingers, ears almost brittle—and tried to recall what he'd done before to stay warm. What was before the cave? The question swirled in his head for the short time it took for him to get to the spring. After a cautious look around, he got down on his belly and drank, then got up and hurried back.

Inside again, he kicked scattered leaves, moss and grass on the cave floor into a pile, arranged a filthy rag over the top, and knelt down in the middle of it. His knees had no sooner hit the ground than the image of a similar nest flashed through his mind—similar, but somehow much different—the vision gone before he could grasp any details. He fought to bring it back, to remember, but his full belly drew him irresistibly down, and he curled up on the warm floor and wiggled into the debris.

Soon, his skinny legs started to twitch, and his arms came up to protect his face. He was running again, fear driving him away from a nightmare. Deeper into the woods, over downed trees, up hills and down again, through icy streams and open meadows—he ran; and he ran; ran until his body would no longer remain upright, and he fell in surrender to the fitful sleep of the terrified.

CHAPTER 3

Dufrey's culinary boast had not been an idle one. He'd offered to make the entire meal, and Lem had been more than willing to let him. For nearly an hour the stranger fussed over the open hearth, skillfully moving heavy pots around, carving two thick steaks from the hanging ham, slicing congealed mush into squares he then roasted over the fire. And finally, he created a brown sauce from the ham drippings and something he took from one of the tins in his pack. The result was food like Lem had never tasted.

"I had my doubts." Lem speared a couple more browned corn cakes and arranged them on his plate. "This gravy is . . . I don't know how to describe it. What'd ya put in there?"

"Called *file*." Dufrey pronounced it *fee-lay*. "Made from sassafras leaves."

"And how about the ham?" Lem puffed his cheeks and whistled.

"Liked 'at, did ya? Red pepper . . . cayenne. Course, ya might not think so highly of it t'morrow. T'other is a mix of spices thet goes good on jist 'bout anything you'd like t' eat."

Lem poured the last of the gravy over the corn cakes. "Where they come from? The spice?"

"Common in Cajun country. M' wife used t' make 'em up."

Lem's fork stopped halfway to his mouth. "Used to?"

"Lost her and all four kids to the fever in fifty-three. Hard to believe it's been two years."

25

"I'm sorry to hear that."

"You got family?"

"Nope." Lem tilted his chair back against the wall and burped. "Haven't had a meal like that since . . ." His eyes closed for a moment, and he sighed.

"Since your wife or mother made it?" Dufrey asked quietly.

Lem nodded and looked down.

"Sometimes helps to talk 'bout it," Dufrey encouraged.

Lem didn't look up. "Sometimes," he replied quietly. A few seconds later, his gaze rose from the floor to Dufrey: "So, tell me what's upriver."

The Cajun leaned forward and put his elbows on the table. "Not a lot different than here. Less people, more Indians . . . peaceful fer the most part." His eyes met Lem's. "The Indians, I mean. 'Fore I was married and moved to New Orleans, I used t' spend a lot of time up here. I was born on the river—on the delta—and I seen most o' both the Missouri and the Mississippi. When my family got took, I was drawn back here—or mebbe pushed away from there—not sure which. This is a good place to forget things."

Lem's jaw muscles tightened as the picture of his wife's face flashed before him. Life had been hard but its rough edges had always somehow been smoothed by her ready smile and relentless optimism. Rhoda and the kids.

Both Martin and Mercy kept well ahead of Lem and his wife, the girl's shorter legs betraying her. "Wait for me!" she hollered to her brother. "I want to find some, too!"

Lem knew Martin was heading for a meadow just ahead that would be covered with light-blue hyacinths, their flowers a cluster of clarion trumpets standing proudly two feet off the ground. After first offering a visual feast of color, a second reward lay just under the surface: bulbs that could be eaten on the spot or gathered for later . . . they'd do both. With luck they'd run onto a few nodding heads of the bright yellowbell flower and its succulent fruit. Though it grew much lower to the ground, its brilliant color gave it away to anyone with a sharp eye, and Martin's was sharp. He'd been his mother's eager student, and by the time he was ten could name and describe thirty different kinds of edible bulbs, berries, shoots, and seeds.

Lem stopped in the trail and watched as the boy paused to let his sister catch up and then, her hand in his, he took off again. As they raced out of sight, the sound of their laughter made his chest ache with pride. He felt his wife's eyes, and when he turned around to meet her gaze he experienced a rare moment of calm. And then the laughter faded, the image of his wife's smiling face disappeared, and he saw himself standing in the forest alone . . . again.

Lem shivered and shook his head when he realized that Dufrey was watching him intently. "Now and agin, I git the haunts too," Dufrey said quietly. "Most of mine are good'uns." His eyes seemed to offer neither recrimination nor judgment.

"How old were your young'ens?" Lem asked.

Dufrey grimaced. "The only girl was two, the oldest boy was seven."

"I'm sorry they were taken."

"Me too. I miss 'em somethin' fierce, 'specially wintertime when I cain't git out and move about. When I was younger, I never thought I'd take up a wife and live in a town, but she made it easy—never a cross word, never complained about my drinkin' and carousin'. She had a gentleness ya could feel without her even touchin' ya. I fight the thought, but sometimes I wonder if losing them was punishment of some sort." A look of pain slipped over Dufrey's face, his lower lip stiffened, and his jaw set tight.

"Don't sound like there was much you could do about it."

"I've thought 'bout thet, and it don't seem to matter much. A fella's mind goes where it needs to."

"I had a wife and children," Lem said, his voice almost a whisper.

"I figgered as much."

A strained quiet filled the small room, and Lem glanced at his guest; Dufrey's open face invited conversation. But his ability to talk freely with this stranger confounded him as much as it brought him relief. He hadn't realized it, but he'd been missing having someone to listen to his thoughts . . . and fears, and this strange man was so easy to talk to. Was it because they shared a common loss . . . kindred exiles?

Lem finally broke the silence. "You mentioned *haunts*. Do you believe in them? Do you think they exist?"

"In my mind, there ain't any doubt they do. We all have souls, 'n our souls are jist like us. When we die, it's s'posed to go ta rest too. But souls kin git lost, same as we do sometimes when we're alive. I think most haunts are that—lost souls—lookin' fer a place to lay down perm'nent, 'r lookin' fer someone to show 'em a way home."

"Then you don't think they're bad?"

"I said *most*. Same as us, souls kin git upset if they've been bad-treated. I been told thet evil spirits only visits them folks what have reason t' fear 'em. Like mebbe folks what carry some guilt." Dufrey give a slight nod and paused for a second. "Like the spirit of a murdered person fer 'xample. They jist might stay 'round and make the one what did them in downright *miserated*."

Lem glanced at the open door. "You said you buried this Percy fella. Where?"

"You been sleepin' on him."

Lem glanced at his low-slung bed and a clammy chill crept

up his neck. "You buried him"—Lem nearly choked—"under the bed?"

"Didn't want animals t' dig him up. And no doubt you've noticed there ain't that many rocks close by."

Lem swallowed hard once . . . then again.

"He ain't gonna hurt nobody." Dufrey said it matter-of-factly.

"How do you reckon he died?"

"If'n it was possible, I'd have to say he got *skeert* to death." Dufrey leaned forward and lowered his voice. "He weren't dressed."

"Barefoot?"

"Bare ever'thing. Him and me was good friends before I took a wife. When I come back up this way, I heard he was livin' out here and found him. I came by ever' chance I got jist to talk. You've probably noticed I like to jaw." Dufrey smiled an apology. "He seemed like the same old Percy . . . funny man, loved to joke. Then 'bout four months 'go I come by, and he'd put thet heavy shutter on the window and barred the door. I asked him, jist jokin', if he was lookin' to keep me out. Know what he said?"

Lem shrugged.

Dufrey looked slightly bewildered as he continued. "Percy peered real close at me, his face ser'ous as a deacon. 'Should I?' he asked. Jist them words, 'Should I?' "

"What'd you say?"

"Didn't know what to say. Jist stood there in the door till he motioned me inside. That's when I saw what he'd done to the window and door."

Lem looked at the open door again, and when he looked back, found Dufrey staring at him.

"You bar 'em too, don't ya?" Dufrey said.

Lem looked out the door. "Down the trail there you said the mule was a might skittish. Well, it ain't just the mule."

"What do ya mean?"

"Whatever's making him nervous is about to run me out of here."

Dufrey's eyes widened as he leaned closer. "What have ya seen?"

"That's just it," Lem replied, frustration raising his voice. "Nothing. I think I hear things . . . no, I hear things, movement in the trees. I go looking, but whatever it is moves too quick. I feel eyes on me too."

"Same as Percy."

Another chill crept down Lem's back, and he noticed the light in the cabin was nearly gone. He went to the fireplace and lit a candle, shielding the tiny flame with his hand as he returned to the table. With yet another glance at the open door he sat across from the Cajun. In the unsteady light of the candle, Lem searched Dufrey's face. He wanted to close the door and lower the shutter, but his sense of pride made him stay at the table. "Your friend heard things too?"

"Yep." Dufrey nodded toward the door. "I told him he needed to git out of here and downriver fer a while."

"How long did he live here?"

"At least four years. Mebbe five or six. Long time, I know that. You've seen how much timber's been cut 'round here. He did all that."

"Was he a good man?"

Dufrey cocked his head. "You askin' if a haunt had reason t' pester 'im?"

"I guess I am."

"Percy was as good as they is. Jist liked to be by hisself, but I know a half a dozen men who've come by here . . . and was welcome." Dufrey lowered his voice and leaned forward a bit. "And I 'spect a woman 'r two. Percy wouldn't hurt a gnat."

Lem shook his head. "Maybe just being alone got to him."

"Nope. Like I said, he enjoyed bein' out here. What come over him was sudden, and it started this spring. I come up the trail one afternoon, figgerin' to go in and fix supper to s'prise him when he finished fer the day. I saw a cloud of dust flyin' out of the cabin and a minute later Percy followed it with a bundle of willow sticks, sweepin' like a whirlwind. Layin' in a pile outside was his bed things, both chairs, three 'r four pots, his winter coat and underwear . . . ever'thing he could git through the door."

"Why?"

"That's what I asked him. He said the place had a foul odor and needed cleanin'. I guess I must have chuckled or somethin', 'cause he looked at me real defiant-like, then started to move the stuff back in."

Lem looked around the small cabin. "Did the place smell all right to you?"

"Ain't no bachelor's place gonna smell like church on All Saints Day, but it didn't smell bad . . . bad—jist normal bad."

Lem absently sniffed the air. "So, when did ya find him . . . dead?"

"I asked him to come with me after the cleanin' incident. Tol' him he needed to spend a few days in Jefferson City. He wouldn't do it. I come back three weeks later and found 'im."

Another chill swept over Lem. "In here?" he asked.

"Nope. Out front."

A sigh of relief escaped Lem. "Naked, ya said."

"As the day he was born. He was sittin' flat on his rump, legs straight out, slumped over his rifle with both eyes wide open. I think he'd died in the night cuz there was a big pile of ashes in front of him. From the size of the circle, he had a fire thet would've lit the whole clearin' and then some. Like I said, he was scared of somethin'. He'd used his rifle."

"But why naked and why out front, and not holed up in here?"

31

Dufrey shook his head. "I've asked myself that ever' day since. I dug him deep in here, and took his rifle, tools and poke to his kin." Lem was looking toward the simple pole-frame bed again. "It didn't bother ya before ya knew, did it?" the Cajun said.

Lem looked back at the smiling man. "I suppose you're right."

"Course I'm right. 'Sides, Percy Mariner knew 'xactly where he was. Nothin' lost about him. He's dead and gone, and what's molderin' in the ground ain't gonna hurt no one, God rest his soul."

"It still sits a little sideways, don't ya think?"

"I suppose it could. Don't bother me none." Dufrey leaned back in his chair and studied Lem for a minute. "So, what brought you out here between nowhere and halfway back?"

"Same as Percy. I wanted to be alone."

Dufrey seemed to ponder Lem's declaration for a moment. "Wanted or needed?"

The question startled Lem. How many times since he'd left had that very question stopped him cold, making his heart race? Does a man *want* a wife and family, or does he *need* them? Or is it the same thing?

Rhoda looked up from slicing bacon as Lem stepped through the door.

"The morning has a chill on it." He rubbed his hands together briskly.

"It's not even the first of May, Salem. Get a good breakfast in you, and you'll not notice it. Is it cloudy, or can you see yet?"

"Looks clear. More important, it's calm. I hate being on the river when it's windy, even when it's moving slow, which it ain't this time of year."

"I don't like you on it in any regard." Rhoda stood. "Your shaving water is hot." She pointed at the steaming kettle hanging in the fireplace. "But get me the molasses jug from the shelf before you start."

Lem shaved every Sunday morning, without fail, and always before he went to Booneville. Rhoda said he didn't have to, but he knew she appreciated it. He absently stropped his razor as he watched her put the bacon on to cook. Before long, the cabin was filled with the smoky aroma, and Lem turned to his task, brushing the thin lather on his weathered face, then sliding the steel carefully down from his ear, over his jaw and along his throat. It always felt good to remove the bristle.

Lem finished shaving, and then took a seat at the table. Rhoda put a plate with four long strips of bacon alongside his coffee cup, then brought a pan of cornbread from the hearth. "Eat plenty, I've got another batch for the children." She sat across from him.

Lem lifted a large square of cornbread out of the pan: it glistened in the candlelight from the bear fat Rhoda used in it. She pulled the stopper from the molasses jug and pushed it across the table. Lem drenched the bread with the dark brown syrup. "I have a favor to ask, Salem."

Lem hurried his mouthful and swallowed. "A favor? Tell me what you want, and I'll do it."

"It's not for me, actually. Would you buy a piece of green ribbon for Mercy's hair? Just a short one, maybe two feet long . . . less if it costs a lot. Her tenth birthday is in a month, and ten is an important age for a young lady."

"Why green? I thought she liked yellow."

"Green to match her eyes."

Lem sat silently for a moment, his eyes on his plate.

"You've never noticed the color of her eyes, have you? Men!" Her smile removed the sting. "She has the most beautiful eyes I've ever seen. Look sometime."

"I'm sorry. I will." Lem speared a slice of bacon and folded the whole thing into his mouth.

Twenty minutes later, he drained the last of his coffee and got up from the table. "Go get Martin." He went to the door and shrugged into his coat.

A minute later, his son shuffled from the other room, rubbing one eye with the back of his hand. "Ready to go, Pa?"

"Yup. I wanted you up and about before I did. How far can the shotgun shoot?"

The boy thought for a few seconds. "About as far as I can throw a stone."

"Good. So how close would you let a man get if it looked like he was up to no good?"

"About half that far, Pa. Just like ya told me before."

"Good. And remember, load again before you do anything else."

"We'll be fine, Salem," Rhoda said. "We've seen no one but the folks who live two miles up."

"I just want to be sure he knows what to do. I don't like leaving."

"I'll take care of them, Pa, I promise."

The earnestness in the boy's eyes made Lem proud, and he wanted to pull him to his side. "I think you will too . . . else, I wouldn't leave." He turned to his wife. "Don't go into the woods any farther than the spring." He wrapped his arms around her shoulders. Her hair smelled of bacon, night-breath and woman. He put his face in the hollow of her neck and breathed deeply, needing the scent for the pleasure of the moment, and wanting the memory of it to last him until he returned. Then, he gave her a peck on the cheek, opened the door, and stepped into the morning darkness.

Lem looked across the table at Dufrey. "I think wants can turn into needs if we place too much store in them. We lived a simple life, a good life, and our needs were few; mostly each other, and a peaceful place to be together."

Dufrey didn't say anything for over a minute; just sat and stared at the fireplace. Finally: "And now you have neither."

"I don't deserve either, friend. I reckon I'm living exactly what I've earned. I'm not fit to be around other people."

Once more, Dufrey let silence prevail for a while. Then, in a cautious, almost reluctant voice, he heaved a long sigh and began. "Ain't no man's place t' tell another what they should feel . . . cain't be done honestly. A man kin, however, git a notion about what he sees and senses in his bones. Folks that live out in the wild like us have a keener sense about that than most." He hesitated again, and ran a forefinger across his pursed lips. "Sometimes, we git down cuz when somethin' bad happens, we reckon someone has to be to blame, and we jist cain't settle on who. In that case, the easiest one to blame is our own self. Well, things happen all the time. Do ya reckon you kin stand in a storm and not git wet? Course ya don't. And do ya question why the first drop o' rain you feel decided to hit you? Nope." Dufrey's eyebrows went up. "Cuz you 'xpect to git hit, and it don't matter which one did it. Same with trouble . . . if yer alive, it's gonna find ya."

"We're not talking about getting rained on." Lem frowned at the Cajun.

"Course we're not, but I figger the whole sky fell on you." Dufrey waited, but when Lem didn't respond, he went on. "I don't know what caused you ta think such a terrible thing of yerself and I'm not gonna guess. What I will say—and before you point it out—I know I wasn't asked, but—"

"You're exactly right. I didn't ask. I have a hard enough time talkin' to myself about this." As soon as he'd said it, Lem knew he'd been too sharp. This friendly, open man had suffered as he had, yet seemed willing to share his thoughts and feelings.

Dufrey nodded. "Didn't mean no offense."

"I know that." Lem turned to stare at his bed. "I'm about ready to turn in."

Dufrey followed his gaze, and then looked back at Lem. "I'll help ya move that bed over here if you've a mind to."

"It really shouldn't make any difference, I know, but—"

"I don't mind sleepin' on Percy. Mebbe he'll whisper me a good joke in the middle of the night. C'mon, you git that end." Dufrey walked over to the foot of the bed and took hold.

CHAPTER 4

Dufrey laid his bedroll where the bed had been, then went outside. Lem listened as his footsteps faded, his own urge demanding attention. He took a look at the night bucket in the corner, another at the open door, then sighed and went outside.

The black wall of darkness slowly gave way to vague shapes as his eyes forgot the light of the candles inside. After a few minutes, he could make out the trail that led to the river, and the tops of the trees, clear silhouettes against the blaze of stars. How many times had he walked out the door of his home, children safely in bed, his wife at the table, hands busy in the lamplight; stepped out, looked up at the same sky, and dismissed it? So much taken for granted, easily overlooked when it's always there . . . or you assume it will be.

Lem stopped in the trail and gave his wife a final wave just as he came to the turn that would take him from view. He doubted she could still see him because her arms remained folded across her chest. Shrugging, he walked on and out of sight of the cabin. He'd gone another hundred yards when an uneasy feeling prickled his scalp and he stopped again. He looked over his shoulder in the direction he'd come: the urge to go back holding him in place.

Go back and do what? He'd left them before, many times. His wife was used to the wild; and Martin knew how to use the shotgun. Was the reluctance caused by a vague sense of guilt at leaving? Maybe. He really didn't have to go, but he wanted to; wanted the see what was new in town, talk to other men, and hear some news from downriver. And Mercy needed a birthday present, isn't that what his wife had said? Green ribbon—and maybe he'd find something for the boy as well.

A busy road crowded with wagons, horses, and people, and lined with stores of all kinds . . . and saloons, superseded the mental image of the cabin that now lay just out of sight. Booneville. With a glance at the stars, now fading rapidly as morning rushed west, he turned and made his way down the path toward the river's edge and his rowboat.

What Dufrey had said about spirits only tormenting the guilty had struck hard. It was plain to Lem that the man was right, because he'd never had a bad dream in his life—until he had reason to have them. He buttoned his pants, and now that his eyes had adjusted to the dark, looked around at the surrounding forest. Did his tormentor only prowl in the daytime, satisfied that nights belonged to something else? The thought of someone or something watching urged him toward the dim light coming through the door.

Back inside he considered not barring the door and window, but after a few seconds, he dropped the heavy shutter and secured it. Dufrey came back just as he finished, looked at the barred window, and without a word pushed the door shut and dropped the oak bar into place.

Sitting down on a chair, Dufrey started to unwrap one of his leggings. "The air is soft tonight. I reckon we're in for a warm spell."

"With winter right behind," Lem replied. "I can use another month of good weather before the cold sets in serious." He moved the candle from the table to the stool beside his bed.

"You mean to winter here, then?"

"Got no place else to go. Or reason."

"I'll be up and down the river a couple more times. I can stop for another visit if you'd like."

"If you can stand my company, you're welcome."

"Ain't the company. I jist don't like to sleep outside." Dufrey grinned broadly. "Now, me and Percy are gonna get some sleep." He lay down on his ground tarp and pulled the blankets up to his ears.

Lem looked at the rounded lump on the ground, shook his head in disbelief, and snuffed the candle.

Lem had gone to sleep to Dufrey's rumbling snore, and now lay motionless in his bed, not quite able to grasp the reality: first, light was filtering through the cracks around the door, and he'd slept sound all night; second, his bed was in the wrong place. The confusion lasted only a moment, and then he remembered his guest. He looked across the dimly lit room for the lump on the floor . . . it was gone.

Lem swung his legs over the edge of the bed, roughly scrubbing his face with both hands. He pulled on his shoes, then, without lacing them, went to the door and pulled it open. Outside, Dufrey's knapsack sat on the bench.

The blue sky still held the milky white of early morning, and the rising sun lit only the treetops. Cool air stripped away the warmth of his bed as he hurried away from the cabin to where, hand on hip, he studied the trees as he wet the ground. Finished, he headed back inside and had just reached the door when the distant report of a rifle reached him. The sound reverberated through the trees, masking its direction. Lem stepped away from the cabin and scanned the edge of the forest. Hearing nothing and seeing no movement, he sat on the bench and waited.

Half an hour later Dufrey emerged from the trees, dragging a small deer by its forked horns. "Mornin' Lem. Shot thet deer like ya asked."

"I'm embarrassed enough that you managed to get up, clear your bedroll, and leave without me hearin' a thing."

"I'm only noisy when I talk." Dufrey hauled the deer to the side of the cabin and dropped it. "Ya got a strong piece of cord or a rope we kin hang this critter with?"

"Just a minute." Lem went inside.

When he came back out, the Cajun had already started to gut the young buck. "I'd have done this out there, 'cept I forgot a tote ta fetch the good bits in."

Lem watched, wanting to help, but wanting to stay out of the way too.

In minutes, Dufrey had the innards on the ground, the hind legs spread and secured, and the deer slung from the pine at the corner of the house. "Lemme git that hide off while it's still nice and warm." Dufrey started in on the legs.

"I can do that," Lem protested.

"I kin too, and have'r done 'fore ya git yer knife sharp. 'Sides that, I hate to sit and watch." Dufrey was as quick skinning the animal as he was gutting it, and soon the hide lay on the ground, wet side up. He pointed at the skin with his knife. "Now, if'n ya want to keep that, ya better—"

"I have no use for it. Tried to save a couple of rabbit skins and they drew every critter for three miles around." Lem added apologetically: "Hate to waste it, but I don't have time to take care of it."

"Got no mind 'bout it either way. Lay the head, feet and guts in the middle and fold the skin up—I'll take it with me and leave it fer the night critters 'n crows. Now the heart and liver . . . 'at there's 'nother thing *all* together."

Lem chuckled at Dufrey's eagerness. "I'll share that with you. I've got a hankerin' for liver like it seems you do. Matter of fact, if you've got time, I'll fry up the liver right now, and we can make pigs of ourselves."

"And the heart?"

"I'll boil it and you can take half with you. I like it cold."

"I'll make ya the same offer on the heart as I did last night."

Lem pointed at the travel pack. "You got something in there that—"

"That'll make ya wish ya hadn't offered me half." Dufrey winked broadly.

The morning was half gone when Dufrey stuck his arm through one wide leather band and slung his pack over his back. "I thank ya kindly fer the night's stay," he grunted as he stooped and shook his shoulders to settle the load up high. Satisfied, he reached through for the other strap, shrugged to adjust the weight, and then offered his hand.

Lem shook it. "I—enjoyed your visit. You're a passable cook and ya left me with something to eat besides salty ham and cornmeal. If you get by here again, I'd be pleased to see you. You'd be welcome to stay as long as you like . . . so long as you cook."

"Oh, I'll be back." Dufrey grabbed his rifle and the gray-brown deer hide. "And I jist might stay a spell. Never kin tell. Cain't seem to abide the town fer more 'n a month 'r so."

Dufrey nodded and then ambled across the clearing to disappear into the forest. Lem stood in front of his cabin and stared at the spot where the Cajun had disappeared, acutely aware that he was alone again. He went into the cabin, reemerging almost immediately with his bow saw, pulled the door shut, and retrieved his ax from the tree.

The weather presented a problem for his meat supply. In the past he'd always waited until the first hard freeze. A deer killed then and hung in the springhouse kept until they'd eaten it all

. . . then he'd shot another. It was going to be too warm for that even if he had a springhouse . . . which he didn't. He started across the clearing, giving the burned circle in front of the cabin a wide berth. A little later, he came to the partially downed hickory he'd found weeks before, and started to work.

About noon, he went for his mule, and by late afternoon he had a supply of wood—half of it dead and dry; the other half live—stacked in front of the cabin. His last load contained a dozen long, slim, green branches, and he now sat on his bench to split the wet wood into thin strips with his knife. The task was easy, the grain straight and even, and after an hour he had the pile of material he needed. Selecting four of the slats, he began to weave them into a four-foot square mat. The work went smoothly, and he soon finished the loosely fashioned lattice. With a satisfied grunt, he leaned it against the cabin wall, picked up his tools again, and went back into the forest.

The sun had been down for two hours by the time Lem had four corner posts firmly planted in a rectangle. He'd notched the tops of the four green saplings to make a hip-high frame that would support the new mat. After cutting the venison into strips, he'd spread them on the clean, white hickory wood; he only hoped the day hadn't been too warm. He went into the cabin.

Compared to the night before, the cabin seemed more like a tomb, and the thought brought a chill and a furtive glance at the spot where his bed used to be. The light of four candles reflected off the dark muscles of the young deer, and cast shadows that danced disconcertingly on the walls. Lem expertly sliced quarter-inch-thick strips of meat from larger chunks taken off the carcass hanging by the door. When he'd finished, a gratifying pile of meat covered half the table.

He arched his back against a stiffness that had set in. The meat still smelled sweet, and he hadn't built a fire to cook on so the cabin was cool. From his spring bucket he splashed water into his washbasin and cleaned the blood off his hands. After he'd dried them on a scrap of linen, he picked up the pan of cloudy-red water and went to the open door to throw it out. The sense that he was not alone seized him, and panic charged the muscles in his legs. He put the pan on the table and grabbed the oak bar. As he slammed the door, he was sure he caught sight of a figure just outside the light . . . a large figure that stood motionless, on two feet.

He dropped the heavy oak bar into place and leaned back against the door. The sense of security that he'd let build all day vanished, and he cursed himself for allowing it. This was the first time he'd seen something after sundown, and he felt in his heart it was going to be this way from now on.

Lem put his ear against the door and heard nothing but his own rasping breath. What had he seen? A man? He struggled to recall the image he'd glimpsed. It stood upright. It was about thirty feet away, right in front of the door. "It's you, isn't it?" he whispered almost silently, and moved away from the door. "You've come for me."

Lem hurriedly snuffed the candles, the last plunging the cabin into total darkness, and for an instant he felt relief. Then the fear roared back, more profound than before, and with a candle in hand, he felt his way to the shelf over the fireplace where he kept the lucifers. Struck on the hearthstone, the sulfur flare brought him a quick sigh of relief, and he moved the shaking flame to the wick.

He didn't want to die, but how did he fight a ghost?

The boy's eyes flashed open, his brain instantly alert, every muscle tense. Perfectly still, he probed the silence with all his might and the emptiness pushed back. Nothing stirred, the air so still it pressed down on him, so calm he could feel his own breath on his face. For several seconds he lay frozen, and then with a start, he realized what had roused him—it was the deathly quiet. The rush of blood in his ears slowed as his heart settled down, and as his muscles relaxed, he soundlessly eased out his pent-up breath. Then, a glimmer on the edge of his conscious-ness teased him—something he should remember, something important—and then it was gone. No! Struggling to grasp what lay just beyond reach, he sat up suddenly and slammed his open hand into the wall beside him in frustration. The pain clamped his teeth tight, and he lay back down whimpering.

Something was missing, something he needed badly. What? Again the sense of the tauntingly familiar swarmed over him. What, for sure, did he know? He was warm; he was safe; he was . . . he was. Pulling his knees to his chest, he crossed his arms, stared toward the entrance of the cave, and with the end of his thumb in his mouth, he waited for morning.

The light slowly overcame the complete darkness at the mouth of the cave, but still he lay quiet. Had the night creature decided to try something different? He swallowed hard. Was it waiting soundlessly just outside? He had no sense of a threat, that intangible something he felt that always came before the smell and labored breathing let him know the stalker was there. Gradually, the light shifted from a promise to enough for him to see the opening clearly, and the boy uncoiled from his huddle. Standing up, he warily inched his way out of the entrance.

The sun had not yet lit the top of the forest and there was something in the air, a subtle hint of change. For three weeks he'd watched the colors of the trees mutate from vibrant green to dull, worn olive, some with tinges of yellow and orange, the sure sign the forest was ready to rest. He sniffed the still air and stretched his skinny arms toward the milky sky. *Pecans.* The word floated into his head, surprising him: *pecans, to put away for later.* The thought was followed by an image of the towering tree: the peculiar color, the impressive height and symmetrical branches. He stood for a moment studying the trees that covered the hillside, and then started off at a fast trot toward the other side of the small valley.

He didn't know why he went toward the ridges southeast, but that's the direction he traveled. He moved quicker as the light grew brighter, darting from shadowy thickets of heavy brush to the shelter of large trees, all the while alert for the somehow familiar shape of the pecan. By the time he came to the crest of a third ridge, it was nearly full daylight, and as he approached the top he caught a distinct scent, a dank muddy smell. His nostrils flared as he sniffed the air, searching his memory, and then it came to him; a river.

He scrambled to the top and was stopped short by the scene below; a mist-shrouded waterway cut the forest from left to right. His eyes scanned from north to south and back again, looking for . . . what? He shook his head and groaned at his inability to remember. Was there a landmark he should recognize? Had he been on the river before, or near it? He closed his eyes for a moment and tried to imagine something—anything.

Dejected, he turned to walk the ridgeline, and had taken only a few steps when the sharp crack of a rifle shattered the calm air. Instinct drove him instantly to his knees, and his head snapped around to make out the direction of the sound. He hesitated for only a few heartbeats, and then, without another look, scrambled down to the safety of the ravine below. There, he turned left and ran.

Looking only ahead, he fled until his lungs started to burn, and then slid to a halt in a grape thicket, his chest heaving for air. There he stood, gape-mouthed, and listened for the sound of pursuit. For several minutes he heard nothing but the irate scolding from the squirrels he'd driven from the copse, and as his breathing slowed, the familiar sound of the rodents helped settle his nerves.

Why had he reacted that way? He sank to his knees on the soft ground of the bower and tried to think. Flight—frantic, and without direction—didn't make sense. It was dangerous to move without looking. He always looked carefully before he stepped into the open. He'd never run mindlessly through the forest, vines clutching at him, branches tearing at his skin—his teeth clicked together as his mouth snapped shut. He gasped as the startling memory of a large form moving stealthily in the trees drove every other thought from his mind.

A chill gripped his clammy body as the scene formed in his mind. He'd felt terror clutch his heart as the shadowy figure searched for him. Then it had moved toward where he hid breathless behind a tree, trapped with no place to run. Desperate, he'd bolted. Within a second or two, something had hissed past his head—followed by the roar of a rifle. The same sound he'd heard on the ridgeline. What had happened then?

He looked up at the tangled vines over his head. When and where did this happen? He searched his mind for more details. It had happened, he knew that for sure; the vivid image assured him he had not dreamed it. Someone had chased him, but who, and why? He remained hunkered down until he felt strong enough to stand, and then got up. His right knee ached and he stooped to massage it a little. Listening over the rodent chatter in the trees, he searched every shadow for some unusual form. Finally, he crept slowly up the ravine and hours later he reached the safety of his cave, his search for a pecan tree forgotten.

Later that day, the boy grasped his belly with both hands and gritted his teeth against the demanding ache. Then he thought about the stripped carcass of the weasel, and his stomach gurgled hopefully. In the dim light he felt his way to the back of the cave and found it, but his work before had been thorough, and there was precious little left on the tiny bones. He broke each joint and chewed the gristle off the ends, but only succeeded in whetting his appetite. One by one, the rodent's bones went back to where he'd picked them up.

He glanced at the light in the entrance, and his heart sped up. Since scrambling back into the cave, he'd managed to keep the sound of the rifle out of his mind, but now the memory returned. The hiss of the rifle ball teased him again, and his groin tensed as a new detail occurred to him: he'd been shot at before, and the man shooting had deadly intent. Why was that so clear to him—but not the when and where of it? The more he thought about it, the less clear the memory of the flesh-seeking bullet became. Had he heard that sound again today, or had he imagined it? And why was he alone? And hunted? That thought made him wince, because he knew it was true, and this new knowledge both thrilled and frightened him; someone hunted him, so maybe they knew him.

He glanced dubiously at the light again. His tongue felt thick, and the back of his throat ached when he tried to swallow. He had to go back out. Instinct told him he could suffer another day without food, but he had to have water. And it wasn't that far away, and the well-sheltered pathway to the pool protected him from searching eyes. But what if the hunter still hunted? He'd just have to be very careful. He hunched down, took up his knife, and stepped out of his sanctuary.

A few minutes later he stopped in the shelter of some brush where he studied the shadows around the water hole and the animal path on the other side. Satisfied he was alone, he crept silently to the edge. The tepid water swept the stickiness from his mouth, and he drank deeply. He had barely started to rise up, water dripping from his chin, when he saw movement on the path. In the dimming light, he made out the hunched form of a raccoon. On his stomach, he crawled away from the pool and into the brush. The coon waddled lazily down the path, stopping frequently to sniff the ground.

The boy turned and hurried away into the forest as fast as he dared, and then, well clear of the pool, raced in a wide circle until he arrived at the path on the other side. He couldn't see where the trail met the pool and hoped he wasn't too late. Hunkered behind a bush, he glanced up at the fading light, locked his eyes on the spot where the path curved out of sight, and waited.

The cold from the ground began to seep into his body, but the promise of the prize kept him motionless. He adjusted his grip on the knife and licked his lips. An animal the size of the one he hunted would feed him for several days, and the skin, with its long hair, might be used along with the one he had in the cave already. His eyes burned as he stared downhill, and the slender wedge of doubt crept in: had he been too slow? He waited a while longer, and then glanced up at the descending darkness. With a heavy sigh, he relaxed his grip on the knife and started to get up.

There! Huffing like a tired old man, the big coon sauntered around the bend and walked straight toward him. Even in the low light, he could see the intense black eyes behind the mask of the egg robber. The animal seemed bent on getting where it was going, and didn't stop to read the scent marks along the way. The boy tensed his muscles, and as the shuffling beast grunted by, he pounced.

He plunged the knife into the creature's back and drove it through to the ground. The animal let out a ferocious growl and tried to spring free. With his free hand, the boy grabbed the raccoon's neck and bore down with all the weight of his slight body. The struggle was as short-lived as it was furious, and the beast went limp. Sagging to his knees beside his prey, the boy pulled the knife out, grabbed his prize by its hind legs, and hurried through the gloom toward his lair.

Outside, he gutted the animal and slipped the skin from the fat carcass; his mouth watered at the globs of fat at the animal's hips. After flinging the guts as far as he could, he glanced over his shoulder one last time before ducking into the cave. Tonight he would sleep with a full belly.

CHAPTER 5

Lem peered through a crack in the door at an eastern sky just beginning to slip the cloak of total darkness; the stars rapidly fading. His eyes burned and his neck had a vicious crick in it. The treetops began to reclaim their identity, and Lem heaved a deep sigh, relieved that his waiting was nearly over. All night he'd sat by the table with his rifle leaning against the wall and watched the door. Several times he'd asked himself what he was going to do against a goblin, but his only answer was to continue to stare toward the door of his cabin. He kept his vigil until he could easily see the trees around the clearing, then lifted the oak bar, pulled the door open, and with rifle at the ready, stepped outside.

The heavy air seemed to close around him, bringing with it the pervasive scent of the river. Hurrying away from the cabin, he looked around the north side, and then moved to see the south. Satisfied, he went to the spot where he'd seen the figure standing the night before. The bare dirt showed his own boot prints, and the moccasin prints of Dufrey's short stride, but nothing else. Snorting in disgust, he returned to the bench and sat to await full light. A little later, another search yielded exactly the same result: nothing. He went inside and made a hasty breakfast of hard biscuits and ham.

After eating he came out, leaned his rifle against the cabin, and carefully arranged the dry hickory between the four posts he'd set the day before. The tinder took immediately, and he spent the next hour feeding pieces of the hard wood to the hungry flames. When they had reduced to several inches of glowing coals, he placed the woven mat over the green hickory frame, and then he moved all the strips of meat from the cabin to the platform. Last, he covered the bed of coals with a layer of green wood, and then sat on the bench to watch as thick smoke engulfed the rack of raw venison. All that remained to do was add more green wood as the hickory burned down to more hot coals. In a few hours—four, maybe six—he'd have jerky. He leaned his head back against the wall, his eyelids heavy from the sleepless night, and dozed.

His unease about leaving his family alone stayed with Lem as he made his way to the riverbank and his boat, a ten-foot, flat-bottomed affair with crude oarlocks and two seats; three if he counted the narrow one in the bow. He stowed his knapsack under that skinny perch, then shoved the heavy craft down the bank and into the river. Jumping on board, he set his oars and moved into the stream. The pair of massive oak logs waited at his timber landing a quarter mile downriver, and he let the current carry him there. Half an hour later, Lem was back on the river, and on his way to Booneville.

Controlling his two-log raft demanded his full attention. A heavy rope connected the stern of the boat to the pair downstream of him. Rowing steadily to maintain tension on the line, he had to anticipate any of the many obstacles that might plague a solitary oarsman. He dared not move too far into the main channel for fear of getting tangled in one of the massive snags that swept by from time to time; whole trees, toppled from an undercut bank, would roll and turn malevolently, their long branches reaching out to snare an unwary boatman. But the safety nearer the shore also made the going slow as the oaks grounded with maddening regularity. Twice already he'd had to get out of the boat to manhandle the logs off a mud bar, and the two hours he'd traveled saw him less than halfway to Boone-ville. Worse, his shoulders and back already ached with fatigue. He leaned back against the oars, favoring the left to pull himself wide of an upcoming bend. A turn in the river always posed the risk of running aground on the inevitable bar, and he watched closely for the telltale slack water.

Lem groaned aloud as the upstream end of the pair of logs started to swing out. Despite his attention, he'd grounded the heavy butts again, Rowing furiously, he steered toward midstream hoping the current would help him pull the load free. The rope yanked tight and he moaned as his boat swung toward the shore, downstream from the stranded oaks. Shipping his oars in disgust, he let the boat come to a stop in the backwater, and then, hand-over-hand, he hauled on the rope until he could touch the grounded troublemakers. Taking off his shoes, he reluctantly climbed out and stood waist deep in the murky flood.

With mud sucking at his bare feet, he sloshed to the upstream end of the logs. The smaller of the two was closer to the bank, and he felt a surge of optimism when his toes slid under it eas-ily; it didn't seem too badly stuck. The last time they'd been hard aground, and he'd had to untie them from each other before they'd budge. That situation offered a real chance that one could get away while he tended the other. Lem leaned over the smaller log, reached as far under it as he could, and lifted. It shifted ever so slightly, and Lem, for the first time since he'd left home, smiled.

Almost an hour later, cold to the bone, covered in mud and no longer smiling, Lem steered his boat to gently drift the logs up against the bank only forty yards below the bar. The first slight shift had been a tease, and what had promised to be an easy task had turned into a frustrating battle among him, the logs, and the mud. With a heavy sigh, he stepped out of his craft and onto dry land; he was exhausted and needed rest and something to eat. The bank made a gentle slope, and he tugged the boat into some willows and tied it up.

Sitting there wet and eating cold food did not appeal to him, so he went into the trees a little farther up the shore and dragged back a large dry tree branch. A little later, Lem sat naked on the dirt and watched wisps of steam lift off the clothes he'd draped across planted sticks. The heat from the fire and early spring sunshine felt wonderful, and for the moment, he was at peace with the world, soaking the welcome heat into his river-chilled body.

Lem's head snapped back, cracking hard against the cabin wall. Startled, he scrambled to his feet, struggling to gather his wits. The jerky! The smoke had stopped rising through the drying-rack, and the four green logs that had supplied it were now gray ash.

"Dammit!" He hurried over and poked around in the dampened fire with a stick. Maybe it hadn't been that long, and he glanced at the sun: not long at all. With the tips of his fingers he gently probed the knob starting to form on the back of his head, cussing silently. Four more chunks of green wood went into the ashes; and almost immediately, wisps of smoke started to rise again. He gingerly touched a few of the meat strips—still soft—and with a satisfied grunt, went back to the cabin. Instead of using the bench, he settled on the ground with his shoulders against the wall, careful not to bump the back of his head. All too soon, his mouth dropped open, and he started to snore.

Lem's riverbank nap had felt good and his clothes were almost dry. He rustled around in his rucksack for something to eat. The sun stood high in the sky, and close as he could reckon, he'd floated about halfway to Booneville. Summer made the trip a lot easier; with the river not so high, he could just float down the middle. Flooding like this meant getting back home would be hard work. He was already dreading the hours of rowing; some stretches in slack water were not so bad, but others, when the river bent against him, could be agonizingly slow. Still, a trip to Booneville had its rewards. He licked his lips as he pictured a full whiskey bottle, but a twinge of guilt pricked his conscience, reminding him of the danger posed by his absence.

Finished with his food, Lem got dressed, put his tote and rifle in the boat, and was scattering the remains of his fire when a large canoe hove into sight downstream. A canvas-wrapped bundle stowed in the center held the craft low in the water, and two men on board hugged the bank, their paddles flashing in the sunlight. Obviously intent on making way upstream, they hadn't seen him yet. They spotted the bar that had grounded Lem, and steered wide, digging deep with their paddles as they moved into faster water. *River trash:* he'd seen their like on the waterfront at Booneville, rough characters a wise man avoided if he could. Lem ducked out of sight.

The man in the bow, though big, was the smaller of the two, and wore a black frock coat. A flop-brimmed felt hat with a bright-red bandana around the band hid most of his face. The huge man steering looked almost ridiculous perched on his knees in the frail-looking craft, the long paddle toy-like in his hands. He wore a striped shirt, but most striking was his beaver hat. It had a high crown and sat atop an unruly mass of tangled black hair that merged with an outrageously long and disheveled beard.

"Pull harder, ya queer bastard," the big one shouted. "Kin ya not see the bleedin' bar? Put us on it and, by God, I'll drown ya like yer mother should've."

The man in the bow glanced back, and dug his paddle deeper on the left side of the canoe. They pulled abreast of Lem's boat, and still hadn't given any sign that they'd seen it or the pair of logs hauled up along the shore.

"Farther out, ya lazy sluggard," the big man growled and dug hard on the right. The canoe responded sharply. "Pull, ya worthless git."

The smaller man struggled to comply as the faster water caught the bow. A few more strokes and the canoe moved past the bar, then turned sharply left and pulled closer to the bank again. Lem remained hunkered down until the big man's sulfurous swearing faded away completely as they rounded the bend and disappeared. Heaving a sigh, Lem stood up, hurried down to his boat, and retrieved his rifle. He stood looking upriver for a while, and then sat on the damp shore.

He held his head, his elbows leaning on his knees. If he left everything and carried only his rifle, he might make it home ahead of the brigands . . . might. It was a long way with no trail; it was even possible he might not be able to find the cabin right away because he'd have to travel well inland, away from the river bluffs. And were they up to no good? There was no way of knowing. His place contained nothing of value and they'd see that . . . if they even happened onto it. None had in the past, so why should this pair be any different? They were obviously on their way with a purpose, and they carried cargo. The big man had cussed constantly as they passed, urging the smaller man on, hurrying him. They probably wouldn't even see his little landing. It was on the fast side of the river, and two experienced river men like these would have instead crossed to the opposite side.

No, they'd not even see his place. And the boy's on guard. The boy—soon a man—and he's armed. They'll be all right— even if the ruffians should stop—which they won't—it's the wrong side of the river. Lem sighed, stood, and went to his boat. He'd have to hurry to get to Booneville in time to start back today.

The boy stirred, tugged at the ragged cloth covering his skinny chest, then drifted back to sleep. He'd waited for the stalker until his weary body had overcome his will to stay awake. Now the realm of night creatures held sway, the silence disturbed only slightly by the rustling foragers, or occasionally by a short, sharp death-squeal from one of the unwary. Dreamless, the boy slept soundly.

Come morning, he actually felt rested and couldn't remember ever feeling this good. Light streamed through the cave's small opening, and he sat up and rubbed his eyes. Then he remembered the raccoon, and spotted the creature's misshapen remains lying on the bare rock, just out of reach. He licked his lips. To be able to count on a meal for the day, several days for that matter, was an unusual treat. What was he going to do until dark if he wasn't foraging for food? Until dark—this was the second night that the stalker hadn't found his hideaway. And who'd chased him yesterday? He recalled the frantic scramble off the ridge and the long, slow trek home. It had taken him all day, and he hadn't seen or heard anyone in pursuit. Had he been chased, or had he only imagined it? At that moment, his body reminded him of his needs and he stood, stretched long and hard, and then ducked through the opening into bright day.

The sun was well above the trees, and as he wet the ground, he turned his face from side-to-side, soaking in the heat. The river! He'd only seen it for a few seconds, but the sweep of it, and the smell—he'd recognized the smell. He hurried his duty, then went back into the cave where he sliced a long strip of meat off the raccoon, hefted the knife for an indecisive moment, and then laid it down by the carcass. Emerging from the cave with the glistening strip of flesh, he took a deep breath of the fresh air, and started off.

Chewing on the meat as he walked, the boy followed the same route he'd taken the day before, only this time more slowly. If someone had chased him yesterday, they hadn't been very good at it, so he'd be safe if he were careful. He was aware of the chance he was taking, but there was something he could learn from the river . . . he just knew it.

Two ridges away from his cave, the boy eagerly anticipated the third. The cool morning air felt particularly good, and for the second time, he caught himself almost strolling along. Silently he chastised himself, and slowed his pace as he deliberately scanned the shadows. Moments later, he realized his luck when he spotted a dark form in the forest ahead. The hair on his neck rose. He'd almost run headlong into disaster. There was only one thing he instinctively feared, and there it was, less than a hundred feet away tearing a rotten log to pieces—a black bear. As silently as a falling leaf, the boy sank to the ground and shifted sideways into the cover of a bush.

The bear, intent on ripping the punky wood apart, flung large pieces through the air with its powerful paws. The boy had seen this once before, and knew what the bear was after: grubs, white and fat, with a small head the color of a roasted wheat kernel. Right after arriving at his cave he'd discovered a nest of them. He remembered studying them a long time, hungry as he was, before he'd stuffed two of the larvae in his mouth and chomped down. The taste had surprised him; not nasty as he'd expected, they had an earthy nut-flavor. He'd then eaten all he could find, exactly as the bear was doing.

Snuffling through the decayed wood, the animal used its tongue to lap up the treasure. A few more swipes with its paw, and some airy explosions as it cleared its nose, and the bear finished off the last few stragglers. It then sat back on its haunches as though thinking of what to do next. The boy, flat on his stomach, willed his body to be absolutely still as the bear looked his way. He could clearly see the animal's eyes intently searching the area. The boy's breath caught when the unblinking eyes settled on the very bush that hid him. The bear paused. Then it shifted forward to all four feet, and with a huff, lumbered up the slope and out of sight. The boy breathed a deep sigh of relief and laid his face on the damp earth.

He rose slowly and listened for further sounds from beyond the ridge. Hearing nothing, he hurried over to the ravaged log and picked around in the rubble. The bear had been thorough. He found a few maggots, not even enough to cover the palm of his hand; but he'd learned the hard way to eat whenever he could. The taste brought a slight smile, and with a quick glance at the sun, he resumed his journey.

It pleased him that he was able to find the exact place he'd been the day before, and knowing what lay beyond the ridge, he boldly crested it and looked: the river. The mist was not low on the water today but hung thin and milky blue-gray over the treetops. Pockets of brilliant red and orange identified patches of maples. And almost hidden in the hazy cover, the thin column of white could have easily escaped his attention . . . but didn't.

The boy studied the scene for a while before deciding that the white against the blue-gray was smoke. A chill crept over him despite the warm sun on his naked body; smoke probably meant others and others meant danger . . . did they not? It was some other who stalked him at night; it was some other who had chased him yesterday; some other who had . . .

He fought to recover a memory that hung just out of reach. Some other had—he shook his head. Maybe if he saw who had made the fire? The smoke wasn't that far away, he guessed he could be there before the sun reached its peak. As with the bear, his instincts told him to avoid contact, but something else pushed his fear aside.

Today he'd managed to escape the bear's notice; yesterday, he'd eluded the hunter—quite easily, in fact—his chest swelled a little. He settled down on his heels and pondered the telltale wisp some more. Could it be natural? The rolling landscape stretched unbroken as far as he could see except for a high rocky outcrop on the shore directly opposite. The sheer face dropped straight down to the river's edge where the solid stone thrashed the water to foam. He counted the ridges between himself and the lifting column of white, took a deep breath, and stood.

Moving up the near side of the next ridge he realized the forest here grew more thickly than it did around his cave, and that gave him pause: the thicker brush offered more cover, but that same protection was given to anyone, or anything, that might be watching him—his skin tingled. As he crested, he was able to see the river again. He stopped only briefly, checked the direction of the smoke, and hurried down the far side.

He moved faster now, aware that the farther he went, the more at ease he became . . . and he wondered why. The terrain was about the same, if more tangled and overgrown. He had to be watchful for side draws angling off the larger ridges. It would be easy to mistake one for a main ridge and be diverted off course. When he'd studied the smoke from the last height, the amount rising had seemed about the same. He'd already considered a natural fire, but there'd been no lightning for weeks. The steady nature of the smoke made him think it was controlled, and that surely meant white people.

White people? The thought stopped him in mid-stride. He was white! Which was different from—Indians! He looked at his hands. Why hadn't he considered that? The feeling of ease he'd started to enjoy vanished, and he took a quick look all around. The fact that he had not thought about Indians at all until just now shocked him; somehow he knew they could mean trouble. But how did he know? Because someone had warned him. The fact dawned so clearly he had little doubt it was true. But who? The urge to hurry back to the safety of his cave was strong.

But the fire starter could just as easily be white . . . no, he probably *was* white. It seemed to make sense to him, but he couldn't understand why. And that made it safer . . . or did it? The boy peered into the shadows some more, then slipped into some nearby bushes, thoroughly confused. New details were coming to him every day: the vague memory of being chased; the smell of the river; and now he knew someone had told him to be wary of Indians. He felt compelled to see who was making the smoke, and to see if they were like him . . . white. With another careful look around, he stepped out of the thick brush and headed for the top of the next ridge.

The boy moved more cautiously, the source of the fire just ahead. His whole body trembled as he approached the top of the last slope. Looking for the best cover, he crept on his hands and knees through the brush until the view of the small valley opened up below: the roof of a small dwelling set at the back edge of a stump-filled clearing, smoke rising in front of the place, his angle of sight hiding the fire itself. He grimaced in frustration, and looked for a way to get closer.

Two distinct paths led away from the hut: one toward the river on the far side of the clearing, and another that led into the trees to his right. That meant the left side was the safest route. Carefully he stole through the brush, angling down to the bottom of the shallow valley. His body ached with tension by the time he'd reached the left edge of the clearing and cautiously parted the bush he hid in.

The boy's nostrils flared and his eyes widened when he spotted the man: legs stretched out, bearded head cocked sideways, apparently dozing, his back against the cabin wall. To the left stood a solitary pine tree, and the sun glinted off a big ax stuck in it at about the height of a man's head. For several seconds he couldn't take his eyes off the heavy-looking tool. There was something ominous about it, the bit buried solid and deep in the wood, the long smooth handle parallel to the trunk. A shiver crept up his back, and he jerked his attention away from the sight.

The smoke came from a smoldering fire under a wooden rack, and he had to study the setup for several minutes before it made sense: the man was drying meat! A smoky taste came to him, and his mouth filled with saliva. He'd seen that before! In fact, he'd seen this *place* before, he was almost sure of it. His heart pounding, he searched for a way to get closer to the shack . . . he had to. Slowly he backed away from the edge of the clearing, and once in deeper cover, started to make his way around the clearing.

The trek seemed to take forever as he darted from tree to tree, and from one bush to the next. At last, he came to the path leading to the river. There he stopped to study the man some more. He hadn't moved. He judged the distance across the path; he'd be in the open for three long strides. With a final glance at the man, he took a deep breath and bolted for the safety of a tree directly across. There he carefully looked around it toward the cabin. The man was still stretched out except now his head was no longer cocked to one side. The boy ducked back.

Was the man watching? He'd only been in the open for a heartbeat or two; surely, if he'd been seen, the man would have gotten up and started his way. He took another panicky look and heaved a sigh: the man was still sitting, perfectly still, apparently asleep. He let his heart settle down before he continued his circular route to the southeast side. He came to the second path he'd seen. Much narrower than the first, it paralleled the river, and he couldn't see the cabin. One stride took him across.

Angling back, the boy slowed to a crawl, remembering how close to the edge of the woods the cabin stood. After each step, he stopped to look through the trees and undergrowth, but sight of the cabin's rear corner and the stack of split firewood along the wall still took him by surprise. He was nearly upon it! Shaking his head, he realized he was too far to the rear to see the man and the fire. Dropping to his hands and knees, he crawled slowly to his right, eyes on the cabin, feeling his way across the debris-covered ground. At last he came even with the front of the cabin, and carefully raised his head for a good look. The solitary pine blocked his view, and for some unknown reason he looked up at the ax.

Even as his breath left him in a gasp, his bare feet churned the ground as the awful truth flared in his brain—the ax was gone! Charged with strength only terror can lend, he leaped behind a nearby tree as he caught movement: the glint of sun on polished steel. The big ax flew past his head, the handle making a whooshing sound as it turned in the air, and crashed into the undergrowth.

An outraged voice hollered, but shocked by the sight of the flashing ax, the boy heard nothing as he picked the thickest tangle of brush he could see and dove blindly into it. Dropping to his hands and knees, he took advantage of the game trail he knew would be there. Scurrying like a rodent, he followed the track until he emerged on the other side. There he stood, glanced over his shoulder, and sprinted away, letting his feet find their own way. He hadn't seen the man, but knew where he was: the crashing in the underbrush sounded like two fighting deer. He ducked instinctively as a rifle shot split the air. Swatting down branches that clutched at him, he ignored the pain as those he missed tore at his body. A voice boomed through the forest, howling words he couldn't hear, but he could feel the rage and he ran even faster.

The man's raving grew fainter as the boy moved at right angles to the ridges. He was aware when he crested the first ridge, and drove headlong down the other side. Through the thick trees he ran, slowed as he charged up another ridge, and only when he'd reached its crest did he stop and listen. The dead calm air brought no sound of pursuit; and the boy leaned heavily against a tree, and retched.

There had been no reason for Lem's eyes to open at the exact moment they did. The sun felt wonderful, the fire was doing well, and his need for sleep had been somewhat satisfied by his morning naps. No sudden puff of air, no calling hawk, no curious insect inspecting the hairs in his nose had roused him—his eyes had simply opened. And there it was, for a fleeting moment: a figure in mid-stride, bounding across the river trail. His first instinct was to scramble to his feet, grab his rifle and give chase, but that urge was instantly quelled as he recalled his last encounter: the thing had simply sunk into the earth. No, this time it would be different; this time he'd catch it unawares, handle it on his ground.

He sat still and watched for movement, his eyes nearly shut. His caution paid off when a dark thatch of hair briefly showed around a sycamore, then disappeared again. Through barely open eyes, Lem caught movement twice more as the creature circled the clearing, moving right. He calculated the time it would take the intruder to get to the far side of the cabin, and waited that long before he stood.

Reaching inside the door, he grabbed his rifle but then stopped short. The rifle might misfire . . . it had before. No, the big ax was better; one solid blow and there could be no doubt. He went to the tree, leaned the rifle against it, and pulled the ax free, feeling the satisfying weight of what was now a weapon drop into his powerful hands. The creature was coming to him; it had before, and there was no reason to doubt it this time. He tried to estimate the size of it, recalling the glimpse he'd had. In his mind, it was big, at least his own size, maybe slightly larger, so he'd have to be careful. He stepped close to the tree. The beast would make for the cabin wall, and then try to sneak around to the front and catch him sleeping. He gripped the ax in both hands, and waited for a sign.

All he heard was a gasp, and it was nearby. How could a creature the size of this one have gotten so close and he not hear it? Lem spun around the tree, arms extended, the ax swinging in a wide loop. He let go when something moved toward a tree on his right—a man? In the instant he released the handle, he knew he'd missed and rage turned his vision red. "I'll kill ya for good this time!" he hollered.

Grabbing his rifle, he charged into the brush. The tangled thicket of berry bushes and grape vines stopped him almost immediately, and frustration boiled his blood. Backing out, he fired into the thicket where he'd seen the form disappear, then dropped the rifle and charged the thick growth again. Tearing blindly at the vines, his rage mounted until finally the futility struck him, and he stepped back to see where else the creature might have gone. Across the open to the side of the cabin? Not likely. That meant the thing fled to the left, and Lem turned that way and bulled his way into the forest, stomping deadwood under his feet and batting wrist-sized branches out of his way. Suddenly, he stopped and listened; too late. "I seen ya and I'll have ya," he howled at the silence. An echo mocked him in his own voice.

He clenched his teeth and mentally railed against his stupidity; while he'd been crashing through the underbrush, his tormentor had simply walked away . . . or had it? He searched, twice turning completely around, and saw absolutely nothing.

The reality of the situation struck him: he'd thrown the ax wide when he had his chance to end the stalking, and now the watcher was that much wiser.

CHAPTER 6

When the sun dropped out of sight, the boy finally admitted to himself that he was completely lost; a fact he'd known for some time, but denied. In the failing light he could see what looked like the crest of the ridge ahead, and he forced his nearly defeated muscles to continue on to the top.

The view on the other side, though shrouded in the settling gloom, promised to be nothing but another, higher ridge. He moved slowly to the base of the biggest tree he could see, a wide-spreading oak, and sank to the ground, back against the trunk. Peering into the rapidly deepening shadows, he wished he'd brought his knife.

When he'd spotted the smoke this morning, the river had been on his left and swung around to the right, which fixed the river north and east. At least he'd be able to find it in the morning. But how far south or west had he traveled, and how far from the river? And the ground here was much more broken, ridges and ravines crossing one another at odd angles. He'd tried to keep his bearings, but steep bluffs and deep gullies had turned him so many times he'd given up, intent on putting as much distance as he could between himself and the crazy man.

He recalled what he'd seen at the cabin. The man had a scraggly beard that bushed out around his face. Though he hadn't been close enough to see his eyes, he did see that the man's hair hung to his shoulders beneath a floppy hat. His shoulders, wide, his arms, enormous—he looked powerful and dangerous.

And the ax! The image of the gleaming tool, set in the tree, filled his mind. He felt sure he'd seen it before, and the same with the cabin, almost. Rough-hewn logs, low sloped roof, a door, and one window on the left. But the ax stood out. Thinking about it brought a strange thrill, a feeling of stepping across some forbidden boundary. It was just an ax; why did he have such an attraction to it?

A rustling sound off to his left interrupted his reverie. Senses alert, he stood slowly, legs and back protesting; he needed a place to hide. He'd chosen to sit under an oak tree. Enormous, with a base as thick through as he was tall, huge branches splayed off in five different directions, each forking six or seven feet up, and then splitting yet again. The bottom crotch was only about head height off the ground and he easily climbed into the natural nest . . . too easily. A little higher, the heaviest branch sloped off to his left, and he dug his callused toes into the coarse bark and climbed. The first fork shot a branch off almost parallel with the ground, and farther out it forked again, sending a big limb angling gently skyward. He scooted out on the level one, leaned his back against the angled limb and let his legs dangle on either side. He felt quite secure, and the feeling of being above the ground and safe—vaguely familiar.

As the sweat on his body dried, the cool night air raised gooseflesh on his chest. He hugged himself; it was going to be a long night, but tomorrow he'd find an open space in the sun and have a nap in some dry leaves, or against a big tree trunk. He'd done that before. His head snapped erect as his mind grabbed at the idea before it faded: he *had* done that before. He'd stayed in a tree many nights, every night until he'd found the cave. Suddenly wide-awake, he looked down at the ground, then into the deep shadows that pooled under the trees. He'd been chased by a man before. The incident of the rifle shot two days ago confirmed that. Was that why he'd hidden in the trees?

That didn't make sense; once he'd climbed off the ground, he'd have been at the mercy of the man hunting him. That meant he hadn't been chased up a tree, but rather chose to stay above the ground for safety—from animals? He couldn't remember how many days he'd traveled before finding the cave, but he knew it had been a lot.

The boy's heart raced as he realized he knew just a little bit more about his past. He no longer felt the chill as he drew his right leg up to his chest, hugged it tight, and settled his head in the crook of his arm. The warmth soothed the dull ache in his knee.

Lem hurried back to his cabin, went inside and got his hunting pouch. A few practiced moves later, he leaned the reloaded rifle against the cabin wall and stood by the pine tree. There he judged the spot where he'd seen the intruder, walked past it, and found his ax in the underbrush. He laid it across his shoulder, and searched for the spot where the creature had been hiding. It was easy to see where it had lain; the leaves were disturbed, damp sides up.

"So, *this* one's not a ghost," he said aloud.

He noticed as well the dozens of small branches and twigs lying about. Whoever it was knew how to be quiet. But what of the earlier visits, such as the one by the water hole? And the other night, standing in front of the cabin? The first apparition had simply vanished, swallowed up by the ground; the second had not left a trace, even in bare earth. He studied the ground and found another place where the debris was disturbed. A stride away, he found more sign, and they all lined up with the bush he'd gone to. He hurried to it, then knelt and studied the bare ground under the overhanging foliage. There, plain as a three-foot stump . . . a footprint! A bare footprint.

"I've got an Indian visitor," he mumbled. But why now? Dufrey said they were all friendly around here. Just a curious hunter? Lem backed out of the undergrowth and stood. Maybe one looking for food. The jerky! Lem turned on his heel and hurried to his fire. It was still smoking nicely, if not as vigorously as he liked, so he put some more green wood on and settled down again. This time, he didn't doze, but listened and watched the forest around him, ax by his side.

The jerky didn't fill a quarter of a cornmeal bag; but, Lem reasoned, it was more than he'd had that morning. He hefted it and reckoned he'd probably need five times as much to get through even a short winter. Unless, of course, the supplies he ordered were deposited on the riverbank in time, in which case he wouldn't need any at all. A gamble. He reached into the bag, took out a piece of the dark meat, and bit off a chunk. He chewed the tough morsel slowly for a few seconds to reintroduce moisture, then went out the door and into the evening. Around the corner of the cabin, he glanced at the drying-mat he'd hung on the outside wall; he'd left the four posts stuck in the ground. Absently, he unbuttoned his pants and relieved himself. Tomorrow he'd get up early and see if he could ambush a deer like Dufrey had. The Cajun had told him that the secret was to get up before the deer went to bed. He grunted at the simple wisdom. With a last look around, he went back inside, closing the door, and dropping the heavy bar into place.

Lem picked up the single burning candle from the table, and went to the mantel for another. Tilting the wick into the flame, the added light of the second taper helped push the shadows back a little more. He sat at the table, and his hand went to the silver bell that stood in the middle. With a single musical note, it protested lightly as he picked it up. Slowly, he turned it in his hand and marveled at its smooth surface, caressing it with his rough thumb from the bottom edge to the angel motif tooled in the handle. With the intricate design between his fingers, he gently tipped the bell to one side and back again. Tears welled up at the sound. He fought to push the images aside, visions he didn't need just before he went to bed.

He passed his sleeve over his eyes, and as he reached to put the bell back on the table, he caught a flicker of movement out of the corner of his eye. He stopped breathing, hand frozen in midair. Ever so slightly, he turned his head to catch sight of a cause. He knew precisely where his rifle and ax were, and a butcher knife; he just needed to know which to go for first. Inhaling shallowly, he continued to turn his head—there!

In the corner, by the window—a man! Lem went cold, and the hair on his back bristled. In an instant, he dismissed both rifle and ax; the intruder was closer to them than he was. The knife was on the hearth, to the left of the skillet. Three steps after he stood, it would be his.

His breath came in short puffs, his mouth dry as dust. How had he not seen the man in the light of two candles? Had he not looked in that direction since closing the door? He couldn't be sure. The man hadn't yet moved, even slightly. Lem slowly filled his lungs, tensed the heavy muscles in his thighs—and bolted from the table, only to tangle his feet in the chair and pitch face-first on the dirt floor. He fought to get his hands and knees under him and then scrambled to the hearth where he grabbed the familiar wooden handle. Rolling into a squat, he twice slashed the blade back and forth in the air as he tried to locate his attacker. And found nothing.

In disbelief, he leaned his back against the fireplace and searched the four corners of the cabin, knifepoint following his gaze. Nothing! But he'd seen it! It *had* been standing in the corner, and now it was gone!

Slowly Lem got to his feet, found a lucifer on the mantle and struck it. With the flaring match held overhead, he searched again: empty. He touched the flame to a candle, lit another from that one, and from it, another. The light of five tapers banished all the shadows. Lem sank back to the floor, his legs unable to hold him up. He buried his face in his hands and started to tremble. The demon, it seemed, had moved in with him. He sagged back against the wall by the fireplace, drained.

Once more, Lem's head jerked upright, and he frantically looked around the dimly lit room. The candles! He grabbed for a fresh one from the stack by his side, but stopped when he realized daylight was filtering through the numerous cracks in the cabin walls. He let out a shuddering gasp and scrambled to stand up. At his feet on the hearth were six greasy pools of tallow; in four, short candles still burned. He stooped, snuffed them and shuffled to the door.

Outside he hurried away from the cabin until he stood by the old fire ring near the center of the clearing—Percy's fire ring. His eyes burned in the early light, and a catch in his back refused to let go. The night had been a trial, his second without much sleep, and his mind seemed numb. How the figure in the cabin had gotten out mystified him. No doubt, he *had* gotten out, because he wasn't there now, and Lem had stayed awake all night—nearly all night—watching the door and the window, and they hadn't been opened. Then how? "The man *was* in there, I saw him!" His own voice startled him and he took a deep breath before turning to stare at the open cabin door.

He shouted, "You're not going to run me out of my own house." He took a few long steps toward the cabin and stopped: "You hear me? Step out where I can see ya, and I'll break your back!" The still forest returned his last word to him, "BACK . . . Back . . . back," fading with each echo.

"I know you can hear me. I know you're there. Come out!"

"OUT . . . Out . . . out."

He strode to the cabin and rushed through the door, fists

balled, blood surging in his ears. He turned, jerked out the pegs that held the window closed, and lifted the heavy shutter. As light flooded in, he dropped to his knees and searched the bare earth for footprints: nothing. Powder-dry dust flew into his face as his heavy fists hammered the earth.

"It can't be," he stormed and slammed the ground again. A sob of frustration escaped his throat. "It can't be," he muttered, his voice weaker. "Can't beeeee."

Shaking his head slowly, he settled back on his haunches, and stared dully at the bare dirt floor.

Excitement surged through the boy at first light. The air, cold and damp, clung to him, and he pulled both knees to his chest to trap heat from his body. His night had been fitful, and once he'd almost fallen off the branch. Desperately, he'd clamped his legs around the huge limb, and ripped a nail back as he grabbed the rough bark with both hands. It was only after he'd managed to catch his breath that he remembered to keep at least one leg dangling. Dawn's full light slowly revealed the last of night's hiding places.

After a trip to the bottom of the ravine for a long drink of water, he went back to the ridgeline and started northeast, keeping just below the crest. With stretches of open ground, some as long as a good rifle shot, traveling proved relatively easy. He couldn't be sure, but it seemed the ridges were becoming more parallel as he went. Constantly alert for any movement, or some shape or form that didn't fit the landscape, the smell of the river didn't come as a total surprise; the odor of mud and rotted vegetation came to him on a breeze wafting up the ravine to his left. He stopped and hunkered down on his heels. If he was that close to the river, he might also be too close to the cabin.

He recalled the terror at the cabin when he'd seen, barely in time, the movement by the tree. Why had the man chased him? He'd meant no harm. The bushy-faced woodsman was three times his size . . . and the ax! He imagined its wickedly sharp blade set deep in the wood, set there by that madman and ready to do its job, be it on a tree or another human being. He felt a chill on his neck, and stood. He knew it was crazy, but he needed another look at the cabin, and the man—and the ax.

Picking his way carefully, a thrill shot through him, when, across the river and upstream a ways, he spotted the tall rock bluff. It appeared a little different at this angle, but he knew it was the same one he'd seen yesterday, and he now knew exactly where he was.

Before the sun had climbed very much, he'd found a good hiding spot in the forest and squatted there, eyes on the cabin. He could see no smoke above the chimney, but both the front door and the window stood wide open. Did the man leave it like that when he went to work? Did he go to work every day? Stomach noises reminded him he hadn't eaten in a while. He squirmed against the discomfort, and thought about the raccoon back at the cave—food. Maybe he should just leave. His stomach rumbled again and he looked down at his belly.

When he looked up the man stood just outside the door, rifle in one hand, a bucket in the other. The boy tensed for an instant, and then relaxed; he had plenty of time to escape if the woodchopper headed his way. The man stood still for a short time looking around, and then he strode to the south side of the clearing and disappeared into the forest. The chatter of alarmed squirrels marked his passage.

The path—the boy remembered crossing it yesterday when he'd circled for a better look. How far did the man go for water? Without further thought, he stood and circled to his right. He soon had the cabin between himself and where the man should reemerge from the forest. The water supply had to be down that narrow trail beyond where he'd crossed it. Add a little time from that spot and the walk back, a bit more to fill the bucket, and maybe a few minutes for morning duties . . . time enough. And besides, the squirrels, now quiet, would warn him. The boy sprinted across the open ground and pressed his body against the north side of the cabin.

The smell of meat immediately caught his attention, and he moved over to the smoke-smudged mat hanging on the wall. Small bits of venison clung to the darkened wood, and he picked a sliver off and put it in his mouth. Altogether different from the stringy raccoon, it tasted smoky and—something else— cooked. He chewed the morsels as he cleaned the mat of all he could find, stuffing his cheeks. The image of a foraging rodent came to mind, and he smiled to himself. He went to the corner, peeked around it, and after listening for a moment, swiftly moved to the cabin door. There, he paused for another glance at the path, then poked his head inside.

The scene was strangely familiar, and the smells—sweat and grease—also struck at something within him. His nostrils flared and he tilted his head back as he sought the source of the aroma. The heavy window shutter on the left stood propped open, lighting a small table. A cloth sack with its top open and folded down immediately drew his attention. He could see the strips of dried meat it contained . . . more of the meat he had in his mouth. Exploring further, he briefly studied the crude fireplace at the back of the cabin—simple hearth, mud chimney, a blackened pot beside an equally black skillet, a small metal pail . . . water maybe. And on the left, a bed. Elusive memories of sleeping in a different nest than the one he knew at the cave flashed alive; and then blinked out again. He continued to look, his heart pounding.

To the left of the fireplace, hanging from the ceiling, was more meat, a large piece; half a leg of something. He cocked an ear for a moment, and then stepped into the hut. The strange aroma grew stronger, and as he moved toward the center of the room, it became clear the source was the suspended haunch. On the other side of the chimney, clothes hung from pegs stuck in the wall, and set against the front wall to the left of the door sat a large trunk. His mind filled with fragments of memories: a lighter place, not so damp . . . bigger somehow. He felt for an instant that he might belong here, but in the next moment knew that this was a strange place, and a dangerous one.

The next object to catch his eye made his heart stutter. The ax, leaning against the wall just left of the door. He moved back to the front and looked out, listening. *Hurry.* Stepping back in, he reached over, took hold of the smooth handle, and lifted. The weight surprised him. Raising the head, he ran his fingers back and forth over the smooth steel, caressing it—*leave it alone!* The warning blazed in his head, and the hair on his neck responded so vigorously that he almost dropped the tool putting it back down. Two steps and he was at the door again, listening above the sound of his pounding heart; for the briefest moment he'd forgotten to pay attention.

His squirrel sentries were still quiet, but his lapse with the ax unsettled him. He rushed to the fireplace and inspected the skillet . . . empty. As he started away, he skidded in a small patch of tallow. He saw the partially burned candles, and then spotted, at the edge of the hearth, a big stack of whole ones. And hard against the mud and stick chimney stood a square tin, lid open, nearly full of matches; he recognized them instantly. *Don't touch!* But countering the warning, he also knew what they meant. He snapped the lid shut and stuck the tin under his chin. Then, dumping the water out of the small pail, he used both hands to grab all of the candles and put them in it. He went to the table where he stuffed his prizes into the sack with the meat. *Hurry!* He unfolded the top, closed the bag with a quick twist, and started for the door.

Light glinted off the silver bell, and he froze. Spellbound, he stared at the small object gleaming in middle of the table. He leaned closer, and his trembling hand reached out as though beyond his control. *Leave now!* The metal was cool to his touch. His fingers gripped the tiny handle on top and he picked it up. Then the sound: Squirrels! Agitated squirrels!

The boy dropped the bell which made one tinkling bounce on the table before falling silent on the dirt floor. He bolted.

As Lem walked across the clearing toward the forest's edge, the sound of the squirrels irritated him; unusual for him, because he'd always enjoyed the scampering tree-rats. They were what he thought a man should be: free, independent, busy, and alert. But right now, they were just noisy. He glanced up, but couldn't see where the commotion was coming from. He took a deep breath of the fresh forest air, it felt clean and—a shudder rippled through him as he recalled the night he'd just spent in the closed cabin. He glanced from side to side and hurried along the path to the trees.

Approaching the spring, he checked the spot where he'd seen the apparition disappear into the ground. Deep in shadow, the morning light played off the low bushes at the base of the tree, and as he moved closer the filtered radiance shifted back and forth in the leaves and branches. A dark patch, illuminated one moment only to vanish within the space of a heartbeat, played on his ragged nerves. He strode the last few yards, and after a close look around, got his water and started back.

He nearly dropped his bucket with the first burst of chatter; so close he ducked his head. More squirrels, higher up in the trees, joined in the scolding, voicing their displeasure. He looked up, and finally saw one; bushy tail twitching with agitation, jumping from branch to branch. Feeling embarrassed, Lem reset his grip on the rifle and continued on. His mind was still on the raucous tree dwellers as he broke out of the forest and into the clearing.

Had the Indian been moving slowly, Lem might not have seen him, but with hair flying and legs pumping, the slight figure shot out the door, slipped to one knee in a skidding turn and disappeared around the side of the cabin before Lem had time to react. Lem's bucket hit the ground with a thud and he ran toward the center of the clearing. Training his eyes on the forest beyond the cabin, he yanked back the hammer on his rifle as he slid to a stop. Nothing moved, the silence broken only by the excited chatter of the squirrels.

"Thievin' devil," he muttered as he searched. "Where did you get to?" Rifle at the ready, he walked swiftly toward the cabin until he came to the footprints. They were plain in the bare dirt, and he followed them as they angled to the edge of the clearing.

From there, he looked back. "Clever little thief . . . lined up the corner of the cabin just right so's I couldn't see ya. Prob'ly done this before." Stooping, he was able to discover more sign, a few scuffs in the debris of the forest floor, but that too soon vanished. Lem stood and looked at the ridgeline above him. Was the little heathen watching him right now? Lem slowly traced the crest with the muzzle of his rifle. "Just give me a look at you," he muttered. "One's all I'll need." Then he turned abruptly and started back to the cabin.

"Damnation!" Lem shouted. He leaned his rifle against the doorframe, and went to the table looking for his sack of jerky, nearly stepping on the tiny bell lying in the dirt. Picking it up, he blew the dust off before tenderly setting it back on the table.

"The jerky . . . and what else?" he asked, scanning the poorly lit interior. The ham was still there. He spun around and sighed when he spotted his ax. Turning back to the hearth, he looked for the knife—still beside the skillet. But the candles! And the lucifers!

"Unholy, Godless little beggar!" Lem roared. "What use do *you* have for them? You've left me in the dark!"

He knelt and carefully gathered up the four partly burned tapers, and put them up on the mantle. Leaning over, he gingerly poked in the ashes with a finger, hoping against hope: cold as stone. Lem stood, took a long slow breath, and then, with a savage kick, sent the skillet flying. It bounced off the wall with a clang and fell to the floor. He stared at it a moment before storming out of the cabin and slumping on the bench in front.

First last night . . . now this. Was he losing his mind? Going mad like Dufrey's friend Percy? The image of the short Cajun striding away across the clearing came back to him, and he glanced toward the path where he'd disappeared into the shadows. Their talk about haunts had left Lem uneasy, and he knew he hadn't been very forthcoming. But to talk about it was to admit it; he couldn't do that, and he knew why: as long as he could deny that the haunt was real, he could live with it. As long as it was just a misty form, or a sudden movement in the underbrush, he could convince himself that maybe it was all his imagination. But last night had changed that. He'd seen it as clearly as he'd seen the little Indian, and he could no longer convince himself he wasn't being watched; because now he knew he was.

Weary, Lem shook his head and slowly let his chin sag to his chest. All night he'd fought with this newfound truth and tried to deny it. He'd struggled to put things in some sort of order, make some sense of that which made no sense. Right now he wished he had nothing to worry about but a shifting shadow, a footfall that made no mark, and a form that left only a fleeting image in memory. Because beginning today, he had something far worse to contend with: since last night, Lem knew *who* was watching, and he knew for sure that person was dead.

CHAPTER 7

As the boy bolted out of the cabin, he saw that the bearded man was looking back, probably at the protesting squirrels. One stride beyond the door, he planted his right foot and pushed away on it. His knee snapped backwards and he nearly screamed at the pain. The leg folded and he went down on it, only to scramble back up and sprint away, every step on his right foot a blinding reminder of how far it was to the safety of the woods.

Instinctively, he cut left to keep the cabin between himself and the man. Halfway to the trees he knew he wasn't going to make it, bright flashes of pain with every step making him sick to his stomach. Grimly, he held the sack tight, and took as much weight as possible on his left leg. *Too many more steps.* His vision started to blur. *A few more.* The image of the rifle leveled, the flash of fire, the ball streaking toward his spine drove him. *One more*—pain beyond imagination.

Shadows closed around him and he choked back a cry. He knew he had to go to ground so he turned toward the thickest undergrowth, fighting to keep his injured leg from dragging while he hopped on his good one. He grabbed hold of anything he could and struggled forward. There! Two feet thick and long dead, a fallen tree offered what he needed. He threw his injured leg across the top of it and with his left sprang up and over. The brilliance of the light behind his eyes shocked him as he crashed to the ground on the other side. Blinded for a moment, he froze, elbows jammed in the soft soil; then the forest dissolved to black.

He felt a dull throb, or at least he thought he did; it seemed a long way away: thud, pause, thud. Then the dull pounding turned to eye-popping pain in his knee, and he realized he'd lost his senses for a moment. He stuffed the bag under the log, and then wiggled beneath the moldy-smelling trunk as far as he could. Gritting his teeth, he stifled the moan that fought for release; then let his head settle back into the dank vegetation.

He heard the man enter the woods and stop. He could picture him searching the ground for sign. Slow steps brought the man closer . . . too close. The boy clamped his teeth against the pain and willed himself silent. The man muttered something he couldn't hear, but he was very close, probably just on the other side of the log. *Trapped!* Thunder would follow, and he felt hot and wetness on his belly as he lost control of his bladder. Strangely, his body relaxed—resigned.

The man mumbled something else—the sound shot into him. And then, he heard footsteps going away. *Leaving!* As the noise faded, he gave himself over to pain again, hoping the blackness would return. But it would not.

The boy marked time as his knee pulsed with each beat of his heart. *"Give me a look."* Was that what the man had said? *"Give me a look."* The words floated back and forth in his mind. Strange-sounding, but eerily familiar. Finally, his ears attuned to the sounds of the forest, he rolled over on his side and sat up. Despair filled him as he stared down at the swollen, shiny lump that was his knee. He gently stroked the swelling with the palm of his hand, and then probed until a sharp pain made further investigation impossible. Willing against the ache, he tried his ankle; first one way, then the other—it hurt worst to turn his foot out. Methodically, he moved all his toes; and then flexed his knee ever so slightly. It hurt, but it did move, and that had to be a good sign. Reaching, he caught hold of a branch stub on the log and pulled himself up. Blood surging back into his knee brought a muffled groan. He scanned the forest around him.

He found what he was looking for: a wrist-thick branch. It was a little longer than he wanted, but a further search produced nothing better. He knotted the sack around the makeshift staff, and leaning hard against it, took his first step and winced. It was going to be a very long journey.

Darkness had long taken over the forest by the time the boy sat down next to the warm spring—his spring—and slowly lowered his body into the tepid water. With the help of a full moon and his knowledge of the immediate area, he'd managed to make the trip in one effort. He scooped handfuls of water into his parched mouth, and spat the thickness that had formed in the back of his throat. The walking staff he'd used was within reach, and he unknotted the cornmeal sack, reached in for a piece of meat, and settled back on the warm mud bank. The water helped ease the pain; or he'd gone beyond it. Either way, the pool felt wonderful, and for the first time in two days he felt relatively safe.

He chewed slowly with his eyes closed, envisioning the interior of the cabin again. The hearth stood out for some reason. He'd been drawn to it; and kneeling on the rough stone, a sense of belonging had settled on him for a moment. The black skillet and round-bottomed pot were familiar. He'd seen them before . . . but not there. His eyes popped open as confusion pushed the vision aside: then where? And the matches? Always on the hearth . . . and always forbidden! But by whom? He'd picked up the entire box, had them now, and there was no one to scold him. Strange.

He shut his eyes again and looked about the single room: the ax. It had stood by the door, and he'd picked it up. Why had the weight surprised him? If he knew about it, how could he have never used it? Forbidden? The gleaming tool stuck in the tree came to mind . . . that's where it belonged. It was always there, except . . . when it wasn't. A rueful smile formed, and then vanished as he remembered the big ax whooshing past his head. Then another image formed, of another tree, different from the one at the cabin. This one had the stub of a cut-off branch sticking out, and in it was an ax! The boy's eyes opened again, this time slowly as full discovery dawned on him.

His own cabin—he had lived in his own place, a place bigger and cleaner—the rank smell of the man's cabin came back to him: sweat and old grease. And a bed set against a wall, covered with a red blanket. A white garment came into focus—it too lay on a bed . . . his bed. His *nightshirt*! That tattered rag in the cave! The other cabin filled his mind: his cabin . . . his home. His and . . . others. There had to be *others*! The warm, clean, rediscovered place of his dreams faded, and gooseflesh formed on his arms. Looking up at the bright moon, a crushing loneliness swept over him. Throat aching, the lunar light took on a shimmer as the taste of salt crept past his lips and into his mouth.

He had to know.

After Lem's fruitless search for the Indian, he'd refilled his water bucket, and now sat on the bench. Weary from lack of sleep, he didn't even have the energy to go in and find something to eat. Besides, looking at the hearth reminded him he was without an easy way to make fire. He could; he'd done it the hard way before. A double charge of powder with no bullet shot more than enough blazing heat to start a fire; and then he'd keep it going. He knew the location of several heavy burls, slow burning and hard as a hammerhead; he'd go get one as soon as he rested a little. Losing the meat irritated him, but he had to make more anyway. "Little thief—I hope you choke on it," Lem muttered.

He stretched his feet out and crossed them at the ankles. Then, hands folded in his lap, he relaxed against the wall. Soon his mouth sagged open, and he began to snore.

Booneville. He spotted the haze above the slight bend in the river long before the settlement came into view, and started to hold to the south side. The lumber mill was on the upriver side of the town, and he needed to be tight against the bank when he rounded the bend. Pulling hard, he coaxed the unwieldy logs out of the mainstream and into the slower water by the shore to let them drift closer and closer to the landing. This time he didn't mind when the heavy oak butts rammed into the mud . . . and stuck. Lem beached his rowboat, clambered out, and started up the bank.

The sawyer's yard was a welter of rough-sawn planks, raw timber, and piles of sawdust and bark, all sitting in what looked like a permanent swamp of black mud and murky water. Lem strode across the muck and into a sturdy-looking log building. Behind a tool-cluttered table stood a burly man talking to someone; probably a customer by the looks of his clean clothes and nearly clean shoes. Both looked his way as he entered.

"Hello, Lem," the big man said. The second man barely tipped his head.

Lem acknowledged the greetings and then addressed the burly one: "Burt, I brought you a couple of logs. I'll be out in front."

Burt nodded, and Lem stepped back outside, nearly getting run down by a team of horses. Their big hooves splashing mud ahead of them, they dragged a twenty-inch log through the muck toward a saw pit at the far end of the yard. A well-spattered teamster, face red with exertion, slipped and skidded along behind them with the reins draped over one shoulder, arms fully extended. As they snorted past, the animals stepped over the planks that formed the walkway to the far side of what was supposed to be the street. The big log caught the edge of one and carried it several yards before it slipped under, mashed out of sight.

He had been outside only a few minutes when the townie emerged, followed by the mill owner.

"I'll get the boys right on that order, Mr. Sprague. Shouldn't be but a week or so."

The dapper man nodded, and then looked across the muddy morass to the other side of the road, dismay on his face.

"Looks like the skidder took out the walk again," Burt said, dryly.

Sprague gave him a sour look. "How's a person supposed to get across without ruining his clothes?"

"Fly?" Burt asked with a grin. "Ain't no way to get across without gettin' mucked up, Mr. Sprague. I put down new boards nearly every day—probably enough planks under all that muck to fill the order you just give me. Sometimes the teams skid over 'em, sometimes not. Just as well step off and clean up later."

The man hesitated, obviously looking for a place to plant his first step, then half leaped away from the building. Burt muffled a chortle behind his hand as Sprague's polished leather shoe disappeared into the muck.

"Damn!" the businessman swore, grabbing a handful of pants leg, and giving up his other shoe to the corruption. High stepping like a wet cat, he squished to the intact end of the boardwalk, turned to glare at Burt, and stomped out of the yard.

"Makes my heart feel good to see someone that clean get that dirty," said Burt. "Don't ya think?"

"Never thought about it, I guess."

"Well now, how can a man say he's been working when he looks like that at the end of the day?" Burt chuckled, and then looked toward the riverbank. "What did ya bring me?"

"Oak?" Lem offered hopefully.

"How big?"

"Come take a look." Lem stepped into the street, Burt right behind.

At the landing the mill owner stood, hands on his hips, and shook his head. "I was hoping, Lem, but didn't expect this."

"I know they're big." Lem's confidence began to crumble. "And I know the big ones are hard to cut up, but—"

"No, no, no." Burt held up a hand. "I was *hoping* for this. I got an order from downriver. They said the bigger the better—thirty-five inches, minimum. That big feller has to be close to four feet."

"Nearly fifty inches, if I'm judging it right." Lem felt hopeful again. "Took me a full week to get 'em down and swamped."

"I'll give seventeen dollars for the two of 'em."

Lem's jaw dropped but he couldn't make a sound come out.

Burt clapped him on the shoulder. "They're paying me extra for the big ones, Lem. Only fair I pass some of that on to you. On top of that, the cutters in that new settlement upriver from you can't supply them either."

"But seventeen? That's . . . somethin', Burt. I appreciate you for the man you are."

"Fair's fair. You going to stay the night, or start back upriver this afternoon?" Burt glanced up at the angling sun.

The image of the two voyageurs returned to Lem along with the uneasy feeling he'd had. "I've got a few things to get, and I'll be on my way. Can I throw my kit and rifle in your place till I get back?"

"Sure. Come on, then, and I'll git yer pay."

Lighthearted for the first time since he'd left home, Lem grabbed his knapsack and rifle and followed Burt back to the operator's log office.

The small town of Booneville appeared as rough as the frontier it served. From the sawyer's yard a street paralleled the river, with several short streets running back at right angles. Away from the riverfront, the roadway turned to hard-packed dirt, congested with people afoot like him, a few horseback riders, and wagons of all sizes. Everybody, it seemed, wanted to be where someone else was, and the noise created as they argued their rights hammered on Lem's ears. He slipped in behind a four-horse freight wagon that was making steady progress, and as luck would have it, soon turned onto the main business street.

One building stood out: the two-story hotel. Single level ramshackle structures made of lapboard, rough-sawn lumber, canvas, and log made up the rest. The first store he needed stood across the street from the hotel, and he followed the wagon until he reached it.

Packed almost wall-to-wall with everything a settler could need from axle grease to zinc-plated buckets, the single-room teemed with customers. Lem shouldered his way to a harried man standing behind a counter, waited until he caught the storekeeper's eye and asked, "Do you have ribbon, green ribbon?"

The man nodded. "How much and how wide?"

Lem shrugged. "It's for my daughter's hair—three feet of it."

With an audible sigh, the man walked around the end of the counter to a tall cabinet, got out a spool of dark green satin and yanked off enough to reach from his extended hand to his nose. He snipped off the length with a pair of scissors. "Anything else?"

"A hairbrush . . . and comb," Lem replied, then added, "For my wife."

The man deftly wound a double-ended loop of ribbon on his fingers as he hurried back behind the counter. Reaching under it, he brought out a box which he opened and presented to Lem. "Tortoise shell, the best," he offered, eyebrows raised. "Two dollars."

"I'll take it. And last, a knife, a real good one . . . and a sheath for it. For my boy."

The man immediately produced both and raised his eyebrows again.

"That's all."

"Three dollars and fifteen cents."

Lem paid, and the clerk yanked a length of paper off a roll to expertly wrap and bind the items. He then handed the package to Lem, and without another look, pointed his finger at another customer. Lem sidestepped his way through the crowd and back out the door.

He headed one street over to the next store he needed. His family would be proud of him for the price he'd gotten for the trees. And now Martin would have a knife of his own to sharpen; Mercy would have more ribbon than she could use; and best of all, his wife would have a new brush and comb for her beautiful hair. Lem was feeling good indeed.

The smell of the whiskey struck him long before he got near to the saloon. He licked his lips and gritted his teeth as he approached it. The door stood wide open and as he came even with it he paused to look inside. The place was packed as the mercantile had been, but a lot noisier. A man let out a long horselaugh, a woman squealed, and Lem felt the urge. He glanced up at the sun, then down at the ground and thought for a several seconds.

"No," he muttered, and continued on.

There were only a few things to get at the grocery store, and he was soon on his way back down the riverfront street with his packages under his arms. The muddy lumberyard was not as busy; all the men were working the saws. He slogged through the slop to his boat where he stowed his purchases under a tarp, then trudged back to the office for his rifle and bag. He entered through the open door.

Burt looked up from a ledger. "That didn't take ya long."

"Didn't need much."

"Then ya got time for a whiskey!" Burt slammed the book closed and stood. "My treat, so I'm not takin' no for an answer." The big man stepped around the desk in a single stride.

"I really should be—"

"You're not going to get back today no matter what, and an extra half hour or so tomorrow ain't gonna make no difference." Burt slapped him on the back. "Right?"

"Right . . . one. We'll have *one,* and then I'll get going."

"Now you're talkin'. Leave your kit and rifle right where they are. Anything ya put in your rowboat will be fine. The fellas will look out for it." Burt maneuvered him out the door. "Hard as you work, you deserve a drink when you get to town."

Lem mused: He's got a point. At least one drink for all the sweat I put into those two trees. Yeah, two trees. Maybe two drinks. They crossed the broken boardwalk and headed up the busy street for Burt's favorite saloon.

He couldn't decide which was more annoying: the gut-turning motion of his bed, or the heat of the sun on the side of his face. Slowly, the fact that his bed should not be moving at all, and that the sun does not shine on his bed emerged through the mental mist: he wasn't in bed! His eyes opened as his head rose sharply from the tarp stuffed in the bow; the pain made him nauseous and he knew he was going to puke. Struggling to get his arms under him, he put his hands on the cold slime in the bottom of the boat, and realized he already had . . . probably several times. *Burt! That damn Bur—my money!* His hand slapped his buttoned shirt pocket, and he felt and heard coins. Not robbed at least; but his head—every heartbeat made it swell and pulse. Oh, to slow *that* down!

He rolled over, got his knees under him, and sat up on his haunches. Two men at the far end of the yard stopped working and pointed; their laughter carried loud and clear in the mid-morning air, adding insult to indignity. He glanced at Burt's office; the door was closed. Lem struggled to his feet, climbed out of the boat as carefully as he could, then headed for the building. His head felt every step of the way, and when he got there, he hopefully tried the door, and it opened.

As Lem had suspected, Burt wasn't there. He picked up his rifle and pack, and went back outside. Two more men were now atop the cradle at the saw pit, and their raucous bellowing almost drove him back inside. He did his best to ignore them as he trudged back to the boat and stowed his rifle and bag under the tarp with his other things.

Untying from the heavy stake in the ground, he threw the coiled rope into the craft, grabbed the bow, and shoved. He muttered a prayer of thanks as the boat moved easily toward the water and then he piled in as it floated free. The cold water felt good and he reached over the side and splashed several handfuls over his head and neck. *Damn whiskey.*

Grimacing against the head pain, and hating the smell of his clothes, Lem maneuvered into the slack water and bent his back to the long and arduous task of getting home. He glanced at the sun and what he felt only made his head hurt that much more. No matter how hard he worked, even rowing into the dark hours—a dangerous thing—he'd be home a day later than he'd said. His wife was not going to be very happy. Worse yet, he knew she'd spend the day worrying. *Damn Burt.*

CHAPTER 8

With a gasp and a snort, the boy wakened with the sting of water in his nose. Confused and frightened, he struck out with both hands, meeting only the water around him. Then he realized where he was: sitting chest deep in his warm pool. A twinge reminded him why, and he reached down and felt his swollen knee. It was better now, he thought, and moved his lower leg gingerly; much better. With a sigh of relief, he relaxed against the bank while his heart slowed, and offered a rueful half smile to the bright moon.

The cabin. Not the one a morning away, but the one he now saw in his mind; he looked at it across a wide clearing. Neat and sturdy-looking, a large wooden tub hung on the right wall. A pair of benches stood in front, one on the left under a window, and another right of the door; on it sat a large bowl and a wooden bucket. *You washed your face there!* The thought brought his wrinkled hands out of the water and he stared at them like they didn't belong to him. The cool night air chilled them. Overwhelmed with fatigue, he sat upright in the warm water; the air was definitely cold.

He turned to one side, got his left knee under him, and braced his hands on the bank to stand up. In the moonlight he could see the knee was still swollen, but not as badly as he remembered. He crawled out of the water, dragging his right leg until he got hold of his walking stick. Using it, he levered himself upright, grabbed the meal sack, and started for his cave.

The bucket in the bag bumped against his leg and he stopped. If he had water he could stay in the cave for two or three days; he had food now, and fire if he wanted it. His common sense argued with the pain in his leg and the need for sleep. With a sigh, he took out the tin bucket. It hurt to stoop, but he ignored the pain, and filled the vessel to the brim. Setting his teeth hard together, he started out again for the cave, sloshing water with every lurching step.

By the time he crawled into his den, he was chilled to the bone and the warm rock felt good on his naked body. He lay down on his bed, pulled the dirty-white piece of cloth over his hips and chest, and before he could think about his discomfort, he fell asleep.

Run! His mind aflame, stark terror drove all but that single thought from his head. Out the cabin door and into the bright moonlight, he sprinted across the clearing, his nightshirt ripping at the side seam as he stretched his stride. He knew any second he'd feel a hand on his shoulder, or hear the rough breath of his pursuer, or—his stomach turned with fear—hear the air-splitting crack of a rifle. Pain ripped across his belly as he charged straight through a blackberry bush. Then he was beyond the edge of the clearing and into the trees.

Which way? Not the path to the river, but into the ridges to the north, the roughest ground he knew about. He was small; he could fit where the monster could not; the thickest woods, the heaviest brush. The thoughts flashed into and out of his mind in an instant, and he turned and dove headlong into a thicket. Under the cover of the vines and leaves, he lay still and listened: nothing. Then he realized he held a knife—a butchering knife, big, with a heavy wooden handle. Still dazed, he turned the long blade to the weak light and gasped at the blood-covered steel.

His attention was torn from the glistening blade by the sharp crack of a dry branch. He strained to hear what he feared would follow: another snap, to his left. He tensed, focused on the silence, and then heard leaves rustling, closer now. Stomach knotted, he fought the urge to scream. Peering through the tangle of vines, he willed his pursuer to reveal himself, to make some move that would show where he was. Then, ever so carefully, the boy reached out with both hands and parted the hanging vines that blocked his view.

Wild hair was all he could see: a devil's halo around the dimly lit visage; black and tangled, it framed a face that wasn't there. It growled, "Arrrrgh!" and a hand shot through the opening.

Powerful fingers clamped viciously on his shoulder, close to his neck. The boy spun free, and ducked as the hand made another attempt to snag him. Tingling with fear, he darted deeper into the thicket. *Small,* the thought flashed, *get small.* He dropped into a crouch, and angled to the right, deeper into the woods. Then he was beyond the heavy cover and in open forest. He stood, and without a look back, ran as fast as his skinny legs would carry him; the full moon was so bright he could see the color of the trees. His bare feet pounding the ground frightened him; could his pursuer hear it too? His nightshirt ripped as it caught a branch, the brief tug at the garment hardly noticed.

The ground rose as he approached the first ridge, and his flight slowed. His breathing rasped, and his lungs started to burn. At the crest he knew there was a line of stunted oaks, and just beyond that a cliff that dropped sheer to a fast-moving stream. The creek was wide there, and shallow, with large rocks exposed in the water, except for one deep, wide hole where he'd fished with his father. But which way to turn? To the left and he'd face an even steeper climb; to the right were thickets so dense that even the animals avoided them—and then the river.

The slope was noticeable now, his speed much reduced as he struggled to keep his feet under him. He slipped often, falling to one knee only to scramble up again and continue. He could not seem to get enough air, and his head hummed with the exertion. The urge to stop and listen nagged him, but he charged ahead, gritting his teeth against the pain growing in his side; he knew it would eventually release its grip on him—he'd run hard before. He glanced up at the treetops, silhouettes against the starry sky. *Almost there—keep going—run harder.*

His foot shot out from under him, and with reflexes too slow to recover: he crashed to the ground. This time he stayed on his hands and knees, head down, air wheezing in and out of tortured lungs. He could not muster the strength to go on, and closed his eyes against defeat. The sound of his hammering heart filled his head, and he felt his pulse behind his jaws. *Rest.* He needed to rest for a little. The thought drifted lazily into and out of his consciousness. Just stay here for a while, his tired body urged, and let the cool earth soothe the hot muscles. He was spent.

Slowly he opened his eyes, and it took several seconds for the dull gleam of the knife's blade to register. He stared at it, still grasped tightly in his hand, and the feeling of total despair he had felt only moments before ebbed slightly. He wasn't completely defenseless. The boy rose to his haunches and raised his weapon to eye level. As he turned it slowly in the moonlight, the sight gave him strength, and he got to his feet. How long had he been down? His throat was so dry it was painful to swallow, but his heart had slowed to normal. He glanced up the slope and felt a surge of hope: almost there! A long stone's throw and he'd be on top. He scrambled up against the steep incline, and soon stood in the narrow line of trees that crowned the ridge.

He had a clear view by the night sky in front of him; a few

strides away, the sharply defined edge of the cliff. Indecision held him fast in the soft dirt of the sheltered summit. Which way to go? Or did he have to go? Maybe he should stay right there; shinny up a tree and spend the night. It would be a lot safer to move around the forest in daylight. He could see any danger before it—

The sound flew up from below and hit him like a punch in the chest; a furious thrashing of brush. His pursuer was right behind him, and charging hard. He considered the rising ridge to his left; he could not climb the steep ground the way his legs felt now: muscles quivering, knees unsteady. And down the ridge? Moonlight made the dense brush look even heavier. He'd likely be trapped.

He glanced down at the knife and his mouth dropped open in surprise; the white sleeve of his nightshirt almost glowed in the moonlight! Angrily, he threw the blade on the ground, jerked the calf-length garment over his head and knelt. Laying the knife on the top part, he rolled it up, folding the ends as he went.

He could hear the pursuer now; rocks kicked loose and clattering down the slope. Desperately, the boy looked for a place to hide; the trunk of a tree near the cliff's edge seemed thick enough, and he ran to it. Ducking behind, he stood with his back pressed hard against the rough bark and listened.

The sound of gasping breaths drifted to him on the still air, and the hair on his neck bristled. As his tracker slowly gained control of his breathing, the boy realized he'd made a huge mistake: he had no place to run, and running was his best defense. He strained to hear anything; the sickness in his stomach returned when he realized that the labored breathing had stopped, and complete silence settled over the moonlit scene. The boy concentrated on not moving; even his chest ceased to rise and fall with his breathing.

A metallic click stiffened his spin. The boy moved only his eyes, straining to see. There, to his left! The dark shape of a man. He looked as big as a bear. With a rifle held across his chest, he approached the edge of the cliff not thirty feet away, moving very slowly, head casting from side to side. In the bright moonlight, the shirt on the man's right shoulder and arm looked wet and dark. The man stopped a few feet back from the lip of the precipice, put his rifle butt on the ground, and leaned the muzzle against his chest. He reached inside his shirt with his left hand and groaned. It was the sound of someone who hurt. The figure turned slightly to his right and something glinted in the light . . . one eye. The other side of the man's face glistened, his bushy beard plastered to his neck: a bloody mess!

Another moan, and the giant drew his hand out of his shirt and struggled visibly to get hold of his rifle with his right hand again. He started toward the boy's hiding place, his head down, moving carefully and slowly; then he stopped exactly where the boy had stood only minutes before. The man dropped his rifle butt to the ground again and stood, his right hand hanging down, and looked at the ground.

The boy knew he was discovered as soon as the man turned and took his first step toward the edge. Two steps more, and he would be in line with the tree that hid the boy; his hiding place had become a trap. If he bolted for the heavy brush, the man would have a clear view of him long enough to shoot; the same was true if he tried to run back the way he came. He shifted his gaze to the top of a tree just beyond the rimrock: it was the large beech that had sheltered his father's fishing hole. Could he?

He'd watched squirrels; and he'd seen some make spectacular leaps. From high in a tree, they'd venture as far as a branch would take them, and then jump. Many times he'd see them miss the first branch only to fall onto the next, and grab hold.

He looked at the treetop again. *Jump and grab hold.* But what if he missed? Would the top branches hold his weight? Would the man see him in time to raise his rifle and shoot? Should he throw the nightshirt and knife ahead of him, or hang onto them?

"Welp!" The single word snapped through the air like a whip.

He jerked around to see the man looking directly at him. No more time to think: he shoved off from the tree with his free hand and took the first of the several long steps he'd need to reach the edge. As he charged across the ground, he heard the ominous mechanical crackle of a hammer being drawn and glanced to his left. The long-barreled rifle rising to the level spurred him on; he tried to stretch his stride, and his legs nearly failed him. Then, two more steps and with all the strength he could summon, he jumped. *Too far!*

He knew it as soon as his feet left the ground. Even as the thought formed, a brilliant orange flash erupted in the dark and a bullet hissed past his head, followed by a clap of thunder. His feet pedaling for balance, one arm outstretched, the very top of the tree flashed under him as he dropped like a shot quail. The first branch he struck slowed him very little, catching his foot and starting to turn him upside down. The second was bigger, and resisted until it broke with a sharp snap and delivered him headfirst onto another one. His attempts to grab hold left him with nothing but a handful of leaves and a certainty that lit up his brain like a flaring match: he was not going to stop until he smashed into the rocks at the base of the cliff. He shut his eyes tight and clutched the rolled-up nightshirt to his chest.

The shock of the icy water was completely lost to the excruciating pain that followed a split second later as his right knee slammed into a sharp rock on the creek's bottom. With the agonizing jolt, he gulped a huge mouthful of water, felt his throat spasm, and then choked. He clawed at the water and stabbed his left leg down in a frenzied attempt to touch the bottom. A cry almost escaped him when he planted his foot on the rough bottom while his head remained above the water. A sharp stab of pain shot through his knee when he tried to set his right foot down.

Looking up at the ridge, he could see nothing but the big tree he'd just crashed through. The current in the middle of the creek pushed hard against his chest, and he let himself move with it. *The knife!* He looked upstream to see nothing, then turned slowly around. To his left, and floating just under the surface, the white bundle appeared almost radiant in the water. He hopped over, grabbed the rolled-up garment, and hugged it. Looking up at the full moon, he could barely suppress a shout: he'd done it! He'd survived the leap. Ignoring the dull ache in his right leg, he started for the far shore, and then stopped. The warm glow of exhilaration chilled as another truth struck him: he'd made it down . . . and so would his pursuer. Reversing course, he started for the cliff side of the creek, moving in the water as quietly as an otter.

He let the current carry him along in the shelter of the overhanging trees and bushes for what seemed like hours. Many times the creek spread wide and he tumbled over the rocks trying to avoid a cracked head, always listening and watching the ridgeline to his right, now dropping much lower. His teeth chattered against the cold, and he began to lose the feeling in his feet. The moon had dropped behind the creek-side trees when he couldn't stand the cold anymore. Numb and shaking, he made for the left shore.

The dry grass on the bank felt wonderful, and the pain from his knee was somehow masked by the numbing cold. Still, he favored it as he crawled toward a large tree with a mass of vines entangled at its base. Dry leaves crunched as he crept into the shelter of the thicket. In the dim light, he scooped together as much loose debris as he could find, piled it up and burrowed into the middle. Pulling his legs up to his chest, he hugged them for warmth. Gradually, his teeth quit clicking, and when his knee began to ache, his fatigued body overwhelmed his desire to stay awake and he lost consciousness.

The cave floor warmed him much more than the pile of leaves he recalled in the last wisp of his dream. He couldn't decide if it was the smell of roasted meat or the dull throb in his knee that had roused him, but his eyes popped opened. He gently massaged his swollen knee. The agony of yesterday's long walk had left him, or so he thought until he tried to straighten his leg—it refused to respond. Steeling himself, he sat up and with both hands forced the leg to extend fully; he held it there. Gradually, the brilliant pain subsided as the bruised muscles relaxed, and he let go the pressure. The relief was immediate, and he let out a sigh.

Now he knew why he was here. The image of the dark man on the ridge returned: wild hair, matted beard, guttural voice rumbling from a face he couldn't see. The monster had wanted him dead, and he'd escaped into the forest. And the dark man had been relentless, pursuing him for days on end; and though never close enough to be heard or seen, never far behind. This was the creature that used to visit him in the night; the thing he knew had waited for him in the darkness. Until it had not anymore. Why? Now it pursued him in daylight; it had shot at him again. Or was it the man with the ax who had chased him?

They were the same thing! His heart raced, and he glanced at the cave's entrance. What if the dark man had managed to follow him here? What if he was waiting outside, rifle trained on the opening to his sanctuary? He recalled the terror of his dream, being caught behind the tree with no place to run. Nothing could have been worse; unless it was being caught in a cave with little water, and no way out but one narrow opening. He stared at the light filtering in, stared until he dropped his head and shut his eyes against the possibility. But the thought would not go away: he was trapped.

CHAPTER 9

Damn Burt. Lem opened one eye and for a few seconds stared across the open clearing, hoping the dream in his head would die. He knew it wasn't Burt who should be damned. He winced as he remembered the day; one he'd relived a hundred times, and one he'd remember a thousand more: the splitting whiskey head, the river's relentless current, and the sure knowledge that he was unworthy of a faithful wife. He didn't want to, but his conscience gave him little choice; his thoughts went back to that late April day on the water.

Lem rowed, his flannel shirt stained dark with sweat. The narrow seat cut into the backs of his legs, and his arms and shoulders threatened to cramp with every stroke of the oars. Salt-blurred eyes kept track of the shoreline, and he steered as close to the bank as he dared, giving thanks for any stretch of slack water. He glanced over his shoulder and groaned; the river was turning again, which meant he had to cross to the other side for the slower water. He strained to make as much headway as he could, and when the current caught the bow, rowed furiously at an angle to the shore, fighting to maintain the upriver progress he'd made.

By the time he reached the other side, he could no longer lift his left oar out of the water; the muscles simply refused to obey his will. Shipping both oars, he glided onto shore, and slumped to the bottom of the boat, his head resting on the rear seat. The sun had just begun its afternoon decline.

The sound of crows woke him. He opened one eye just enough to see them: nearly a dozen in a nearby tree, pecking and squabbling as each maneuvered for the space of another. Lem flexed the muscles in his shoulders, winced, and sat up. The bird in the very top of the roost let out a squawk, and the whole flock took off downriver. "I'm not dead yet, ya black devils," Lem muttered. "Go find something else to eat."

Eat? The word teased his dulled wit. Was it any wonder he couldn't continue rowing? He glanced at the sun. It had slipped a bit toward the western bluffs, but not by very much, so he hadn't slept long. Cursing himself for not being able to remember if he'd eaten last light, he realized it could have been as long as twenty-four hours since he'd had solid food. He dug his knapsack out of the bow and opened it. The cornbread squares in the oiled-paper sack hadn't fared well at all. Digging further, he found a small clay jug full of molasses. He set both on the seat, and found another wrapped package that contained thin slices of hard, smoked ham. Gathering it all up, he climbed out of the boat, and moved into the shade of the crows' tree.

He couldn't remember when anything had tasted so good. Twice, the salty ham drove him to the water, and his hands were a sticky mess, but he could feel energy returning to his arms and shoulders. Fourteen hours of rowing was about what it took to get him home. The hours he'd wasted niggled him, and he resolved to make them up by staying on the river longer and rowing harder. His family certainly deserved that.

Martin would be tickled with his knife. Lem knew that he didn't dote on him much, but then that's how a man was made; that was how his father raised him. Still, Lem smiled as he conjured up the image. He'd wait until after supper; wouldn't even let on that he'd bought the little man anything. He could see the brave face the boy would put on when Mercy got her ribbon. Her eyes—why had he never looked at them? He'd noticed her striking beauty; as young as she was, he could see the shape of her face was exceptional, straight nose, cheeks that narrowed perfectly to a mouth made to smile. He remembered the smile, and felt the mellow warmth as he dwelled on the thought: Lord, she was perfect. He'd be sure to look in her eyes when he gave her the long strip of green silk.

And his wife—she'd be so pleased with the brush. All she had now was a bone comb. Lem imagined her sitting on the end of the bed as she stroked her soft brown hair with it. He loved to watch her, to touch it—which sometimes led to more than just touching. The new brush would make her long tresses gleam. She worked so hard for them, and was such a good mother. God had blessed him three times. Lem heaved a sigh, and had just started to get up when he saw them again.

The same two men, only this time the big one sat in the bow, and he wasn't working. In the stern the smaller man bent to his task, his floppy hat with the cardinal-red kerchief dipping with each stroke as he paddled furiously. The canoe was moving very fast downstream, and soon came abreast of Lem, not forty feet offshore. Lem remembered the striped shirt and tall beaver, but the big man wasn't wearing the hat. Instead, his mop of black hair appeared stuck to his bare head, and his shirt was stained black and red on the left side. He was wounded! The canoe shot past, the smaller man looking neither left nor right, the sun flashing off the paddle as it changed sides. They soon moved out of sight.

A sick feeling rose in Lem's throat as he gathered his things and hurried to the boat. Shoving off, he scrambled into his seat, and then leaned into the oars, bending them as he pitted his strength against the current. The day before yesterday they'd been on their way upriver, probably to a new settlement. Burt had said something about that . . . hadn't he? Yes! He'd mentioned the woodsmen there didn't have any big logs. His angst subsided a little. But they couldn't be coming back already; not time enough. Then why? They must have had an accident; got caught in a snag, maybe, or got attacked and robbed by river pirates. Maybe some Indians took an opportunity. Could have been anything; no reason to think the worst. No need at all.

The tempo of his oars in the water was as regular as his laboring heart. Through the afternoon, shipping his oars only long enough to take a drink, Lem beat his way against the relentless river. The fire in his muscles eventually gave way to a merciful numbness that still allowed him to go on.

As the sun dipped below the bluffs, he started to look for a long sandbar or stretch of beach; to row in the dark was to court disaster. The traders in the canoe were proof of that. The odds were good that's exactly what the two strangers had done. In a hurry to get their pay they'd paddled right into trouble. Lem grunted—one big snag and you fed the fish. Just as the light failed, a patch of bare shore appeared, and Lem nosed the boat toward it.

Ashore, the fire offered some cheer, and Lem tried to relax. His arms and back throbbed dully, and flat ground felt wonderful on his tortured rump. He slowly chewed a slice of the pork, and absently picked five-finger pinches of demolished cornbread from the sack. Transferring crumbs to the palm of his hand, he dribbled the brown treacle on it, and licked it up.

His wife would be cleaning up after supper right now, humming one of those spirituals she loved. Mercy loved them too, and was always after her mother to teach her the words. He wasn't sure it was a good idea before the little girl was old enough to understand the meanings; but he suspected the two of them conspired against him and did it anyway. And that was all right too, he thought. The Good Lord gave him a lot of comfort when he needed it; like now. God surely wouldn't let anything bad happen to his family.

After washing the stickiness off his hands, Lem spread his bedroll and stretched out. Dusk had turned into darkness; the night skies a cathedral with the ultimate vaulted ceiling, arching from the buttresses of the riverbanks through infinity and back again. He stared into the depths of the night's black sky; though perforated countless times by points of starlight, it still maintained its mystery of darkness. Pulling his blanket up to his chin, Lem whispered his nightly prayer of thanksgiving and a request for a good new day. The soft cadence of the lapping water, steady and even, murmured quietly to him; the river's lullaby.

Lem awoke at first light, had breakfast, and was making good time upriver before the sun cracked over the eastern shore. He'd slept undisturbed, and his body felt new, full of life. The morning mist burned off rapidly and he started looking for the landmarks that would tell him he was close to home. It was always a joy to get back to his family, and as he stroked along the left-hand shore, his heart grew lighter.

The money he'd gotten from Burt—Lem felt a little flash of anger as the name popped into his head—made the coming summer a pleasure to think about. Summers were hard; he sometimes cut fourteen hours a day, taking advantage of the fair weather. This year it would pay off; Burt had told him the demand for the larger trees was strong and Lem knew where to find a dozen more of the monstrous oaks. As he rowed he visualized where each of the mighty trees stood, and planned how he'd get them to the water. He glanced at the far shore and a familiar feature—he was making good time.

Eventually, the next bend to the right became the last one, and Lem smiled. A final traverse to the far shore, a quarter mile upstream in the slow water, and then hard across—he'd be home. He leaned into the oars with renewed vigor for the next half hour, and then headed over. The current was strong, but his need to get home felt even stronger, and he fetched up almost directly across the river from the two big trees that bracketed his landing. Difficult as it was, he continued upriver; he had to gain the distance needed to cross back without overshooting his place. The sun was well up when he pulled hard on his right oar and turned his bow into the middle of the river.

Lem didn't let up until he rammed the bow of the boat into the soft bank. He scrambled out, tied the mooring line to one of the trees, and snatched up his knapsack and rifle. His feet raised dust in the winding path as he hurried. Craning his neck, he rounded the last curve and heaved a sigh; the door was wide open. He'd been afraid they might be out in the forest gathering roots and he'd have to wait—but they were home. Hiking his pack a little higher, he hurried across the clearing, a grin growing wider as he came closer to the door.

"Rhoda?" he called as he entered.

The cabin stank and dirty dishes cluttered the table. And the door to the bedroom hung crooked . . . on one hinge! Something was—

"Rhody!"

Lem threw down his pack and sprinted across the room, his rifle crashing to the floor. As he grasped the doorknob, his shoes crunched on broken glass and he looked down. The base of the oil lamp lay on the floor, the chimney smashed; his whole body chilled. Grabbing the edge of the crooked door, he jerked it open.

Blood, black and sticky-looking, covered the floor at his feet and spattered the wall to his right. And then he saw her on the floor. Mercy's unseeing eyes were turned back in her head. Her swollen tongue hung halfway out of her mouth; purple, it displayed a crescent of teeth-marks, blue-black tracks of desperation. Her face and neck carried a mass of bruises, and deep purple formed a band that followed the curve of her jaw. Naked legs, blood-smeared and awkwardly bent, begged to be brought together again. Lem knelt beside her and gently, reverently, righted the violation as best he could, then spread the thin blanket she clutched tightly in her hand over her crumpled body. Tears spurted from his eyes, falling on her battered face, and with a final look, he covered her completely.

Lem knew where his wife was; her bare legs hung over the end of the bed. He got off his knees and went to her. As he came to the edge of the bed, he inhaled sharply, and his head jerked to one side. Slowly, he turned his gaze back. The sight of her face caused his whole body to tremble and he clenched his teeth and bunched his fists. Her lower lip had been torn away, exposing teeth crusted with blood. One eye was swollen shut; the other coldly stared back at him. Her exposed breasts bore teeth marks, deep and savagely inflicted.

Lem grabbed the quilt that lay wadded beside her, then leaned over and touched her hair with the tips of trembling fingers. "Rhoda," he whispered, "how can this be?" He spread the cover over his wife's ravaged body and looked at the scene for a few seconds, strangely calm. His tears had stopped.

Martin! Two strides took Lem to the far side of the room and the tiered bed. The top bunk was empty, its blankets turned back neatly, almost undisturbed. He looked at the berth below, Mercy's. Her straw tick lay half off the bed, and he got down on his knees and peered under it. Nothing. He went to his own bed and looked under it, then left the bedroom.

After a quick look around, he picked up his rifle and went to the door. Clearly visible in the dirt, man-sized tracks led to the house. Looking right, he studied the ground, then dropped to one knee to examine a single, small, bare footprint, and beyond it, another appeared—then another, but coming the other way. Easily, he followed the tracks halfway to the privy. The boy had been out there when it happened. Lem hurried back to the house.

"Martin!" The faint echo returned to him unanswered. "It's Pa!" Lem cupped his hands to his mouth and shouted again. "Boy!" Nothing.

Lem slumped down on the bench in frustration. Where would he go, barefooted? Holding his hands on top of his head, he suppressed a scream. Then he saw more footprints, small ones. Plain as day and right in front of him, they led off to the left. Lem scrambled to his feet. The first one was smeared, the second much farther along than he expected, the third the same. A boy running! Lem followed, his eyes glancing up as he went, trying to figure the general direction. The tracks headed straight for the ridges—smart lad.

He easily followed the trail until he got to the edge of the clearing. The prints led directly into a blackberry bush, and Lem stopped. Nobody ran through *that* on purpose. He stooped over and studied the mark, then took a long stride and looked again. The next print appeared *inside* the grasping vines. Oh, Lord, the boy must have been terrified. Lem found his way around the brambles, and located where the boy had come out the other side. Slowly and carefully he tracked him into a dense thicket. Impressions of the boy's bare feet were plain in the soft soil. Then he spotted blood; not very much, but his heart felt sick as he examined the leaves it stuck to. He'd fought. And he's climbing into the ridges.

Lem cast back and forth until he broke the trail again. A single glance told him where to go. An hour later, he topped the ridge and stood in the line of scrub oak. Where from here? The ground rose sharply to his left, too steep and rugged for a boy. Ahead were the sheer cliffs. That meant he went to the right and into the thickets that stretched all the way to the river . . . of course. He'd get down on his knees and follow the animal trails. Lem had shown them to him when the boy was almost small enough to walk through standing up. He started along the crest, searching the ground. Halfway across an open space between some trees he stopped.

Blood, unmistakable in the dirt, alongside the rounded impressions of the boy's bare feet. Lines of dark purple formed obscene art in the soil as it flowed from the boy. There! A small pool of it where he'd stood still a moment. Lem imagined the boy's blood dripping off the tips of his fingers. And worse . . . trampled over the top were the deeper prints of a man. The tracks led to the cliff, and Lem's heart went out of him as he followed the tracks to the edge. The boy's footprints were nowhere to be seen. *The ogre had thrown him over!* For a moment, Lem looked down at the rock-strewn creek below, and then spun around and went back to his boy's bloodstained track. Fury banished his sorrow, and he slowly closed his hands into fists: "I trusted You!" he raged at the sky. "How could You let this happen?" He dropped to his knees, leaned over and pounded the dirt where his son's life had leaked out.

He didn't remember the walk back to the cabin, and his mind remained blank as he dug two graves beside it. He laid the loves of his life in the ground; his wife with her new brush on her chest; his daughter with a green ribbon twined in her hands; and covered them both with the damp earth. Never again would he touch the gleaming hair; and closed forever, the beautiful eyes he'd never noticed.

The task complete, Lem slumped to the ground in front of the cabin and leaned against the wall. Staring across the clearing toward the river, the image of the hulking brute in the front of a canoe came to him and darkness swept over him. He embraced it; bitterness burned in his throat, and his heart felt the cold touch of hate—he sensed its power; it felt good, and filled him with resolve.

CHAPTER 10

"Mercy!"

The boy heard the scream and bolted upright, soaked in sweat, and stared wide-eyed into the pitch-black. Where? What was it? Chest heaving, he put his hands out in front of him, warding off whatever it might be, but felt nothing. Heard and sensed nothing. There was nothing in the cave . . . his safe cave. *Bad dream.* He breathed a long sigh and put his hands down.

A twinge of pain reminded him of his knee and of the man at the cabin. Feeling around in the darkness, he found the meal sack and took out the tin of matches and a candle. He struck the lucifer on the sand-rough side of the container, and darkness fled before the flash of fire. Putting the flame to the candlewick, he held the light above his head.

For the first time he really saw the inside of his lair. What he'd thought was a solid back wall had an opening in the far corner. The raccoon's carcass seemed to move as he shifted the candle back and forth. He wondered if the meat would stink by now. He had to pee.

Using the walking stick, he got up, gingerly put his right foot down, and was pleased that his knee would take some weight. Holding onto the candle, he hobbled to the back of the cave and over to the breach on the left. The entrance was as square as if cut by a mason. Stepping through, he found the ceiling rose out of sight, and the floor was no longer smooth rock, but a layer of fine sand. He continued, staying close to the wall, and found the gallery turned off to his right. His candle flickered as a draft of air swept past from behind him. Far enough. He leaned his stick against the wall and wet down the sand.

Back at the front of the cave he found a place for the candle, and in the soft glow of its light, he felt the carcass of the raccoon. It no longer felt stiff so he picked it up and smelled it. Not as good as the meat in the sack, he thought, but he'd learned the hard way not to waste anything. Picking up the knife, he sliced off several strips of the fatty meat.

One bite of the raw meat was all he needed. He put the rest down and glanced at the dark cave entrance. Did he dare go out? The one who hunted him used a rifle, and needed enough light to see. There was a large deadfall not ten steps away from the entrance; enough wood to last for weeks. He pictured it in his mind, took a deep breath against the pain he knew he'd feel, and ducked outside. The moon had departed and it was very dark. His leg took the strain well; it hurt, but it worked. After listening for a few seconds, he moved quietly to the tree, and feeling his way around on the ground, started to gather the dry wood.

A few minutes later he was back in the cave, his arms loaded with sticks. He walked through the newly discovered portal, around a corner, and into the more spacious cavern at the back. There he dumped the firewood, and then went back out to gather up everything he had and move it as well.

Layering large pieces on top of small—where'd he learn that?—he assembled a small stack of wood and lit three tiny twigs at the bottom with the candle. He sat and watched as the fire ate hungrily at the tinder, soon creating enough light to show him the entire cave.

The ceiling arched roughly to a height about five times his own and ran back a further twenty paces. The smoke from this small campfire rose straight up and disappeared. Where to? He stepped well away from the blaze, and studied the ceiling in the flickering light. The smoke was definitely going somewhere. He shrugged, and went back to where he'd been sitting.

After the fire had burned to a small bed of coals, he sharpened a suitable branch, skewered three strips of raccoon flesh, planted one end of the stick in the sand, and settled back to watch his meal cook. Soon glistening fat bubbled out of the meat, and dripped into the fire. He rotated the stick to cook the other side, and licked his lips. He felt safe; almost comfortable. This far into the cave his fire could not be seen from outside; he had plenty of wood, a way to carry water, two large pieces of cloth, two coonskins; and his knife. A sly smile slipped over his lips.

He missed the mysterious warmth of the rock out front, but the fire more than made up for it. Gingerly, he stripped the last piece of meat off the stick and popped it into his mouth, sucking air past his teeth to cool it off. While he chewed, he sliced more strips from the coon. It was something else he'd learned: eat all you can, while you can. He speared the flesh, a larger piece this time, and fixed it over the fire.

After his meal, he took the jerky out of the bag, stacked it on the stiffened raccoon skin, and then stuffed the meal sack with some of his original bedding material. He lay on it now, his legs extending past onto the sand. With the dirty nightshirt spread over him, he rested his head on his hands and tried to relax. He was comfortable enough, but . . . ? He knew he'd gorged himself until his swollen belly would take no more, but he'd done that before. He shifted again on his makeshift mattress.

Was it just the change in location? It was the same cave, after all. Eyes wide open and ears alert, he felt the darkness was complete, as was the silence. That was it! Out front, even on the blackest night, some light, even if only a sense of it, managed to make its way in. And occasionally he heard something: an owl, or a night creature of some sort that dared to take a peek at what lived in the dark hole. But back here it was black, and dead quiet. The boy fumbled in the dark until he found both a candle and the tin of matches. Standing a candle up in the sand, he lit it, and then studied the ceiling for a few minutes. Slowly his imagination yielded to his need to sleep, and he shut his eyes. The light continued to play in the shadows above his head as his breathing became slow and steady, his body still.

"Take a light." The words stopped him in mid-step. "I don't want you surprising a skunk." His mother's soft voice floated across the room. "Come over here, and I'll light the lamp."

"It's a full moon, Mom," he whispered. "I'll see them."

"I want them to see you . . . so you *don't* see them."

"Okay." With outstretched hands, he crossed the floor until he bumped into her bed and made his way around to the far side. There he waited until he heard the oil lamp's chimney come off, then shut his eyes against the glare of the flaring match.

"There," she said.

He opened his eyes, took the lamp and left the bedroom, crossing to the door in front, and stepping out into the night. The moon was just topping the trees, casting an even but subdued light across the clearing. Martin loved to be out on a night like this. The urgency that had awakened him hastened his trip down the path to the privy. Too many lily roots; he'd known it after he'd eaten about his tenth. Once there, he went in, left the door ajar, and sat.

His guts settled again, he'd just picked up his lamp when the eerie screech of a night owl stood the fine hairs of his body on end. He instantly knew what it was; but the sound wasn't one that could be taken in stride. His father had told him that small ground dwellers suffered the same reaction. They knew the owl was up high, perched where he could see the forest floor, so they hid. The high-pitched scream was meant to unnerve a rodent and send it scampering from its hiding place to the safety of its burrow. The owl depended on keen eyesight, and the silence of its soft-feathered wings, to see and then pounce on the fleeing prey.

The boy put the lamp on the plank seat and closed the door as he left. He'd watched this nocturnal drama before, and was anxious to see it again. Once more the owl screeched, and the boy made his way toward the sound, moving quietly from tree to tree, shadow to shadow, deeper into the woods. How long could he be gone before his mother would wonder about him? Or did she drop off to sleep after he left? Probably.

The screech this time came from almost over his head. He studied the tallest trees until he spotted the bird; perched near the top of an elm, it looked like an upside-down wasp's nest. The boy could see the clearing that apparently had the owl's interest; he'd been to a patch of wild onions on the far side of it several times. He picked a spot that gave him a clear view and sat down to wait, eyes fixed on the owl.

Screech! The call sounded, and seconds later the bird left its perch as though it had simply tipped over. It plunged headfirst, gathering speed until, almost miraculously, it sprouted huge wings that turned the bird away from the ground and carried it silently forward through the air. Breathless, the boy watched as the owl glided to the center of the clearing, and then dropped straight down. There was a soft thud as it touched the ground; then its wings extended again, seeming to float the predator silently toward the trees, where it vanished.

The boy let out his pent-up breath and grinned. Wait till he told his father . . . or maybe not. Probably not. He got to his feet and hurried back to the privy to get the lamp.

As the front of the cabin came into view he stopped. The

door was open. His heart sank; his mother had come looking for him, and he was going to catch what for when he went back in the house. Why was it he could never get things right? This time, he'd promised himself that he was going to do exactly as his father had told him: stay close, carry the shotgun. Don't let Mercy wander. Cut firewood. Get the water for his mother. He ticked off the list as he made his way to the door; and through it. Wrong! Something's *wrong*. In the shifting light, the door to the bedroom seemed crooked, off one hinge. He raised his light . . .

"No!" The word struck back at him from the cave walls.

The boy sat upright in the sand, head turned away from the flickering candle, hands pressed tightly against his face. "I can't," he pleaded, his voice a whisper.

"But you must," the dancing shadows replied. *"You have to know."*

"No," the boy whimpered.

"Yessssss," the shadows gently assured.

One bare foot in front of the other, he advanced across the cabin floor. A grunting sound froze him in place.

"Mom?" he whispered. The unsteadiness of his voice frightened him.

"The lettle one has to be better than theese cold fish." A man's voice—a stranger who talks different—not like us. The boy looked for the shotgun by the door . . . gone! Panicking, he searched the room for a weapon, and his eyes fell on the butcher knife that lay on the table. He snatched it up, and in three steps was back at the door. He kneed it open, and with the knife held in front of him, lifted his lamp and sought his mother.

Bare legs and one arm was all he could see of her. A hulking figure, buttocks stark white in the lamplight, lay on top of her, and held a wadded-up quilt down on her face. Her hand lay listless as he thrust himself at her.

"The boy . . . I theenk he wants to watch?" the man said.

Another grunt . . . at his feet! He lowered the lamp.

"No! Stop," the boy in the cave prayed.

"*You* must *know*," the shadows replied.

A woolly monster had one massive hand clamped on his sister's throat while the other groped between her legs, his face pushed against her naked belly. Grunting like a rooting pig, he ravaged her, Mercy's head flopping loosely from side to side. It was her eyes that stopped time for Martin; they were turned back in her head, gleaming white.

The beast's massive head snapped up. Hair—masses of black, tangled snarls framed eyes that glinted orange-red in the light. They fixed on the boy for an instant, and then a great mouth opened, exposing a mass of crooked, rotten teeth and gushing air that reeked of stinking carrion; oily rank corruption. "Ar-rrrgh!" it growled.

Martin jerked the lamp away, the chimney falling off and shattering on the threshold. The knife at his side rose and slashed back down in a heartbeat. The dark flesh at the monster's brow split, and the razor-sharp steel sliced across his eye, through his cheek, laid open his lips, and parted his chin. A gout of blood sprayed the boy's blade, the wall, and his nightshirt, and the man screamed. The boy dropped the lamp when the man reached for him, then turned and fled into the night.

"Mercy!" The anguish of his protest filled the dark corners of the cave and it was not enough. "Mercyyyyyyyy. Pleeeeeease." He gasped for air between sobs, the image of her battered face hanging before his eyes, punishing, tormenting. Her head, loose on her neck, broken like he'd broken the weasel's. And his mother's hand—useless, flopping, dead as the raccoon. Because of him; he'd dallied in the moonlight and left them alone. He deserved to die here in this cave, isolated and hunted like an animal. Even if he knew how to get home, he could never, ever face his father.

His racking sobs could not escape the surrounding darkness any more than his soul could escape his guilt.

CHAPTER 11

Lem awoke soaked with sweat, as he always did when reliving that nightmare. He leaned forward and put his head in his hands. How could any human do what they did? What breeds such filth? Should they even be allowed to walk among the innocent? Lem knew the answer to the last question. It had become part of him.

He'd moved half a cord of wood to cover the twin graves, then returned to the cabin. From the shelf by the table he removed a tin of primers and a handful of rifle balls from his supply and put them in his hunting pouch. He picked up and shook his powder horn; then slung it and the pouch across his chest. Retrieving his knapsack from the floor, he stuffed it with any food that came easily to hand, grabbed his rifle and walked out of the cabin, shutting the door tightly.

An image of his son came to him; gray-white and rock-battered, floating down the fast-moving creek to the river. He trembled with rage. From the tree by the corner of the house, he yanked loose his big ax. Without a backward glance, he strode across the clearing and into the forest. Minutes later he reached the meadow where his mules grazed. He undid their hobbles, gave each a pat on the rump, and watched them move off a few feet and start foraging again. Lem headed for the river.

At his boat, he put his pack, rifle, and ax on the ground by the mooring tree and started his search for sign. Old tracks, his, were preserved in the soft bank. The three-day-old mark left by the keel of his boat was there and he studied the ground under his craft. There was no new sign, which meant the miscreants had walked in. It wasn't surprising when he thought about it; set between the two trees the way it was, the landing was not that easy to see. And from across the river, everything blended, except—

The obvious answer angered him, and he aimed a savage kick at his rucksack, then snatched it up and threw it in the bottom of the boat. Gritting his teeth, he untied the mooring line, stowed his rifle and ax in the bow, and shoved off.

Minutes later, his intuition proved correct as he stood and stared at the wide flat mark the canoe had left in the mud. Two sets of footprints went up the bank where he'd slipped his logs into the water. He scrambled up the steep side and followed the tracks toward the trees. He didn't know exactly what he was looking for—blood maybe—so the sight of the tall beaver hat on the ground came as a shock. He stood stock-still for a few seconds, his rage growing. There, discarded for some reason, was the symbol of all his hate. The hat tied the beast in the canoe to . . . what he couldn't even bear to think.

With a trembling hand, he stooped and picked it up. Dried blood blackened its insides. He wanted to tear it to pieces, stomp it in the earth, destroy it; but he steeled himself. There couldn't be too many river runners who had one like that. He'd use it to ask around; someone might know the name of the man who wore it—maybe even his whereabouts. Lem turned and went back to his rowboat. Pushing back into the water, he rowed into the main channel and dug his oars into the fast-moving river. He wanted to be in Booneville as soon as he could.

The smoky haze guided him to the southern shore, where he slammed his craft into the landing he'd left only two days before. Climbing out, he tied the boat to a mooring stake, and stood for a moment looking into the boat. Then, with a snort, he grabbed his rifle and the tall hat, and started across the muddy yard toward Burt's office.

When Lem walked in he found Burt busy at the back. He leaned his long rifle against the wall and started across the dirt floor.

The mill owner turned. "Lem! What'n hell ya doin' back here so soon? Need another drink, do ya? I—" His mouth snapped shut and he stepped away from the rough counter. "Jesus, what's the matter, Lem?"

Words would not come as he stared at Burt.

"The boys told me ya left in a hurry. Guess we had a few too many, huh? Not mad at me, are ya?" The mill owner moved closer.

Burt's face came into focus as Lem repeated in his mind what he'd just heard: "*We* had a few too many?" It wasn't Burt's fault. His friend stood before him, his brow knit, and Lem knew where the blame lay, and why. "Somebody killed my family, Burt, all of 'em." His voice trembled.

Burt's mouth worked . . . and failed him. He waited a few seconds, then stepped closer and put his hand on Lem's shoulder. "How, Lem? When?" He grimaced. "Who?"

Lem took a shuddering breath, and handed him the hat.

Burt's eyes widened as he took the black beaver. "Barron."

Lem's heart raced and he stared into Burt's eyes. "You know him?"

"I know of him. And his partner. They run orders up and down the river for Jason Sprague."

"You say that name," Lem said curtly, "like I should know it."

"Sprague . . . the fella that was here the other day when you come in. Remember? He didn't like the mud."

"Yes." Lem nodded his head slowly. "I do." He took the hat

out of Burt's hand. "Have you seen this Barron?"

"I haven't, but some have. He visited the doctor. He was cut eyebrow to nutsack, they say."

"Who says?"

"Sprague, for one."

"Where can I find him?"

Burt pulled a watch out of his pocket and looked at it. "Wait ten minutes and you won't have to. He's supposed to be here at three to complain about something or other."

Lem glanced at the door, then down at Burt's watch.

"I'm plumb sorry to hear about your family," Burt said quietly. "If there's something—"

"You can help me find these two butchers."

"There's the constable."

Lem sniffed. "He arrests drunks and card cheats."

"The marshal?"

"That hat was at my place and it's got blood on it. I'm not waitin'." Lem walked over to his rifle and was about to pick it up when he heard someone crossing the makeshift boardwalk outside.

A moment later, Jason Sprague stepped through the door and approached Burt's desk. "Let's make this quick, I've got other—"

"You recognize this hat?" Lem interrupted from behind him.

Sprague slowly turned around and looked Lem up and down. "And who are you?"

Burt began: "He wants—"

"I can do my own talking." Lem stepped up to Sprague and shoved the hat into the man's chest. "Recognize it?"

"It's a beaver hat, like any other beaver hat." He pushed it away. "I asked who you are."

Lem moved even closer to the dapper man. "Do you know a river runner who wears one of these?"

Sprague, slightly taller than Lem, wore clothes tailored to fit, and one of the newly fashionable bowler hats sat squarely on his head. Smooth shaven, he smelled to Lem of lilac and pomade.

Sprague took a step back. "No. I don't consort with"—he gave Lem another slow appraisal—"that kind," he said with a sneer.

Sprague's eyes betrayed his mouth, and Lem had a hold on his lapels before the startled man could blink. "I want to know what you know." He yanked the surprised man closer. "And I want to know it now!"

Jason blinked rapidly for a moment, then reached up and took hold of Lem's wrists. "Unhand me," he muttered through clenched teeth. "Now!" He jerked down on Lem's hands; and his eyes flared as the shiny broadcloth lapels ripped. Sprague glanced down at his torn coat and as he looked back up, Lem spun around, dragging the surprised man with him, and shoved. Sprague took three awkward steps back, hands flailing wildly, as Lem pushed him out the door. Before he could catch his balance, Lem was on him again. One of Sprague's polished boots went toward the river, the other straight out in front of him and he landed flat on his back—in the mud.

Lem jumped astride him. "I'll ask once more, mister—do you know a man who wears a hat like that?"

"I don't have to—"

Lem's work-hardened fist smashed the man's nose like a grape.

Sprague howled and crossed his hands in front of his eyes as Lem drew back to hit him again. "No!" His head rolled from side to side. "Barron. Jake Barron."

Lem leaned closer. "Where is he?" Half a dozen workers clattered across the boards to take positions on either side of Lem and his victim, jostling each other for a closer look.

Sprague's eyes flicked from one group of onlookers to the other, and then focused on Lem's face: "I paid them. They left."

"Them? Who's the one that wears the red scarf on his hat?"

"That be Guy LeFarge," one of the bystanders volunteered.

Lem glared down at Sprague, who was nodding emphatically. "Do you know where they went?"

Sprague shook his head.

"Downriver, be my guess," another onlooker said.

Sprague nodded.

"Why's that?" Lem asked.

"Jake's got a whore he stays with in Careytown sometimes," said the spectator.

"And I hear he's got a place on the river somewhere," another added.

Lem pushed off of Sprague, stood, and moved back just as Burt picked Sprague's muddy bowler out of the mire, dropping it on the man's chest.

One arm went wrist-deep into the muck as Sprague pushed himself up into a sitting position, his other hand clamped to his nose. "You had no—"

"I'd leave it be, Jason," Burt said, and went back to his doorway.

The spectators all chuckled as they turned and headed back across the boards. One turned around and addressed Lem: "Don't let the Frenchman get behind you, mister. He'll offer you your gizzard, and stick ya again before you can take it back."

Sprague struggled to his feet, apparently trying to keep as much mud off as he could. He took a white handkerchief out of his breast pocket and pressed it against his nose. With a wince, he glared at Lem, jammed his filthy hat on his head, and started across the boards. On the other side, he stopped and looked back. "You'll hear further of this," he called and headed for town. The workers at the end of the yard howled with laughter as he passed, hurrying him along.

Lem stepped past Burt and went inside the office.

"Careytown ain't a good place, Lem. No law there at all." Burt followed him in.

"If there's someone there who might know where Barron and the Frenchman are, that's where I'm going." Lem picked the beaver hat up from the floor. "I want you to give this to the constable and tell him what I told you." He handed it to Burt, and picked up his rifle.

"Be awful careful, Lem. Those two ain't got much to lose."

"I don't either, Burt," Lem replied and walked out.

Lem put his rifle aboard and pushed his boat out into the current. Immediately below Booneville, two large, wooded islands, lined up end-to-end, split the river with most of the volume flowing around the east side. Lem chose the wider and faster channel, and less than a half hour later had Careytown in sight.

Smaller and located about four miles downriver from Booneville, it might have grown as big had it not been built on low ground. Every few years the town endured a thorough cleansing by a flood, and as Lem drew closer he could see it was overdue. A single landing served the village and ramped up only slightly to lead directly onto the main street. As he beached his craft, Lem studied the several boats already tied up. The only canoe didn't look like anything to be trusted on the river.

He climbed over the prow, adding his line to several others lashed to a stake some thirty feet to the left. With a final tug on the knot, he started up the bank, rifle in hand.

"You gonna leave yer kit right there?"

Lem turned to find the speaker, a tall man sitting in the shade of a large elm. "You think it won't be safe?" he asked.

"I know it won't, 'less someone looks after it." The man, dressed in wool trousers and a rough pullover, stood and rested the butt of a double-barreled shotgun on the toe of a heavy brogan.

"Someone like you?"

"Not like me . . . *me*." His grin showed a mouthful of gleaming white teeth. "I don't hanker after loose women and can't tolerate hot drink. Don't leave a lot for me to do 'round here."

"How much?"

"Twenty-five cents till sundown, or half a dollar till sunup next."

"You stay here all night?"

"Me, or someone who gets along just as well with this shotgun."

Lem shifted the muzzle of his rifle toward his boat. "You guarantee it?"

"I guarantee the boat and everything in it will be gone if ya leave it like that. You pay me, it'll be there till you want it back." Lem looked at the other dozen or so craft pulled up on the gentle slope. The man smiled again. "They all paid."

Lem dug his purse out of his pocket and took out a quarter. "I don't expect to be long."

"Give me the half-dollar now and you won't have to worry about it." The guard winked.

"I'm here to find someone. Won't be long, one way or the other. Maybe you can help me?" Lem dropped the coin into the man's hand.

"I make my living lookin' after other folks' property, and I can do that without knowing their names. I don't know yours and don't want to . . . understand?"

"Plain enough. Where would a man ask to find out who comes and goes around here?"

The man shrugged and nodded toward the town.

The settlement consisted of about a dozen one-story, rough-hewn timber structures. Most had just a door in front, no windows, and a nearly flat board roof. One, a little farther up the street, had a layer of sod over the boards and was larger than the rest; two horses were tied alongside. The first place along had a corral, and beside it stood three men. One wore a leather apron and looked every bit a blacksmith; the other two, shabbily dressed, eyed Lem suspiciously. He went over to them. "I'm looking for someone."

The two scruffy-looking men exchanged glances, and then looked to the blacksmith. "This fella have a name?" the smithy asked.

"Jake Barron."

"Ain't seen 'im."

"But you know who he is?"

"Yep."

"And his partner?"

"He's had lots of partners."

One of the rough men chuckled. "Yeah, lots."

"A Frenchy named LeFarge," Lem offered.

The blacksmith shook his head. "Ain't seen him either."

"Humpin' Bridget, ain't he?" the second roughneck offered.

The smithy glared at him, then looked back at Lem. "Nobody comes off that river without I knows it. You didn't . . . and neither would Barron and LeFarge. Did you see Clarence at the landing?"

"I talked to a man with a shotgun."

"That'd be Clarence," cackled the first scruffy.

"You ask him?" asked the smith.

"He said it was none of his business."

"Sounds jist like 'im," the second scruffy snorted. "He's a peace-lovin' man, but if you mess with 'im, he'll split yer noggin with that big ol' scattergun."

"Clarence has a good point, mister," the smithy said. "There's enough trouble in this place without a man goin' lookin' for it.

Neither Barron or LeFarge are here—so why don't you take your squabble somewhere else?"

"Squabble?" Lem barely recognized his own voice: it sounded strangled. He gripped his rifle with both hands. "Squabble, ya say?" The two rough men backed away a full step.

The apprehension that had first appeared on the smithy's face changed to arrogance as Lem simply stood and stared. With a confident smirk, he rocked on his feet, jaw jutted. "Yeah, squabble." He sniffed derisively. "You've got yer back up, and yer lookin' to make trouble for some friends of mine. That means you start with me." The man flashed a wink at his two companions.

Had he not been looking at his friends, the smithy would have seen the color flooding Lem's face; he might also have had time to fend off the muzzle of the long rifle heading toward his belly as hard as Lem could shove it. The dismissive sniff was followed by an explosion of air as the steel rammed into the man just below his sternum. He hunched his shoulders as the pain paralyzed him and the sudden lack of air struck terror; slowly he sank to his knees, mouth gaping as he struggled for breath, his eyes wide.

Lem watched for a moment, then turned to the two dumbstruck men. "Where can I find this . . . Bridget?"

One pointed up the street at the sod-covered building. "The big place . . . Murtaugh's," the man mumbled and immediately dropped his gaze to the ground.

Lem started around the smithy, now prone, his lips turning blue.

"He gonna die?" one of the two asked.

"He might." Lem headed for the building.

Two men standing outside Murtaugh's paid no attention as Lem walked through the door and stopped just inside. The assault on his senses came from all directions and all at once. His hand went reflexively to his nose and mouth, blocking the fetid humid air. A long plank counter, supported on both ends and in the middle by whiskey barrels, stood directly opposite. In front of it men jostled each other, shouting obscenities and laughing raucously. Serving them from the other side of the bar stood the biggest man Lem had ever seen. Murtaugh? A glowing lamp hung above the giant; and like a wind-sniffing bear, the barkeeper scanned the entire room, dark eyes flicking from group to group, man to man. They settled on Lem for an instant, narrowed slightly, and then moved on; but for that brief moment, Lem felt like the only one in the room. The hair on the back of his neck bristled.

The meager light of late afternoon filtering through the door added little to that provided by a dozen dingy oil lamps hanging from the ceiling and attached to the walls. Slowly, Lem's eyes adjusted, and he could see both sides of the room. Three tables stood at each end, and around them more men were drinking and talking, or playing dominoes, or cards; and at one a boisterous arm-wrestling contest was going on. At that table stood the only two women in the place, and Lem studied them for a moment before he walked over to the crowded bar. Using the butt of his rifle, he made room for himself beside two men who stood talking.

"Hey, Goddammit, watch who you're shovin'," the closest man protested, but allowed Lem the spot when their eyes met. He shifted closer to his barmate.

The big man behind the bar was in front of him before Lem's belly hit the bar. "What'll ya have?"

"I want to talk to Bridget."

He gave Lem a sly wink; then slapped the bar with a hand the size of a hearth shovel. "Three dollars."

Lem glanced at the two men standing beside him. "I just want to talk to her," he said to the bartender in a low voice.

The short man he'd butted out of the way nudged his friend; both turned to face Lem.

Murtaugh's massive eyebrows climbed the slope of his forehead and a wisp of a smile appeared. "Sniff it, kiss it, finger it or fuck it. I don't care. Hell, just sit 'n look at it if ya want to . . . it's three dollars just the same." His eyes twinkled as the two men next to Lem chuckled. The barman rubbed his first finger against a thick thumb as he held out his hand.

"But—"

"That too, if it's yer fancy." The barkeep guffawed at his own wit, and slammed his open hand against the shoulder of the short man next to Lem. The two men and the bartender roared with laughter as Lem felt heat rise in his face.

"Now look here," he shouted and started to lift his rifle.

A hairy-knuckled hand shot out, grabbed the barrel, and jerked the weapon out of Lem's grasp. "You won't need that, no matter what you decide to do. When you're goin' out the door you can have it back." The twinkling eyes were gone, replaced by a dead stare. "Three dollars." Again, he held his hand out.

"Bridget!" the man hollered above the noise as Lem gave him the money. The smaller of the two women looked toward the bar. "Git your scrawny ass over here."

Bridget opened the first door in a short hallway that led off the left end of the bar, stepped back, and let Lem go first. A double-wick lamp burned on a small table by a narrow bed. A single chair and washstand completed the furnishings of the dirt-floored room. The door closed, the crude wooden bolt slid, and then she brushed past him.

The woman wore a plain cotton dress, and before Lem could say a word, he discovered it was all she wore as she deftly hiked it over her head and threw it on the chair. With her hands resting on narrow hips, she looked down at what Lem was staring at; small breasts that sagged slightly on her skinny chest. She cupped and lifted them both. "This what you want?" Her tired smile lasted only a moment.

"Uh . . . you . . . no!" Lem rushed past her and yanked the dress off the chair. His eyes fixed on the woman's dark mystery for a few seconds, the small wedge of hair a startling black against her pale skin. With a sharp intake of breath, he threw the dress at her. "Put that back on!" he almost shouted, then turned his back, furious at his weakness and the stir he felt.

"Whatever draws the smoke up your stack, mister," she muttered.

Lem heard the whisper of the dress, and then the rustle of the straw tick as she sat on the bed. He turned around. "I just want to talk to you."

"You ain't gonna get your money back." Her sad eyes blinked slowly.

"I want to find Guy LeFarge. Know where he is?"

"He's not here."

"I know that, but someone said he stays with you."

"Not my choice, mister."

Lem realized he was talking to a young girl. Her homely face, filthy with smoke and grime, was unlined; and her teeth were still white. He could see fear in her eyes. "He killed my family, missy. My wife and two children. Do you know where he might be?"

A wince flickered across her face. "I do." Then she took a deep breath. "He has a bark shed on the first island this side of Booneville. Know where that is?"

"Yes. I passed it. Are you sure?"

"I'm real sure, mister." She stood and turned around.

Lem could not take his eyes off the back of her legs as she lifted the hem of her dress. Puckered skin disfigured her from the back of the knees to as high as he could see: burn scars, and not that old.

"He took me to the island once." She spoke matter-of-factly. "He likes to hurt people."

Lem could not take his eyes off the puffy red flesh. He swallowed hard to clear the lump in his throat as she turned back to face him. "Good Lord," he murmured.

"Not here, mister." Her lips trembled. "The Lord don't care 'bout a place like this, or about me."

Lem fumbled in his pocket and took out a gold eagle. "Thank you for your help, missy." She took it silently; then her eyes widened when she glanced at it. She stepped close and kissed his bristled cheek, tears glistening in her eyes. She swiped at them angrily. "Thank you, mister. You kill him good."

CHAPTER 12

The smell of smoke startled the boy, and then he remembered: he had fire now. His knee stiff, his legs cold, he missed the warm floor in the front of the cave. But this was better; he could have fire . . . and light. He felt around until he found the tin of matches and stack of candles he'd arranged the night before. He lit the wick, and the blaze of light brought a sigh of relief.

Last night's fire had left a rough circle of gray on the dark sandy floor. His roasting stick stood where he'd left it, leaning against the wall, tip charred; and farther down, greasy. His stomach complained and his tongue stuck to the top of his mouth, but first he stood, and with the nightshirt draped over his shoulders, went to the back of the cave. The single candle by the cold campfire offered little light, and he hurried with his duty.

The warmth of his bed felt good on his rear as he sat and pulled his knees up to his chin. Clutching the nightshirt close around his legs with one hand, he reached back and grabbed a handful of jerky. Quietly he sat and chewed, his shoulders slumped. He knew who he was now; at least, for the most part. The horrific image of the bedroom tried to intrude, but he pushed it back. He glanced at the knife lying beside the nearly stripped carcass of the raccoon. The knife had lost its edge.

The image of his father appeared—Pa. They were home, out front, waiting for supper. The big man reached up on a shelf by the door and got down a long, pinkish-gray stone and held it out. "Take good care of this," he'd said gruffly. "Don't leave it on the ground, and never drop it."

"Okay, Pa."

"Get some water, there." Pa pointed at the bucket. "Keep the stone wet, otherwise it's ruined." He poured a trickle on the stone and laid it on his leg. "The edge comes toward you, and you pull it across the stone like you was cuttin' slivers off." He drew the knife-edge completely across the stone. "Do that six, seven times, then turn it over and do the same. Ya watchin'?"

"Yeah. Cuttin' slivers off. And don't drop the stone."

"And one other thing . . . the back of the blade stays up the same every time." He tilted the back of the knife up and down. "Keep it the same. Think you could do that?"

"I think so. Want me to try?"

"Not now. I'll finish this one and then show you again later, maybe next week. Then I'll let you." He finished with the stone, then drew the knife back and forth over a piece of leather. "Now watch." He wet his arm, and drew the knife along the wet spot like a razor.

"That's sharp, Pa." The boy was impressed.

"Best way to keep 'em. Dull knife will cut ya faster than a sharp one." Then his father had looked at him closely, the deep-set eyes clear. "I'm going to Booneville tomorrow. You know I trust you to be the man when I'm not here."

"Yes, Pa."

The candlelight shimmered as tears welled up.

I trust you to be the man, you know?

"Yes, Pa," he said quietly and a sob escaped.

I trust you, you know?

"Yes, Pa," he whispered, pleading.

And his father had gone to Booneville and his mother and sister had been killed.

I trust you.

"No, Pa," he sobbed, his shoulders shaking. His mother and sweet, gentle Mercy were gone; and with them, he'd lost his father too.

Lem was tired, yet sleep had no appeal, and his unfocused gaze settled on the forest across the clearing from the cabin. *"Kill him good."* The image of the young girl—he could not think of her as a whore—drifted into his mind. Did her desperate need for revenge, rightful and justified, absolve him? How many times had he lain on his bed and wondered about that? Was he seeking an answer to her need . . . or his? "Vengeance is mine . . . unless." But it didn't say *unless.* "Suffer the little children." Suffer? Suffer and die? His children?

The fire that made his blood hot—and his mind see nothing but black—flared up again as he sat on the bench and stared at the trees, remembering.

Lem had closed the door to the girl's room, walked down the short hall, and into the noisy saloon.

"There's the sonofabitch." The voice, little more than a croak, came from a man at the bar, a whiskey glass halfway to his lips. It was the blacksmith, his two cronies right behind him. "He tried to kill me, Murtaugh," he squawked at the bartender, pointing a shaky finger at Lem.

The customers at Lem's end of the room quieted and, to a man, all turned to look at him. Their eyes followed him with catlike curiosity as he made his way toward the big barkeeper. In a voice steadier than he felt, Lem announced: "I'm leaving. Give me my rifle."

Murtaugh nodded toward the smithy and his two companions. "They don't seem to think so."

Lem looked around. Except for the three glaring at him, the

faces in the crowd looked neutral. He'd located his quarry; and these mud rats were not going to stop him. He glanced at his rifle leaning against the wall behind the giant.

"They ain't armed," Murtaugh said.

"That's right," one of the scruffy pair said over the blacksmith's shoulder. "Now it's even."

The bartender grinned at Lem. "He's right, if I get your measure."

Lem scanned the place as silence rippled across the room, his heart picking up speed, his mouth chalk-dry.

"Your only concern is these three." Murtaugh reached back and picked up Lem's gun. "When you're ready to leave." He put it back down.

"I don't want any trouble with you three." Lem took two steps closer, holding his hands in front of him, palms out.

"Ya already got it," said one from behind the blacksmith.

"If that's the case—" Lem took two more quick steps and slammed his fist into the exact spot he'd jammed the rifle muzzle before. As the air again rushed out of the smithy and he sagged to his knees, a shout went up from the crowd. The two followers looked down at their stricken leader for a few seconds, then glared at Lem, but made no move. Lem glanced at the saloonkeeper.

"He never *wuz* very smart." Murtaugh gave the crowd a broad wink. They started to laugh as he handed over the rifle.

A path opened to the door when Lem took hold of the stock and turned. He strode toward the dim light of the doorway.

"Look out!" someone shouted, and Lem ducked. A thick-bladed knife flashed over his head and bounced off the door frame. He spun around in time to see one of the smithy's friends reach down to his boot as the other stepped out of the way. Lem turned and ran out the door.

He didn't remember it being so far from the river as he

sprinted across the ground. He could hear several men at a dead run, and not very far behind. Pulling the rifle's hammer back to full cock, he tried to increase his speed. As he ran down the slight slope to the river, the tall man with the shotgun moved away from the big elm and stood in plain view. Lem glanced over his shoulder—his pursuers had nearly caught up. He ran past the man, to the mooring stake, and frantically tore at the knot in the rope.

"Get his boat!" someone shouted.

The roar of a shotgun dropped Lem to one knee and he ducked; a howl of pain followed the blast. He whipped the muzzle of his rifle around and pointed it at his closest pursuers—four men. Two others, the blacksmith's cronies, were farther down the landing, close to his rowboat; one held his thigh and hopped up and down.

"Gawdammit, Clarence, ya shot me!" the wounded man hollered.

"Keep away from the man's boat," the tall guard said in a loud voice.

The man quit hopping and held on to his partner's shoulder.

"You know my rule," Clarence said.

"He tried to kill Kincaid!"

"Tried? I reckon if he wanted that so-called blacksmith dead, that's the way he'd be. Just like you—couple pieces of shot in your leg is just bein' friendly. Now git up the bank with the rest of 'em." He motioned up the slope with the muzzle of the shotgun.

The two started up the bank and Lem called to the guard. "Thanks, mister."

"It's nothin' to do with you. Now, if you was leavin' . . . leave."

Lem finished with the balky knot, coiling up the rope as he went to his boat. With a nod at the tall man, he put his rifle in the bow, and pushed out into the river.

"Kill him good." The simple imperative, spoken quietly by a simple girl, occupied his mind as he rowed. He wished he'd had twenty dollars to give her, though the ten would give her a chance of getting out of there. And whether she left or not, pretty soon she'd never have to worry about the Frenchman again. Nobody would have to worry about him—nobody.

The last soft glow of twilight had given up to darkness the hour before, and his neck ached from craning to watch the shore. The river channel from Booneville to Careytown was a straight one with little slack water on either side—hard rowing. It also meant snags weren't confined to the center or to outside bends; they could be anywhere. He glanced over his shoulder again, corrected course a little, and hauled back on the oars. Straining against the current, he tried to dismiss the image of the girl. Only now . . . it was Mercy he saw.

The full moon he'd been expecting finally rose, and the light allowed him to see farther upstream. As close as he could reckon, it was near midnight when the lower isle appeared on the far side of the river. Straining, he came abreast of it, and then pulled hard, oars going deep, and rowed across the water. He judged it right, and the boat settled into the slack water on the lee side, where he ran it onto the exposed tip of the island.

As soon as he climbed out, he caught the strong scent of wood smoke in the nearly dead air, and knew the girl had steered him *almost* right. They were just ahead of him, so close he thought he could sense their presence; not on the first island, like she'd said, but right here. He took his rifle out of the boat and drew the hammer back to check the primer. Snugly set atop the nipple, the dull copper cap reflected in the bright moonlight, and he carefully let the weapon back to half cock. He'd never felt the need for a pistol, but wished he had one now. There were two of them, and given a chance, they wouldn't go down without a fight.

Lem stood for a moment, then retrieved his horn and bag, slung them over his shoulder, and started out. Picking his way silently through the sparse bushes at the end of the island, he stopped every few feet to listen and sniff the air. He moved into the moon-shadowed trees, the smoke smell still plain, where he stopped. Straining to see any sign of fire in the darkness ahead, he listened intently for any sound, and then moved on.

The woods soon closed in around him; with most light now shielded, he moved even more slowly. The faint sound of the river lapping at the shore assured him he'd hear voices if they were talking. He placed one foot carefully before the other, feeling the ground before he set his full weight down. His tongue stuck to the roof and his eyes burned as sweat seeped into them. Where were they?

He glanced up at the moon again; it had shifted some. Several times he could have sworn firelight was filtering through the trees, but then he hadn't been able to find it. Dim shadows took on life as he moved, and his arms burned with tension as he gripped his rifle. He stopped to rest his eyes and quiet his nerves. How long had he been sneaking through these woods? He took another look at the night sky. They had to be close. He took a deep breath, blinked hard to clear his vision, and started off again.

He stepped around a low-hanging branch and his breath caught in his throat. Water! A few low bushes gave way to a narrow band of mud that bordered a shimmering expanse of open river. Damn it!—they *were* on the other island! He shrank back into the cover of the branch. Were they in those trees at the edge? The two islands narrowed to points that missed touching by a stone's throw. He'd be totally exposed to anyone watching, but who would that be? They weren't expecting him. They'd be wrapped in their beds. Was it shallow enough to wade? He took another anxious look at the sky. He could go back for the boat, then row it up the slower narrow-channel side . . . and have them hear the oars rattle in the locks?

Lem slipped out of the trees, snaked through the bushes, and stepped onto the muddy bank. Kneeling, he washed the stinging sweat off his brow and out of his eyes, then cupped both hands and lifted water to his parched mouth. He felt the cool liquid all the way down his throat. The stretch of water before him seemed to be still—flowing neither left nor right. Taking off his pouch and horn, he wrapped the straps tight around his wrist, hiked them and his rifle to his chest, and stepped away from the bank.

He heaved a sigh as water slowly inched up his leg. Ten steps, calf high; fifteen more, knee high; twenty more, and the water reached his waist. He lifted both hands into the air and took ten more steps, chest high; ten more, and still chest high. Lem glanced over his shoulder and his scalp tingled—*halfway*. He took another step, a longer one this time and hurried the next.

In a heartbeat Lem knew he was lost. His forward foot found nothing, and he sank to his neck as his trailing foot slipped off an underwater bank. Thrusting his rifle as high as he could, he tried to turn back. One foot caught a vague hold on the slippery bottom, then slipped, and Lem was submerged. He dragged the rifle down to his side, and grabbed at the water with his free hand. The pouch, wrapped tightly to his wrist, acted like a paddle, and Lem felt a surge of hope as his head cleared the surface for a second. He managed a gulp of air before he went under again. He took another grab with his paddle hand, and another gasp for air. He continued to struggle as a slight current moved him toward the narrow strait to his right. Then he felt his rifle butt strike bottom, followed by a touch with the toe of his shoe. Then both feet found mud.

Lem crawled across the narrow bank and flopped down in

the bushes. Chest heaving, he rolled over on his back and spread his arms flat on the ground. As he lay there, gathering his strength, he silently cursed his stupidity. Two islands . . . a channel, however narrow, separated them; and he'd just stepped in it. Now he was soaked, it was half a mile to his boat and back, and the night was wasting away. He sat up. Still time to do it if he hurried. A ball in one and a cracked skull for the other. One shot and . . .

Lem slammed his fist into the mud. Untangling his powder horn, he pulled off the top and tipped it. A black slurry poured onto his leg. With a groan, he lay back down. Now what? He took a deep breath and tried to slow his thoughts. *Think,* he urged himself, *think about it.*

They'd be asleep for sure, so he could take the first one. Lem hefted his heavy rifle. It would have to be precise. Neck? Or head? Would one blow with the steel butt-plate kill him? Maybe. No, probably. The first one would have to be sure—dead sure. One he could do. But two? Could he get to the second before he was aware? Maybe—and swing the rifle like a club. But would it break? Was that sure? If he hit him just—

His plan materialized in a flash of insight, and Lem scrambled to his feet. He hurried into the woods behind him, moving quietly, but not so slowly. He could not be sure attacking with the rifle, but he could with the tool he'd used all his life. Lem needed his ax.

The trip the length of the lower island went quickly and he threw his sodden gear into the boat. His soaked shirt drew heat from his body, so he shucked it, then sat down and took off his shoes. Rising to stand bare-chested in the moonlight, an overwhelming urge to fight inflamed his body. He strode to the boat, snatched the ax out of the bow and stood on the narrow beach, arms raised over his head. The chill he'd felt vanished, and his hot muscles grew tense. Teeth clenched tightly, he shook

the heavy steel tool at the sky, and suppressed the scream forming in his throat. Raging in silence, he put the ax back, grabbed
the mooring rope, and started the hard slog through mud and
shallow water to the other end of the island.

Lem soon stood looking across the water where he'd almost
drowned. He figured less than an hour had passed since he'd
crawled out on the mud bank, defeated. Now he was eager to
get to the other side. With one oar lying in the back of the boat
so he could grab it easily, he lined the bow up with the far shore
and shoved off. Using the oar as a paddle, he silently moved the
boat across the narrow passage, aware of how conspicuous he
was. He grunted with satisfaction when the craft slid silently to
a stop on the gently sloped bank. Lem made his way to the
front of the boat, picked up his ax, and stepped ashore.

He moved barefoot across the soggy shore to the trees and
stopped in the shelter of one, his heart pounding furiously. The
campfire smell was stronger now, and Lem concentrated on
containing his urge to charge ahead. Taking slow, deep breaths,
he waited and thought about the best way to go. He wished the
girl had been more specific about the lean-to. Where would he
have put it? Simple. He'd find the thickest trees, and those were
in the middle of the island. Lem started out, one stealthy step
after another, pausing often, eyes and ears straining. The silence
of the night folded in on him and he felt part of it.

Then, he couldn't believe his ears. He stopped breathing and
held his breath. His head started to spin, and he was about to
inhale when he heard it again: the sound of a man talking. And
then a louder voice, almost a shout, shattered the calm. He sank
to his knees and stared toward the sound. From the volume,
one sounded angry.

Lem stood again, and even more carefully now, moved in
their direction. Scant minutes later, a flicker of firelight appeared through the trees. They were still awake, and had a blaze

going. He smiled in the dark; all the better. Taking a firm grip on his ax, he made his way closer until he could see the camp. The big man, Jake Barron, sat on the far side of a small clearing. His head wrapped in a bloody bandage, he picked at the edges of it with a grimy finger. The Frenchman, his back to Lem, sat facing Barron across the fire.

Moving even closer, he got to his hands and knees, and crept to the edge of the clearing.

" 'Twas more than a catfish in the mud," Barron grumbled. "I tell ya it was someone in the bleedin' water."

"And I'm telling you, my friend, eet was nothing."

"You limp bastard, you were'na gone long enough to git a look."

"There is nothing to stop you from seeing for yourself."

"Don't ya be gettin' smart with me. One eye or no, I'll sort ya out."

LeFarge's hand found the rifle that lay beside him. "I looked. There was *nothing*. I am going to sleep. You will be up till the dawn seeing that fire die."

"Aye. And providin' that woodchopper doesn't creep in here and cut yer worthless throat. We're lucky Sprague told us he was lookin'."

Lem's scalp contracted; they'd been warned.

"I'm not afraid of some booney with a busted shotgun," the Frenchman sneered.

"You go to bed, then," the big man chided. "I'll wake you with me new toy."

Barron reached over and picked up something setting atop a piece of firewood. Lem's eyes went wide as the man held it head high and shook it. The pure tone of his wife's silver bell rang in the night. Every muscle in Lem's body reacted at once: focusing on the nearest man, he started to slowly rise to his hands and knees. Suddenly, the Frenchman picked up his rifle and stood. Lem sank back to the ground.

Slowly, the man turned, looked directly at Lem, and spoke: "Ya keep ringin' that damn bell, and you'll have that damn fool over here for sure." And then, to Lem's horror, he started toward the very bushes where he hid. Gripping the ax, he was again preparing to strike when LeFarge stopped, laid his rifle across a bush and unbuttoned his pants. His stream arced onto the ground, the sound dwindled, then stopped, and LeFarge grunted with satisfaction as he repaired himself and picked up his weapon.

The Frenchman's bed lay beside a sapling, and he leaned his rifle against it. Sitting, he opened his bedroll, took off his hat, and turned into his blankets. After shifting around a bit, he soon settled down flat on his back with his arms by his side.

"Frenchy bugger," Barron grumbled and shook the bell once more before putting it back on the wood. Then, groaning, he got up and went to his bed, directly across from LeFarge. He stood tall in the moonlight, and tugged at the bandage that swathed his head. Black whiskers and long hair hid the neck and massive shoulders that slumped as he moaned, "The skinny little bastard, I hope he burns in hell." He put his coat on, buttoned it, and lay on his covers. Grasping the edge under his shoulder, rolled over once, and wrapped himself in the heavy wool blanket and canvas rain tarp. He, too, lay flat on his back, a huge lump on the ground.

Lem could not take his eyes off the silver bell. Glinting faintly in the firelight, the tiny ornament became the most precious thing in his world. He would have it back . . . but first, patience. He let go his grip on the ax and allowed his muscles to relax. The moon was well over halfway on its slide to the horizon, but he had plenty of time to do what he had to do . . . what he wanted to do.

It took a long time for Barron to settle down; several times he moaned out loud, or cursed. But now, the two lumps were making a lot of noise as deep sleep held them. The low, wet rattle was the big man; the higher nasal wheeze, the Frenchman. The fire burned down first to a shimmering mass of glowing coals, then to a sulking gray with orange hot spots that occasionally flared.

Lem was ready, and rose like a ghost out of the ground to stand silently, studying the camp. The shed was to the left and beyond the Frenchman, well out of the way. He couldn't see Barron's rifle, if he had one; and when he'd been standing, there'd been no sign of a knife. Their stack of firewood lay well to LeFarge's right; nothing else stood in Lem's way. A moan came from the big man as he turned slightly, then he snorted and continued to snore. Sleeping like . . . babies. The thought flashed into Lem's mind before his could stop it. Baby. Mercy: naked on the floor, savaged, cold and still. And his wife . . . his family. Lem stepped out of the bushes and into the clearing.

The Frenchman's face was turned to the sky, his arms still straight down beside him. Lem glanced over his shoulder at the big man across the fire, and then looked back at the sleeping man at his feet. Hefting his ax, he swung it with the fluid ease of long practice.

The sound came, dull and sodden; the reaction of the decapitated man violent and instantaneous: LeFarge, incredibly, sat straight up, and for a few seconds bright blood spewed out of his neck. The heat of the man's life drenched Lem's chest and face as the stream erupted. Then the headless body slammed back to the ground and started to flop. Jerking convulsively, it slipped from the blankets and moved across the ground toward the glowing coals of the campfire. Transfixed, Lem watched the senseless body dance into the searing embers. Its clothes burst into flames, flaring up until all Lem could see were legs, twitching as the hungry tongues of fire licked flesh.

A grunt from across the camp tore Lem's gaze away. Barron had started to stir. With four long strides, Lem was to him, his ax climbing above his head as he moved. An arm came up to shield the big man's face, but it slowed the descending ax little as it struck. Barron screamed as he fought the wool cocoon that bound him. He rolled to his belly and got his knees under him. Blood spurted from his severed arm and like a green grass-crawler, he tried to hump his way out of danger. Lem's ax caught him in the center of his back, and with a single massive blast of breath, the crawler sagged flat and was still.

Lem's heart turned as cold as Death's breath, and the emptiness he sensed in his soul chilled his blood. He stood a moment, the ax still buried handle-deep, while flickering light from the burning corpse played in the surrounding trees. He jerked the steel free, and a scream roared from his throat, rising as a curse into the dark.

Head aching with pressure, he swung his ax with singular purpose, chopping at anything that looked to be part of a human. With his bare feet stomping in the gore, the pressure in his head continued to build, until, finally, the blackness in his mind slowly dissipated and light reasserted itself. He stopped. Shuddering from exertion, he lowered his bloody ax and looked around.

At first, his fevered mind refused to register the scene, and his eyes squeezed tightly shut. But a need to know forced them open, and in the shadowy light of the smoldering body, Salem Greene, man of God, took account for the first time the awfulness of his work. The taste of bile rose strong in his throat.

"*God* damn you," he screamed at the darkness. "God *damn* you. God damn *youuuuuuu*," he moaned. Then he sank to his knees in the blood-soaked dirt and bowed his head. "God damn me," he prayed, and a mighty sob ripped from his throat and escaped through his clenched teeth.

CHAPTER 13

Damned! Lem got off the bench and walked over to the big fire circle. Had Percy also been damned, made to pay a price for something he'd done? Dufrey didn't seem to think so; but then Lem had seen things that Dufrey never would. Lem had learned where demons dwell; and it wasn't in some dark, cold place underground, or skulking in the forest shadows. Lem thought he knew what Percy had discovered, and knew because his own education had begun that night on the riverbank as he stood staring at the far shore.

The waning moon laid a path of light across the narrow channel that ended at Lem's feet. He stared at the silver bell he held in the palm of his bloody hand. His ax lay in the shallow water where he'd dropped it. In the deathly quiet, his mind reeled at the enormity of his deed. Could the loss of his family justify compromising one's soul? His soul—was it not already compromised? His family had been his soul. So he had decided to be the judge and the executioner. Who better? God? He who'd allowed a mere girl and her mother to be raped and murdered? An eye for an eye; two deaths, one for each. But he hadn't simply killed them; he'd butchered them like a demented madman—a madman killing mad men. The stench of loosed bowels and scorched flesh still filled his nose, and the sticky corruption on his body knotted his stomach. Lem reached down, retrieved his ax, and went over to the boat.

He put the ax away, and placed the silver bell on the seat in the bow. The cool air chilled him as he stepped back to the water's edge and slowly walked into the river. He soon stood chest deep, the current gently moving against him. Slowly and methodically, unmindful of the frigid water, he washed the blood away. He ducked beneath the surface and let the water move through his hair. How easy it would be to inhale sharply, and sink into the mud at the bottom. That's all it would take; and then he'd drift with the slow water out and away into the main stream, soon becoming only a dim memory in the minds of the few who might care. So easy. He started to feel light-headed and set his teeth in his lower lip . . . *just a little bit longer.* His arms felt weightless and drifted away from his body, spreading like the wings of a soaring hawk.

A charge of energy stiffened his spine, jerking his head erect, eyes open. With a gasp, he stood up straight. The bright water of the moonbeam's path swirled and danced as if alive, yet the river on either side remained placid and smooth. Pressure began building on his chest. Gentle at first, it soon felt like a huge hand pushing down on him. Then a dark form, like a shrouded coffin, moved straight at him from upstream. Terrified, but unable to move, he watched the black shape draw closer. Then it was on him, and in an instant the hand became a fist that slammed him with a force that took his breath away. Knocked on his back, the hand again found his body and forced him under the water. Struggling, he sucked a mouthful of water into his lungs and, in that moment, knew death had come to find him.

A brilliant burst of light filled Lem's vision, and the roiling water became still and calm. Air, sweet as honeyed milk, passed his lips and filled his lungs. Batting at the water—confused but no longer afraid—he looked for the source of light, which faded rapidly as he stared; drifting away, the coffin blended with the dark water and disappeared. Then, utterly spent, he sensed a presence—someone or something beside him, and he relaxed. A feeling of being lifted up overcame him, and he closed his eyes.

The eastern sky was gray when Lem woke—flat on his back in his boat. His shirt lay across his chest, and his mud-caked feet were propped on the rowing seat. He turned his head to see the silver bell in the dim light. Vaguely, he remembered standing in the water; and then, more clearly, the terrifying dark form that came at him. What had tried to kill him? And why was he still alive? A sense of foreboding gripped him, and he scanned the far bank. His gaze fell on the handle of his ax standing upright toward the middle of the boat; and he instantly resisted the vision that began to form. *Not now.*

The edge of the small seat cut into his neck, and he couldn't feel his legs. After a struggle, he got an elbow down and levered himself into a sitting position. His pants were still damp, although he wasn't particularly cold. But he was hungry . . . really hungry. He climbed out of the boat, grabbed his shoes, limped over to level ground, and sat. There was enough light now to show the mist hanging over the river. He knocked the dried mud off his feet and put his shoes on. Should he go back to Booneville and let the law know what he'd done? Not much they could do to him that was worse than what he felt coming. Burt deserved to know that he'd made it back from Careytown.

And Jason Sprague needed to learn that too, and in such a way that he would not forget.

Lem beached the boat and went directly to Burt's. There was no one there, but the door was wide open, so he went in. His eyes were drawn to a water bucket behind Burt's workbench. He had drained his fourth dipper full when he heard steps on the boards outside.

Burt, carrying a package, entered the room and stopped.

"Been wondering about you. Looks like you went in the river. Trouble?"

"I took care of it. Now I have a little here that needs attending to."

Burt cocked his head. "Here? What about Careytown?"

Lem took a deep breath. "I found 'em, Burt, and I killed 'em both. First LeFarge and then Barron."

Burt's jaw dropped. "In Careytown?"

"Nope. They had a place on the big island just downriver and they knew I was coming to Careytown."

"How's that?"

"Sprague told them."

Burt walked over to his desk and put down the package. "Jason? I find that hard to believe, Lem. He's a skunk . . . but he don't stink *that* bad."

"I heard Jake Barron say so. Where can I find Sprague?"

"Not sure I want to tell you, Lem. I mean, you've got *fire* in your eyes."

"He knew why I was looking, Burt. He knew—yet he gave them a chance to get away. I think if I hadn't found out about the island in Careytown, they'd be gone. My wife and kids slaughtered and those two in Saint Louis."

"But—"

"I want Sprague to tell me why he'd do that, Burt. That's all I want . . . just him to tell me why."

"If I thought—"

"You're with me on this or against me, Burt. There is no middle way." Lem dropped the dipper in the bucket with a splash and started for the door.

"I'll go with you, Lem. I'll take ya to him . . . but first, can't we sit a minute and talk about this?"

"Nothin' to say . . . I'll do what I have to do, and then I'm going home." Lem walked out the door and crossed the boards to dry ground, Burt right behind him.

As they passed the end of the sawyers' pits, half a dozen workers dropped their tools and followed, chattering excitedly. The entourage walked down the center of the street, and as they went, more people fell in with them, until nearly twenty were marching up the road. The constable's office was in the middle of town; and as they approached, the lawman stepped into the street and raised his hand.

"Stop right there, Salem Greene. I've heard enough to know you're up to no good, and it's my sworn—"

"If you've heard, then you know what I've done," Lem said through clenched teeth. "And you know I have nothin' to lose by going past you, one way or 'tuther." A murmur went through the crowd, and the paunchy lawman swallowed hard. He dropped his hand to the small pistol stuffed in his waistband.

"He just wants to talk to Sprague," Burt said, stepping in front of Lem.

The constable looked past Burt and studied Lem for a second. "You armed?"

"No."

"Then you can talk in there." The constable nodded toward his office. "Go on in and I'll find Jason."

He stared at the dumpy man with the round badge but didn't move.

Burt wore a hopeful half smile. "Let's do as he says, Lem. Sounds fair."

Lem walked into the squat one-cell jailhouse and went to the single window where he stood, looking out.

Burt came in and sat. "Have a seat, Lem."

"I'm in no mood to sit. I just want to be out of here. I've got no business here anymore."

"You'd better sort this out now. Otherwise, the marshal will come looking for ya."

"All I want is to see Sprague. He needs to know he's made an enemy."

"But you have to tell the constable about LeFarge and Barron."

"Nothing to tell, Burt. They're dead. Let the crows have them."

"That's not very—"

Lem spun around, eyes narrowed: "Don't you dare say *Christian*, Burt. They weren't. And neither am I."

"But—"

Lem took two quick steps toward the sawyer and poked a finger at his face. "They got what they deserved. And I'll get what I've earned. But it's not for you to hand it out, Burt. Not you, or the constable, or the Goddamned marshal."

Burt slumped back in his chair, lowered his head, and stared at the floor. He was still staring when the constable entered, followed by Jason Sprague.

The constable went to his desk, and Sprague had reached the middle of the room before he saw Lem. He paused, and his eyes, both bruised, narrowed for a second before he continued to the constable's desk. There he turned to half sit on the front edge of it. A sniff creased his swollen nose, and he winced as he dabbed at it with a handkerchief.

"You said I hadn't heard the last, Sprague," Lem began. "Well, neither have you."

"Say what you've got to say." Sprague looked up and down at Lem's grimy clothes.

"Your two friends are dead."

"What?" A shadow flicked over Sprague's face. "They're not my . . . who are you talking about?"

"LeFarge and Barron. But not before Barron said you'd warned them I was looking for 'em."

The constable gulped. "You've killed two men?" He rose

152

from his chair.

Lem glared at Sprague. "Two murdering beasts who nearly escaped . . . because of you."

"Ill-bred peasant, you better—" Sprague started.

Burt was out of his chair in an instant and stepped in front of Lem. "Don't!" he shouted and put his hand on Lem's shoulder. A muttering came from the crowd just outside the door.

"Constable," Sprague sputtered, stepping away from Lem. "Keep that criminal away from me."

"Greene!" the paunchy lawman shouted. "I'll not have you making threats. Now, you've killed two men, by your own admission. And for no reason that I can see."

Lem looked at Burt. "The hat?"

"I haven't talked to him yet, Lem." Burt grimaced.

Lem shrugged off Burt's hand and stepped closer to the constable. "I found Barron's hat at my place, bloodstained. And you know Barron had the doctor sew up his face. At their camp, I heard Barron cursing my boy for cutting him. And I found this." Lem reached inside his shirt and took out the tiny silver bell. "Barron had it. He called it his new toy." Lem swallowed hard and put it back. "It belonged to my wife."

"I'd have done the same," someone outside shouted; and the crowd murmured agreement.

"Sprague knew about the hat—I showed it to him. He knew I was looking for them. And he knew I was going to Careytown."

The constable started toward Lem. "You're under arrest, Greene, for killin' two men." He turned and pointed at Sprague. "And for assaulting him."

Ferret-quick, Lem stepped around the lawman, grabbed Sprague by his cravat, and yanked him into the middle of the room. His face screwed tight, teeth bared, he jerked the man close. "I want to know why, Sprague." Lem pushed and Sprague backed toward the door. "And you'll tell me or I'll break yer neck." The crowd parted as Lem shoved him out the door and into the street. "I want to know why you'd help swine like that."

"Greene!" The constable hustled through the door, pistol drawn. "Take your hands off him!"

"Tell me, Sprague." Lem twisted the blue silk cloth and Jason's color changed from chalky white to florid red. "Now!"

"Needed . . . them." Sprague squeezed out the words. "Useful."

An angry mutter rippled through the townspeople. Lem heard them somewhere deep in the back of his mind, and vaguely heard his name again. *"Greene!"* He focused on Sprague's terrified eyes, and struck as hard as he could with his tightly bunched fist. The ripe nose erupted in a spray of blood and mucous, and Sprague sagged to his knees. Lem hit him again in the side of his head.

"Greene!"

Lem jerked up on Sprague's necktie, and drew back his fist once more. Burt grabbed it and twisted the muscular arm behind Lem's back. "Stop, Lem! He's had enough."

Lem fought to shake Burt off, but the hold on Lem's arm was strong and sure. He ceased to struggle, and let go of the unconscious Jason Sprague. The dapper man, now a bloody mess, flopped back into the dust like a disjointed manikin.

"Put your hands up, Greene," the constable ordered, his voice shaky. "Put 'em up and turn around."

Lem couldn't tell if it was fear or anger that caused the lawman's voice to quaver. And it didn't matter; it simply didn't matter. He stepped over Sprague's body and started down the street. "I'll be at my place if the marshal wants me."

"Stop right there!" the constable shouted.

Lem kept going.

"Stop, or by God I'll shoot you!"

The crowd, which now filled the street from side to side,

parted as Lem walked through. Several nodded sadly as he met their eyes; but most simply bowed their heads and stepped back.

"Stop, I say!"

Lem walked the length of the street without looking back, through the lumberyard and to the landing and his boat. Taking the bell out of his shirt, he carefully put it in his knapsack. Then, shoving the bow back, he jumped on board.

"You have to pay for this!" the constable shouted from the shore. "You have to pay!"

"I am," Lem muttered, and with another look at Percy's fire circle, walked slowly back to the cabin and went inside. The story relived, Lem felt drained, and went to his bed. "Demon be welcome," he thought as he lay down.

CHAPTER 14

Lem's ax made quick work of the small branches as he swamped a tree he'd laid down that morning. After the Indian had stolen his jerky, he'd spent three unsuccessful days hunting for another deer; but chill evenings reminded him of the certainty of bad weather to come, and of his need for more firewood. So now he usually brought his rifle along in case he saw an animal. That had been over three weeks ago, and he was beginning to wonder if a boat was ever going to pick up the last fifteen cords he'd stacked.

The autumn sun felt good on his back as he slammed his ax into the stump and picked up his saw. He'd no more than set the teeth into the bark when the piercing scream of a steam whistle ripped the air. From the meager shade of a nearly defoliated beech, his mule fluttered its lips as the boat sounded again; longer this time, with a final trailing wail. The animal started braying.

It was the first time Lem had heard a boat make that much noise. Another blast came with the same ending note. Was it meant for him? Three quick blasts came in short order, then three more. They *were* calling to him.

"Now what would they want with me, Mr. Mule? They've never done that before." The beast turned its ears toward him for a moment, and then set them back to attend to the boat. Lem wiped his brow on a damp sleeve. "Guess we better go see what they want." He put his saw down and approached the mule. "Stand still now." Lem knelt by the mule's hobbled front feet. "Let me get those off." He put the thick leather straps by the tree, and then hooked the towing traces to the collar before swinging astride the animal. The creature looked back at him and shook its head. "C'mon now, don't get that look." Lem nudged its ribs, and the mule started down the slope toward the river.

The steamer moored bow-on to the riverbank. Two ropes, each thick as a man's wrist, reached to a couple of mature trees. A gangplank connected the vessel to the shore, and several men were busily moving Lem's neatly stacked wood aboard the boat. They were arranging it on both sides of the lower deck, and it looked to Lem like they were already nearly a third done. A bearded man, smartly dressed in a dark blue coat, white shirt and wearing a billed cap, stood at the peak of the second deck. The captain? Lem wasn't sure, but he instantly recognized the diminutive second man who stood there dressed in brown buckskin: Dufrey!

The Cajun saw him, waved, and then spoke to the bearded man. A moment later, he disappeared on the far side of the boat, emerging a minute later on the lower deck. He paused for a break in the line of black men carrying wood, and then strode down the gangplank.

"Good to see you, Lem Greene!" he almost shouted as he walked up.

"Likewise, Dufrey." Lem shook his outstretched hand. "What's all the ruckus with the whistle?"

"I wanted to make sure you were still here. Looks like you are." He chuckled. "Decided to see if your offer was a good one."

"My offer?"

"To stay a bit." The Cajun cocked his head. "If I was to come back?"

"Of course." Lem clapped him on the shoulder. "Yeah, offer still stands. Welcome."

Dufrey smiled and nodded at the boat. "The skipper has your provisions. Soon's they git the wood on board we'll git our things off."

"*Our* things?"

"Sure. I won't be gobbling up your winter stores. Brought some of my own." Dufrey patted the mule's shoulder. "I see you're still cuttin'."

"More for something to do than necessity."

They watched the men load for a few seconds and then Dufrey looked back into the forest.

Lem followed the Cajun's eyes. "He's still here, if that's what you're wondering."

"Uh-huh."

"Just not so regular as he was. And now . . . I've got another one."

"Another haunt?"

Lem grimaced. "I don't know if I'd be better off if he was. Nope, an Indian. Come right in my cabin and took that deer you shot."

"Be damned! Did ya track him?"

"I'm not very good at that. I saw where he went into the trees, but even if I'd picked up his trail, he was already well on his way."

"Hmmm." Dufrey scanned the forest again. "Ain't been back?"

"Well, that was actually the second time he'd been here."

"The second—and the first?"

"He was just lookin', I guess. Sneaked right up to the place. I damn near had 'im. I was smokin' that deer in front of the cabin. Waitin' like ya do, I was half dozing when I saw movement across the clearing. I kept my head down, and he circled around to the south side. I waited till I heard him and then threw my ax. He disappeared—quick as a marten."

"He'll be back." Dufrey pursed his lips and lowered his gaze to the ground.

"I don't think so." Lem had seen the expression on the Cajun's face. "What ya smirking at?"

"Tryin' not to, Lem, I swear I am." Dufrey put his hand to his mouth.

"He thinks I'm easy to get around . . . is that what you're sayin'?"

The man's eyes sparkled. "I ain't sayin' it."

Lem could feel his face getting hot. "Yeah, but you're thinking it."

"I just know Indians. Nothing to do with you, Lem—they're sneaky. He got away with it twice, and he'll be back. Probably already been here a time or two."

"Then I'll catch him at it."

"Maybe. Maybe not." Dufrey looked back at the boat.

With the last of the wood aboard, the captain had his men off-load Lem's supplies, and an almost equal amount for Dufrey.

The skipper came back down the gangplank and extended his hand. "It's good to meet you, Mr. Greene. Don't often get to see you folks ashore."

"We're usually well back." Lem shook the captain's hand.

The man counted Lem's pay and gave it to him. "I'll leave this order with my chandler." He stuffed Lem's list into a breast pocket. "Will you have another ten cord or so in three weeks?"

"Ten?" Lem considered.

"Sure we can," Dufrey said, and poked Lem in the ribs.

"Good. I'll bring your goods back, and count on that. Must be off." He half raised his hand, and hurried up the gangplank.

Soon, the loading boom had the ramp slung, and the huge

stern wheel started turning in reverse as men dragged the mooring ropes onto the deck. The steamer backed away a bit to let the current catch the bow, then the whistle let loose two short blasts, the wheel reversed, and the boat slowly gathered speed. With twin stacks belching sparks, soot and smoke, the great paddle beat the water to foam as the vessel moved to the center of the river.

"You didn't have to volunteer your hands to cut wood, Dufrey. When's the last time you worked a saw?"

"I could use a week or so of that kind of abuse. Been gettin' soft. 'Sides, I like to earn my keep."

"That mean you ain't gonna cook?"

"Oh, I'll cook. Just to *preservate* myself, if nothin' else." The Cajun laughed out loud. "Well . . . ya ought to see the look on yer face." He continued to chuckle.

"I can see it's gonna be a long three weeks." Lem shook his head, turning his face to hide a smile. "Let's tie what we can on the mule, and then come back for the rest with a pack saddle."

The boy slipped out of his cave in the early morning, and hurried, bucket in hand, to the water hole. It had been more than two weeks since he'd taken the jerky, and during that time he'd worked hard, bringing in as much deadfall wood as he could manage without an ax. He'd also made forays into the forest for roots and bulbs, and accumulated a good store of them. This morning's air had a definite nip to it; he hurried along, ragged nightshirt flapping around his legs.

The move to the back of the cave had been a good one. He felt safer, and the occasional drafts that used to wake him could not be felt in the larger room. With a good fire going, it was actually quite pleasant. What worried him now was the weather. The last two days had been cloudy and cool, almost cold; the first hard freeze was not far off. Could he survive a winter?

When he hadn't been doing something else in preparation for winter, his father had kept him busy with the small ax on the woodpile every day but Sunday. It seemed everything they did was to prepare the cabin for winter. *Home.* He felt a twinge of loneliness. Could he even find the cabin if he went looking? How far had he traveled after—he shook his head against the thoughts that started to form.

He slowed his pace and crept to within sight of the pool. The water hole was deserted, so he stood and walked directly to it. He'd killed three rabbits in the past week and hadn't touched his supply of dried meat since then. He knew there wasn't enough to last, but he was forming a plan to take care of that. First he had to make sure his knee was better; he flexed it and smiled. Soon he'd go find what he needed to get him through the coming cold. Stooping, he filled his bucket, and then hurried back to the cave. There was plenty to do before he visited the woodchopper again.

The boy stood on a slender limb and jumped up and down while shaking another branch with his hands as hard as he could. Pecans, most still wrapped in their hulls, but some free, clattered down around him and showered the ground. He'd literally tumbled into the small grove, clustered on the edge of a large meadow at the base of a steep hill. He'd been chasing a raccoon down the slope, tripped, and fallen head over heels. The coon had escaped, as they usually did; but the sheer number of nuts he saw in the trees dispelled any feeling of defeat. Even though it was distant, he'd gone back to the cave and brought back the jerky sack. The bag was proving almost as valuable as the meat he'd taken.

He shook down only a tiny fraction of the nuts, but those left behind would not be wasted; a dozen squirrels, perched high in the surrounding trees, noisily condemned his thievery. The warm floor at the front of his cave was going to be perfect for drying the nuts; he imagined hundreds of them spread out.

He was interrupted by the high-pitched shriek of a whistle in the distance, and the hair on his neck stood. Another piercing call. It came from the northeast. Then one more. He'd heard boats before, but never one that sounded quite so insistent. Was it hailing someone? Maybe another boat? Was it in trouble? Then he heard three short blasts, followed by three more. Was it calling the woodcutter? He stuffed the partially filled sack into the crotch of a tree, picked up his knife, and took off at a fast jog toward the river.

For weeks he'd thought about going back to the woodsman's cabin, but foraging had kept him busy. This was just the excuse he needed. He was only about a quarter mile from the river, and it didn't take him long to get it in sight. He scrambled over the bluffs until he saw the rock cliff on the far riverbank, then slowed down until he caught sight of smoke. Easing to the top of the last ridge, he spotted the blue-and-white steamboat, nose-on to the bank. Black men were moving the last of a stack of wood from shore to the deck. Near the end of the gangway stood two men; he recognized one: the shaggy woodsman.

He lay on the ground and watched. Though he could hear an occasional loud voice, he couldn't make out any words. Then all the wood was loaded, and the men started to take bags and packages off the boat. Supplies! The woodsman's winter food. What had he bought? Tempted as he was to get closer, his last close call remained fresh in his mind. Then another man appeared on the ramp, walked ashore, and joined the other two. They stood and talked.

The boy studied the pile of supplies, and tried to imagine how many trips the woodsman would have to make to move it all to his cabin. A smile crept over his face, and he eased himself back off the ridge. Out of sight, he stood and hurried toward the cabin, keeping just below the crest. He ran the half mile and settled down in the familiar spot on the edge of the clearing. A whistle blast alerted him minutes later, and he strained to see the woodsman. He'd wait until the man started back for the second load and then he'd get a look at what the boat had delivered.

Unexpectedly, a short, thickset man dressed in brown appeared on the trail, and right behind him was the woodsman, leading a mule. Where had the mule come from? A puff of exasperation escaped the boy as he watched them cross the clearing to the cabin. He tried to imagine how much was left at the shore. Maybe he would still get a look at the treasures they carried.

The men reached the cabin and went inside with their bundles, but reappeared almost immediately. The short man took two hams off the mule and went back in, while the woodsman took the harness off the animal. He replaced it with a wooden rig he had hanging on the outside cabin wall. Soon, the two men headed back down the trail with the mule in tow. The boy watched them move out of sight, then stood and sprinted across the open ground. With one quick glance over his shoulder, he opened the door and stepped inside.

The enormous hams lay on the table, and on the hearth were the tote sacks the short man had carried. On the floor at the foot of the bed lay the paper-wrapped package the woodsman had brought in. He went to the table, put down his knife, and bent over to inhale the delicious smoky aroma. Salivating, he wrapped his arms around one of the cloth-wrapped delicacies and lifted it off the table, but immediately put it back down: it was heavy and awkward!

Next he went to the sacks in front of the fireplace and dropped to his knees. The first bag he looked in had many smaller parcels inside. He took one out, sniffed it, and jerked his face away. The second one he retrieved didn't smell any better, and he put both back. The third made his heart skip; it made the crunching sound that only chunks of sugar can. He took the package out, and then opened the second sack. It contained bags of beans, rice and flour. After hefting a bag of beans in his hand, he took a second one, and stood. He put the prizes on the table, and then went to the package by the bed.

He knew what it was as soon as he picked it up . . . clothes. Tearing the heavy paper open on one end, he immediately found something of use: two pair of heavy wool socks. With his new footwear tucked under one arm, he returned to the center of the cabin and slowly looked around. He knew what he needed, but he couldn't see it: the sharpening stone. It had to be there. A long plank shelf was fastened to the left wall, extending over the bed and beyond. Standing on the bunk, he felt with his hand where he couldn't see. Just past the end a red coffee grinder was attached firmly to the wall. The low mantel over the fireplace allowed him to view the top, but he found nothing of interest on either shelf.

The right wall was festooned with hanging garments: shirts, trousers, a large wool overcoat, an oilskin slicker, and long underwear. The boy glanced down at his ragged nightshirt, then went to the wall and unhooked the heaviest plaid wool shirt he could see. Draping the socks over a chair back, he held the shirt up to his scrawny chest; the hem reached the middle of his shins. He gave the trunk by the door a passing look—its big, forbidding hasp clapped shut—then picked up his knife and carved off the biggest piece of ham he could manage, taking cloth and all. With a last look around, he put the meat, beans, sugar and socks on the shirt, bundled them up, and tied the long arms together. As an afterthought, he went back to the fireplace and grabbed a small pot. With his booty slung over his shoulder, he stepped back outside, and moments later he was in the trees, jogging toward his cave.

CHAPTER 15

On the way back to the cabin with the second load, Lem had decided not to go back to work and felt a little foolish at the reason. He was eager to see what the Cajun had brought. He speculated about that as they walked into the clearing. Dufrey's hand touched his arm—Lem turned to face him. The Cajun, finger to his lips, signaled silence, and then moved out front. The long rifle swung up and was at the ready before Lem could follow his gaze.

"The door's open," Dufrey whispered. "Stay here with the mule."

Without waiting for a response, he angled sharply off to the right, skirting the edge of the forest. His short legs carried him a lot faster than Lem would have thought possible. It took him less than half a minute to reach the front of the cabin and flatten himself against the front wall. With his rifle pointed toward the door, he sidled sideways, and then turned his head as if to listen. A few seconds later, Dufrey stepped into the doorway, and went inside. He reappeared almost immediately and waved for Lem to follow.

"The thievin' devil's got brass, I'll give 'im that," said Dufrey as Lem came in.

Lem's eyes followed the Cajun's nod; a quarter of one ham was missing. He spun around and looked at the trunk by the door. "Anything else?" he asked as he went to it and tried the locked hasp.

"Don't know yet." Dufrey went to his parcels by the fireplace. Lem continued to look around.

"Hope you have some spare sugar. He got that and looks like some beans." Dufrey continued to rifle through the packages.

"And my little pot," Lem added as he looked over the fireplace. "He must have been watching us."

"Told ya he'd be back. You weren't the only one who heard that boat. Wouldn't surprise me if he was out there right now, smilin'."

Lem glanced at the open door, then rushed for it. "Damn."

"I already checked," Dufrey said. "Yer rifle's there."

Lem swung the door half-closed and took his rifle from behind it. "That's all I'd need now, an Indian with a rifle watching me."

Dufrey got up from the hearth. "No sense starin' at a busted crock. Let's unload the mule 'n git on with our business." He walked past Lem and went outside.

With everything inside, Lem rode the mule to the worksite, picked up his tools and the hobbles and then took the mule to the meadow. When he got back to the cabin, chimney smoke lifted into the afternoon sky. He entered to find Dufrey kneeling at the hearth. "I see there was enough heat in the ashes to get a fire going."

"Yep. Gonna make you up a pure Cajun delight. It'll take a bit, but we have an early start and I think you'll find it worth the wait." Dufrey glanced around the cabin. "Where's yer water bucket?"

Lem felt his scalp react. "Indian took it."

Dufrey glanced up. "Ya said he got the deer. Yer bucket too?"

Lem exhaled loudly. "Yeah. And my matches, and the bag the jerky was in," he admitted, and could hear the irritation in his own voice.

Dufrey looked down at the knife in his hand. "And he left

your knives?" He glanced at Lem's bed. "And the blankets?"

"I told ya: jerky, matches and bucket." Lem's good mood was wearing thin.

"Hmmm. So where's your water?"

Lem sighed. "It's outside," he mumbled and went out the door, returning immediately with a heavy wooden bucket, which he set on the hearth.

Dufrey looked at the clumsy receptacle for a moment, and massaged a smile off his lips with one hand. "Handy," he muttered, then used the ladle to fill both the black kettle and a smaller pot about half full. Opening the two cloth bags that lay by his knees, he hand measured some red beans into the kettle and white rice into the pot. "There. Let that soak for a while, and then I'll start on the other."

The "other" had Lem's curiosity aroused. He could smell whatever it was and the aroma was like nothing he'd experienced before.

Dufrey looked up at Lem. "Tell me how you've been." He settled on the hearth, his back against the chimney.

"Off and on. Some good days, some not so."

"Ya seen your visitor out in the woods again?" Dufrey's hand shot up. "You don't have to say if ya don't want to."

"No, that's all right. You'll see. He's moved in here."

Dufrey looked taken aback, and then scowled. "I don't follow ya."

"I've seen him. Standing right over there." Lem pointed to the corner by the window. "Plain as day. But he wasn't there. And his face shows up on my plate, in the fire, in the water bucket. He shows up, and then vanishes. I'm getting used to it. Sick to death of it, but used to it. You'll see."

"I 'spect I won't. I'm figgerin' this is just 'tween him and you." Dufrey's eyes narrowed as he spoke. "Could be wrong, jist the way I see it."

"You sayin' it might all be in my head?"

"I see with my *own* eyes enough peculiar things to not question what other folks see."

Dufrey was saying things that Lem had thought about and dismissed; the spirit was too real to be imagined. But why did it never leave any sign? A cool breeze didn't either, yet there was no doubt when it was around. Lem stared at the glowing coals in the fireplace and watched the heat play. Any second he expected Barron's face to appear. He became aware of Dufrey's gaze and shook his head.

"And the Indian?" the Cajun asked. "Ya didn't see any sign of him till today?"

Lem paused a second or two. "No. But like ya said, I'm not very good at seeing things I should."

"That's not what I said. I said he's sneaky." Dufrey glanced at the pots, and then pushed himself off the floor. He went over to the door and picked up his rifle. "The way to get him is to go where he is. I'll take a look around tomorrow; see if I can find where he's been. If he's makin' a habit of watchin' you, I'll see the sign and maybe work out how often he's comin' around. And then one day I'll wait for him. A rifle ball from two hundred yards will show him who the sneaky one is." He put the gun down and went back to the hearth. "That'll take care of one of yer troubles."

While Dufrey fussed with his fixings, Lem went outside to work on increasing the size of his woodpile. He'd sawed more than enough sections to last the winter, but was behind on getting it all cut into manageable pieces. Splitting wood had always been a time of contemplation for Lem, and as he set the first billet upright on the chopping block, his conversation at the river two hours before came to him. "I decided to see if your offer was a good one." Dufrey's statement had taken Lem by surprise.

He'd been thrilled to see the short man standing on the deck of the steamer. The last few weeks had been a succession of desperate, sleepless nights, and weary days. The Cajun, or anyone, for that matter, might just be what he needed to break the hold that Jake Barron had on him. Though he still believed that he was unfit to be around other people, he knew that his mind was close to breaking.

Lem had no doubt that Barron had tried to drown him that night in the channel by the island, the facts of the matter be damned. He'd spent countless hours reliving the experience, trying to remember what had changed the almost-certain outcome. He never got further than knowing he'd lived, but he no longer cared if he died, evidenced by what he'd done at Booneville later that morning. He'd wished then that the lawman had pulled the trigger and relieved him of his grief. He flexed the muscles in his shoulders as he felt again the almost-physical impression of the constable's pistol pointed at his back. But the constable had held his fire, and for that Lem was grateful . . . most of the time. His thoughts drifted back to the spring.

The lawman's shouted orders to stop echoed in Lem's head as he had pushed his boat away from shore and headed upstream. He'd realized that he was not escaping—he was going to meet his just reward. He had no idea what that might be, but knew he could endure anything if only he could be near his wife.

When he arrived a day and a half later, the cabin was as secure he'd left it, and he went directly to the stack of wood that covered the twin graves. They were undisturbed, and Lem sat on the ground beside his wife and wept. The morning sun found him slumped against the pile, emotionally drained and confused.

He spent the first day burning everything he could find with blood on it, and tried to put the house back into the same order she'd have wanted. He became discouraged and infuriated in turns as he realized how little he knew about his own home, and how much he'd depended on her to do things for him. That evening, he burned his first batch of cornbread, and nearly destroyed the pan taking out his frustration on it. For the next month, he worked from sunup to sundown, punishing his body to relieve his mind of the memories. And then, late one afternoon, the US marshal had arrived.

The mule alerted to someone working their way up the hillside, so Lem put his ax down and waited. A gray, wide-brimmed hat hid the approaching man's face. He wore a shirt the same color as the hat, and dark with sweat under his arms. His riding boots had to make negotiating the uneven ground even more difficult.

"I hope . . . yer Salem Greene," the man panted. He took off his hat and wiped the inside of it with a big blue handkerchief, then plopped down on the ground.

"I am," Lem replied.

"Good, cuz I ain't got another climb in me. I'm US Marshal Caleb Beech." He turned back his vest to show a silver badge attached to his shirt pocket.

Lem looked downhill. "How'd you get here?"

"Horse. He's at your cabin."

"You've got a horse, and you walked up here?"

The squat man kneaded his lower back with both hands. "I've been on her all day, matter of fact, two days. You're hard to find."

"I'm not hiding."

"I know that, Mr. Greene." The marshal gave Lem a wry smile. "It wouldn't do ya no good anyhow." The marshal pointed at the downed tree Lem was half sitting on. "Are you nearly done with that for the day?"

"I can be."

"This sun is about to scramble my brain." Beech settled his hat on his head. "What do you say we go down to your place and we can talk?"

"If that's what you want."

"That's what I want." The marshal got up off the ground.

Lem picked up his ax and stuck it in a tree, hung the saw on it, and went to the mule. All three headed down the hill.

At the meadow, Lem suspended the harness on a branch— well out of reach of salt-craving varmints—hobbled the mule, and then walked to the cabin with the lawman puffing along beside. As soon as they got there, Beech sagged onto the bench in front, took off his hat and wiped his forehead with his arm.

Lem picked up the water bucket and moved it closer to the lawman. "Help yourself." He handed him the dipper.

After he'd slaked his thirst, the marshal handed the ladle back. "Appreciate that. For as green as these forests are, it's hard to stumble onto a spring."

"Is there a trail that leads from Booneville to here?"

"Several. That's the problem. A coon-skinner drew me a map of sorts from memory. I'd have been better off relying on dumb luck. Burt said you lived about fourteen miles upriver. I made four trips down before I found your cabin. The trail goes on by, about two miles back in."

"I wasn't sure. I use the river."

The lawman went quiet for a minute as he looked over the clearing. "I assume that's your family's grave under the pile of wood."

Lem swallowed hard. "It is."

"I'm sorry for your loss, Mr. Greene. All I've heard is what Burt and the constable told me. No sign of the boy?"

"He's gone," Lem said simply. "If you'd just tell me what you've come for, I'd like to say the same of you."

"Ain't no need for that, Mr. Greene." The marshal stood.

"I've seen folks lose kin before, and I understand that they usually see the law as ineffective and useless. That don't mean they should take the law to themselves."

Concern lined the lawman's brow and Lem felt shame. "That was hasty, marshal."

"That's what I think. But I understand. I've got some news you'll be glad to hear, and some thoughts I'd like to share with you."

"Let's take care of your mare first. She looks tired."

Beech flexed his shoulders with a groan, then went over and untied his horse. He turned to Lem with a question on his face.

Lem nodded toward the east. "If you've got hobbles, you can take her to the meadow and she'll be fine with the mule. There's plenty of water."

"Hobbles are right here." The marshal lifted the flap on a saddlebag and took out the leather straps. A minute later, he pulled the saddle off the horse.

Before Beech could put it down by the cabin, Lem pointed at the door. "You'd better put that inside. Pine-pigs will chew it up."

Lem followed the marshal in. "I'll fix us something to eat and we can talk."

"Sounds good." Beech dumped his rig in a corner. "I'll be back shortly." The lawman shuffled out the door, and Lem went to his store of food.

An hour later, Lem pushed his plate away, picked up his coffee cup, and watched the lawman finish the Spartan meal. The marshal crushed half a pilot biscuit with his fork and soaked up the bean juice on his plate.

With a satisfied sigh, Beech sat back in his chair. "That kind of grub will stay with a man."

"I'm not going to apologize, or compare that to what used to be put on the table." He tried to shrug off the twinge of pain.

"I'm just happy I have canned beans, some bacon, and that hardtack."

"Coffee's good." The lawman took a sip, and then paused for a moment. "I had a look at that campsite. Want to tell me how that happened?"

"Some . . . most of it's not very clear."

"Tell me as best you can."

"First, I want you to know what I found here," Lem said firmly.

"You don't have to. I've talked with three or four people who know you, and I don't doubt the story you told Burt."

"I didn't tell Burt all of it, and I need to tell someone," Lem replied. He stood up from the table and walked over to the bedroom door. "As soon as I stepped into the house I could feel something was wrong." He pointed at the floor. "The oil lamp lay there, the chimney smashed. My little girl was just inside the door. She was nine years old, Marshal, and as sweet as spring clover. Helpful to her mother, kind to her brother, just pure joy to be around." Lem set his teeth in his lower lip for a moment. "She was naked, Mr. Beech, beaten, bruised and bloody. And she'd been raped . . . raped." The last word was barely audible and Lem turned to face the hearth, his left hand to his mouth.

Lem had relived the scene many times, yet each time it was newly offensive, and his heart raced to keep up with his rage. Why did he feel compelled to tell this stranger the story, when by the man's own words, it was a story he didn't need to know? Lem knew the answer to that; the same one he always came up with. He needed someone to tell him what he'd done was good, or at least justified, and his need angered him.

He turned to the lawman, and could feel the heat in his face. "My wife's fingernails were torn back," he snarled. "And she had been bitten several times; her lower lip chewed clean through." Lem strode to the table, and planted his balled fists on top. "Did she do that to keep from screaming?" he shouted. "Or did Barron do it because she cut him? Either way, can you imagine?" Spittle flew from his trembling lips. He stepped back, his breath ragged gasps, and stood still for several seconds, his chest heaving.

The marshal looked back at Lem, his lips pursed, concern furrowing his brow. "You've given me the answer I came for, Mr. Greene. You don't need to tell me any more."

Lem went on as though he'd not heard a word. "They cut my boy, and he ran. I can see it. He left his blood from here to the top of the ridge to the west. But they caught him, and then threw him over the edge of a cliff to the rocks in the creek below. He's gone, Marshal. They're all gone!" shouted Lem and he slammed his fist onto the table.

The lawman winced but remained seated. "I was duty-bound to come talk to you, Mr. Greene. I didn't know what I'd find. Considerin' what I saw on that island and what the constable told me, I fully expected to find a madman."

"And you did." Defeat sounded in his voice. "I see my family. I see those two foul animals. I imagine my boy. They're all in my head, day and night. I have condemned myself to hell, Marshal Beech. I'm not fit to live among others."

The marshal stood. "Those two you . . . handled, were wanted in two states for a dozen crimes and one murder. The Frenchman especially; his warrant said dead or alive. There will be an inquest, and by law you need to be there, but I'm inclined to give you your head. Leave here, Mr. Greene. Go somewhere else and try to put this to rest. Most men would have done what you did, God knows."

"That's just it, Marshal. God does know, and just as bad, so do I."

★ ★ ★ ★ ★

Lem felt someone's eyes on him and he turned around.

Dufrey stood in the doorway. "Hate to disturb a man that deep in thought, but supper's ready."

Lem stuck his ax in the stump. "Thinking back about . . . just thinking, I guess." He followed the Cajun into the cabin.

The aroma flared Lem's nostrils, and he went to the fireplace to look in the big kettle. Slowly bubbling on the side next to the fire, short lengths of sausage half floated in a bath of red beans. Cooked rice filled the smaller pot to its rim.

"Sit down and I'll load ya up a plate of that," Dufrey said.

Lem did as he was bid, and a minute later Dufrey put two full plates down on the table, and took a seat opposite.

"That's sure 'nuf Cajun, Lem. The sausage is called andouille." Dufrey drawled the *awn-doo-ee* and grinned, his face full of pride. "You'll like it, guaranteed gratisfaction."

Lem speared a piece of the sausage, looked at it closely for a second, and then bit it in half. The flavors filled his mouth and nose as he chewed. "That's special, Dufrey. I mean, really good." The remaining bite went into his mouth, followed by a forkful of the beans and rice.

The day had faded away by the time they'd eaten everything Dufrey had cooked, and they now sat in front of the cabin in the gathering twilight. Lem stood studying the changing colors of the trees, his mind more or less empty for the first time in weeks. He actually felt contented.

"I stopped in Booneville on my way up. Don't usually do that," Dufrey said absently.

Lem's sense of peace vanished like a wisp of steam, and he looked sharply at the Cajun. "You mention that for a reason?" He sat on the bench.

"I guess I did." Dufrey turned to look directly at Lem. "Heard a couple of things farther downriver."

"Like what?" Lem felt a slight twinge of panic. He liked this short, swarthy man, and didn't want to ruin what seemed to be a building friendship. But then, as with the US marshal, he realized that Dufrey might be another man who could help him find the answer to the question that was slowly destroying his soul.

"I heard about what happened there," Dufrey said. "And I can see where your haunt comes from."

Lem sat silent.

"Do ya want to talk about it, Lem? Ya might not think so, but I listen real good."

The compassion in the Cajun's eyes made Lem's throat seize, and he tried to swallow it away. "It's a bad story, Dufrey. Nobody comes out of it good."

"I'm thinkin' it ain't ended yet, Lem. Gimme a try."

CHAPTER 16

Lem stood and walked away from the cabin a little ways, into the gathering darkness that he'd come to dread. He stopped and turned around. "I've decided that the thing I keep seeing can't hurt me physically."

"That thing, as you call it, is Jake Barron, Lem." Dufrey sounded emphatic. "And I wouldn't be too sure of that. Look what happened to Percy."

"You said Percy shot himself."

"I said his rifle had been fired. T'weren't nary a mark on him."

"But—"

"He was dead, stark nekked, and sittin' outside by what had to be a very big fire. Somethin' unnatural 'bout that. Down on the Delta, they's folks who know about haunts and curses 'n such, mostly nigras. I learnt not to laugh at 'em."

A chill crept up the back of Lem's neck, and he took a couple of steps toward the cabin. "That's devil talk, Dufrey. You don't believe it that stuff do you?"

"You don't think the devil exists, Lem?" Dufrey cocked his head sideways. "You think he ain't pokin' around stirrin' up mischief?"

"It says in the Bible that—"

Dufrey cut him short. "You saw this haunt before you got here, didn't ya?" A slight scowl ghosted over the Cajun's face.

"How'd you know?"

"Just seems to fit with what I've heard. Haunts go where they're invited."

Lem bristled.

Dufrey stood and put his hands up, palms out. "When I heard what happened on that island, and that one of the men you . . . fixed, was named LeFarge, I remembered something that happened to a feller back home. This LeFarge man? Did he talk like me? I mean, did his talkin' sound like mine?"

"I didn't hear him say much, but, yeah, it did."

"Then he weren't a Frenchy, like a Canada Frenchy, he was the Cajun kind."

"Meanin'?"

"This feller back home was a slave master in the cane fields. One day, he pushed 'em too far, and several had at 'im with their cane knives. They tried to hide what they'd done by scatterin' him all over the parish. Some say his spirit is still runnin' around down there, lookin' fer parts. Others say he's there to torment folks who've done somethin' bad wrong, folks with a guilty mind."

Lem puffed his lips dismissively. "That's ridic—"

"I learned not to laugh," Dufrey said seriously.

"This thing I'm seeing don't look like LeFarge."

"From what I hear, you didn't treat either of 'em very gently."

"Dammit, they had it comin'!" Heat rose in Lem's neck.

"I ain't sayin' they didn't. Factly, I think they did." The Cajun paused for a moment. "The problem is, yer not so sure."

Lem felt like he'd just been kicked in the chest by his mule. In a few short minutes of conversation, Dufrey had been able to put his finger on exactly what was plaguing him. He wasn't sure he'd had the right to do what he'd done. He knew the difference between justice and vengeance, and he knew one was not his to deal. At the moment Lem felt confusion. Dufrey had no reason to suggest he'd been wrong to go after those filthy beasts.

But wasn't that what he himself thought? He didn't know how to respond.

"The haunt come after you that night didn't it?" Dufrey asked.

"Yeah," Lem said quietly.

"But you got the best of it, didn't ya?"

"No." Lem shook his head. "Something else did."

Dufrey turned his head slightly sideways. "What?"

"I don't know." Lem studied the treetops for a few seconds. "One minute, something dark and heavy held me under the water. I was drowning for sure. Then, I see light . . . no—no, I feel bright light . . . or I'm in that light—I don't know. I just know I didn't drown, and woke up later in my boat." Lem shook his head vigorously.

"Something wanted ya to live, Lem."

He looked at the Cajun. "What?"

Dufrey shook his head slowly. "I can't know that, Lem. Only you can."

He walked over to the bench and sat. "Do you believe in God, Dufrey?"

"Same as I believe in the devil, Lem. Ya can't ignore either one."

"But you don't seem to put a lot of . . . ya don't seem too concerned what He thinks, I mean talking about evil spirits and haunts runnin' around and—"

Dufrey turned toward him. "If ya knew my thoughts, you'd be me."

Dufrey's face was nearly lost in the dim light, but Lem had the sense that he could feel the Cajun's eyes, and they were friendly and caring.

"I had no right to kill those two, Dufrey. I lost myself in the dark. I think God means to leave me there."

"Maybe you was doin' what He wanted you to do."

"Killin'? That can't be."

"Sure it can. If you'd asked me two years back whether I believed or not, I'd'a give ya the shortest answer they is. I lost my whole family, jist like you. Ain't no god that I'd claim do that to young'ns. Since then, I've seen things happen for reasons that ain't got no reason . . . 'n that goes for both good and bad. That's why I say you can't ignore either God or the devil, they both just are." Dufrey stood and moved into the doorway. "And they both use folks like us all the time." He stepped into the dark cabin.

Lem sat alone on the bench for a few minutes. He could hear Dufrey inside, rummaging through some of the supplies. He wished he could put things straight in his mind as easily as the Cajun seemed to. Many nights, when sleep was only a promise, he'd searched his soul for the flaw he knew existed.

Lem was startled by a flare of light that shot out the door.

A moment later, Dufrey stepped out with a burning candle. "No need to sit there in the dark. Come on in and I'll make us a cup of coffee . . . with chicory."

"Chicory? More Cajun?"

"That be true." Dufrey turned and went back inside.

Lem got off the bench and followed.

Dufrey knelt down on the hearth and put a big skillet on the glowing coals. After pouring in some coffee beans he covered them with a lid and started shaking the pan steadily. It wasn't long before the heady aroma of the roasted kernels spread throughout the cabin. "Ya like it dark or not so?" Dufrey asked.

Lem snorted. "I usually scorch 'em good, but I think that's more by accident."

"We'll git ya in between, then." Dufrey worked on the roast, shaking the skillet gently to begin with. When the first bean cracked, he started to agitate the batch more vigorously. Shortly, the continuous snapping noise slowly decreased tempo, and then came a sizzling sound. He waited a few seconds, then lifted the pan off the coals and dumped the smoking beans into a wooden bowl. He hurried out the door and shook the container while he blew the feathery chaff away into the dark. A minute later, he came back in. "There's enough for the mornin'. You do have coffee in the mornin' don't ya?"

Lem sniffed the air. "I do now." He reached out. "Let me have that." He dumped about half of the piping-hot beans onto the hopper of the red grinder near the foot of his bed. Turning the crank, he ground the beans into a small tin can.

Dufrey took the coffee and shook about half the contents into the boiling water, followed by a small handful of flakes he took from one of his mysterious bags. The pot immediately overflowed with foam, hissing into the hot coals. "That smells so good, I can't believe me."

Lem held out two enameled mugs, and when the Cajun had filled them both, went to the table and took a seat.

"Do ya have sugar?" Dufrey asked as he stood.

Lem pointed at the shelf. "Plenty. There's most of a busted-up cone in that small square tin by the grinder; two or three more whole ones in the trunk over there."

Dufrey pried off the lid and took out a thumb-sized piece of the light brown treasure. "You want some?"

"Never learned to like sweet coffee." Lem blew across the steaming brew he'd lifted to his lips.

The Cajun came over, dropped the chunk of sugar into his own cup and sat. Reaching into the top of his soft boot, he took out a short knife, slowly stirred his coffee with it for several seconds, and then took a sip. He smiled as Lem followed suit. "That'll put you in a mood for some good news I brought from downriver."

Lem swallowed and looked at Dufrey over the rim of the cup. "That gives it a different taste, that's for sure."

"Do ya like it?"

"I think I do." Lem took another sip. "Ya say good news?"

"Yep. That marshal who was here . . . Leech? He said if I was to run onto you to tell ya that the judge took yer side."

"His name was Beech. Whatcha mean my side?"

"Ya killed the right man first, Lem. The Frenchy was wanted for murder and that warrant give anybody the right to capture him—dead, if that's how it worked out. The judge also said that the way you told it, Barron was awake and trying to escape when you stopped him. He said his death was a missed adventure. I don't understand that part. Anyhow, you ain't got nobody looking for ya now."

Lem put his cup down. "You're saying the law—a judge—believes I did right?"

"More 'n that. The US marshal's office in Natchez, Mississippi, has five hundred dollars gold in their safe fer ya. LeFarge had a reward on hisself."

Lem sat quietly for a few seconds and stared at his steaming cup.

Dufrey leaned over the table. "Yer still thinkin' you had no right, ain'tcha?"

Lem sighed and looked across at the Cajun. "That's what I believe. It's what I taught my family, as it was taught to me."

The Cajun snorted and leaned back in his chair. "What if it was time for them two ta git stopped? What if you was the one to do it? What would ya think then?"

"I can't be judge and executioner, Dufrey."

"You weren't the judge, Lem. That's what I'm saying. They was both judged already, one in Mississippi, the other in Tennessee. You was jist the man who give 'em what they earned."

For the first time since the day before he left his family, Lem felt the guilt stop gnawing for a few seconds. Could he have been made an avenger? He'd tried, unsuccessfully, to find the place in the Good Book that talked about that; a man could put a kinsman's murderer to death when he caught him. Dufrey had said the same thing; both God and the devil used people. Could he have been right to kill them both?

"Ya know I'm right, don'tcha?" Dufrey interrupted Lem's thoughts.

"If just to stop the ache in my guts, I might. I'll have to think on it some more." Lem's eyes caught those of his visitor. "I'm glad you came here, Dufrey."

"Maybe I was supposed to." The Cajun gave him a wide wink and took another long slurping swig of coffee.

The next morning Lem awoke to the sound of water being poured. The door stood open, and only a faint light came through. He sat up.

"Ya sleep jist like a possum," Dufrey said without looking up from the hearth.

"I can't remember the last time I did that." Lem stomped his feet into his shoes and stood. "I can make us something to eat."

"If that's what ya want, but I surely don't mind. Factly, I enjoy it."

Lem headed for the door. "No, no. Told ya I hate it. I'll go get some more wood." Lem glanced at the wet wooden bucket. "Looks like ya already been to the spring."

Dufrey turned to look at him. "Yep. That's a deal, then. I cook, you fetch wood."

Lem chuckled and went out the door.

By the time they'd finished eating, it was almost full daylight. Lem picked up his nearly empty cup, and leaned back in his chair. "So, we start on ten cord of wood today?"

Dufrey nodded. "Yep, we can, but I'd like to take a look around first."

"For the Indian?"

"Uh-huh. He's camped out near here, but I don't think he's gonna stay much longer."

"How do you figger that?"

"He's stealin' a whole lot less than he could. Two bags of beans, instead of just taking both sacks of ever'thing. Took yer small pot and left the big kettle. Had a slice of ham, mind you a big slice, but not the whole thing. Nope, he's jist lookin' for something to eat. Maybe he's on one of them journeys they go on when they's young."

"Do you think he means us harm?"

"Don't care. He's a thief and I can't abide one. They're not to be trusted. What if you was to catch him red-handed? Think he might fight? No need to take the chance . . . dead'ns can't." Dufrey drained his cup and stood. "I'll find ya when I get back. Won't be past midday."

The Cajun grabbed his long rifle and shoulder bag, and left.

The boy released a fluttering burst of gas into the darkness and immediately felt another surge start to build in his guts. He blew a puff of air through pursed lips and got out of bed. The night before, he'd not waited for the beans to cook through and was paying for it now. However, along with the ham, they'd tasted wonderful, and he felt quite pleased with himself. He made his way out of the rear of the cave, and into the better-lit front. There, he paused at the entrance and listened carefully. All the sounds were familiar and normal, so he bent down and made his way out into the morning air.

A few minutes later, he reentered the cave, finished off the rest of the beans and another piece of ham, and then left for the pecan tree. The morning air moved coolly over his skin, but not so much that he needed his ragged nightshirt; he jogged along the faint trail naked. The forest seemed alive with squirrels and birds. Several unseen ground dwellers scurried to safety as he rushed past. He was in tune with all of it, secure in his knowledge of the area. The dreaded beast that used to come in the night was now a dim memory, and he felt safe in his cave. He smiled as he hurried along—the woodcutter was going to be handy. But his smile was short-lived; there were two of them now. Was the second man just a visitor? That could be dangerous.

The sack was in the crotch of the tree where he'd left it, undisturbed. A greeting party of several squirrels took up positions in the trees, and started their protest. He picked up a nut, chucked it at the nearest one he could see, then laughed as the rodent scampered a little way away and stopped, tail twitching indignantly. The boy dropped to his hands and knees, and started to gather the nuts. It didn't take him long to clear them all up, and his sack was nearly half full. Content, he leaned back on his elbows, and sat still for a few minutes and enjoyed the warm sun on his skin. He studied the branches in the pecan tree and selected the one to work on next.

The limb was on the side opposite of the one he'd shaken yesterday and he tromped hard and shook the branch over his head at the same time. The shower was as impressive as the cacophony of chatter from the squirrels. Satisfied, he climbed back down and moved his sack into the thick of the bounty. There were more today than yesterday, and he felt a charge of excitement. It occurred to him that more squirrels than before had raised a ruckus, and he paused to listen and look. Then he realized that the rodents on the far side of the meadow had joined the fray. They were settling down, now that he was out of the tree. "The selfish little devils hollered for help," he said quietly and chuckled. As he snatched the pecans off the ground and put them in the sack, the squirrels across the way started up again. He stood back up and searched the trees. Deer? In mid-morning? A bear, then? He glanced back over his shoulder at his escape route. The brush beyond the pecan grove beckoned. Safer out of sight.

Just as he stooped to pick up his sack and leave, something else caught his attention and he froze, his stomach turning. How could he have missed it? The short man, dressed in light brown, blended well with the background and he could have missed him, except for the glint of sunlight on metal. Even as his muscles tensed for what he knew must come next, he also knew he was too slow. He saw the puff of white smoke.

CHAPTER 17

Dufrey made his way to the edge of the clearing near the river path, and then moved slowly left, along the tree line. Near one particularly large bush, he dropped to one knee for a few seconds, then got back up and continued. He was due north of the cabin the next time he stooped to look. A slight smile spread over his face and he glanced back at Lem's cabin before he stepped into the woods.

The savage he tracked was young and small, and his evenly spaced footprints barely showed in many places. The sign indicated he was unhurried, and moving in more or less a straight line—like someone going home. The Cajun moved confidently up and over the first two ridges and through the shallow valleys in between. The occasional footprint spoke clearly in the game trails. Then he ascended the far side of the third valley and his confidence evaporated. The track disappeared into a spine of windswept rock, and on the other side, a steep drop-off made forward progress impossible. Right or left; which way had his quarry gone?

After only a moment's hesitation, Dufrey turned right and started toward the river. A larger man would have left some sign in the rocky ground: a stone disturbed, a patch of lichens scuffed up, a small impression in the occasional patch of sparse dirt. The Cajun tacked back and forth across the ridge, and after walking nearly half a mile and finding nothing, he stopped. Either the Indian had been tracked before and was naturally cautious, or he'd gone to the left, away from the river. Dufrey hurried along his back trail and renewed his search up the ridge.

He'd gone only a few hundred yards when he found his answer, a sloping slab of granite showed a scuffmark that ended with an unmistakable impression in the shallow dirt beside it. But was the print made by a human's foot? He got down on his hands and knees and studied it. Fresh for sure, it was just a depression, the soil crushed smooth. He'd followed too many tracks, man and beast, to know not to make a quick judgment. He stood and looked farther along the ridge.

"Give me jist one little slip," Dufrey muttered out loud. "One more sign and I'll have ya."

Moving quickly again, he watched until the precipice on his right gave way to a passable slope into the ravine below. He slowed, looking carefully for a game trail that led down. He soon spotted one, and felt the ancient hunter's thrill when his guess proved right; footprints, plain as the scrub brush they skirted, led downhill.

"Now you've answered another question. You live away from the river, so you have a spring nearby. Yer makin' this easy." He smiled and started down.

The first narrow valley had no water, so he hurried up the ridge and down into the next. It, too, was without the telltale trickle in the bottom. The tracks still led in a straight line to the northwest, and Dufrey increased his pace, going farther and farther before slowing to find another footprint. And then he couldn't locate one.

Dufrey let out an exasperated snort, and started back down his own trail until he located the last sign. Slowly, he resumed his search, looking for the change in direction. He found it in a thick stand of small trees that huddled in the bottom of the canyon. The game trail he'd been relying on continued straight out the other side, while the footprints turned abruptly west, along the bottom of the dry ravine. A hundred yards farther on, the tracks intercepted another animal path and fell in line with it. The Cajun stood in the bright sun and shook his head.

"You've been here longer than I thought. Knew right where to turn and find another deer trail. And you feel safe enough to not worry about yer tracks." Dufrey chuckled softly. "That's yer undoin'."

The trail led up the valley and then turned to climb over another ridge. The Cajun stopped at the crest to survey the landscape. More ground, just like he'd traveled for the last two hours, advanced to the west, ridge after ridge sloping down to the river he couldn't see, but knew was there. The next ravine was wider than most he'd seen, and a quarter mile away was a nearly circular meadow. He imagined the game trails meandering to it, a natural feeding place, and plotted its location in his head. He'd come back later in the week and shoot something in the early morning. But that was for later. He started down the slope.

Several times during the chase he'd disturbed animals, especially squirrels, and they'd let him know it. The excited chatter as he moved onto the more even ground at the bottom sounded familiar, but unusual—it wasn't nearby. He stopped and pinpointed the noise; they were down the valley. And there were a lot more than just two or three. He looked at the tracks. Had the Indian circled around? Headed for the meadow? For roots maybe? The ruckus got louder. Dufrey picked a landmark, a large oak with a lightning-blasted branch off to his left, and started in the direction of the clearing.

The trees thinned abruptly, and the Cajun slowed his pace as he came to the open area. The majority of the noise was coming from the far side of the meadow, but several squirrels right over his head had joined in the protest. He stopped next to the trunk of the largest tree he could see, stood perfectly still, and watched as he waited for the rodents to quiet down. Then he saw the reason for the disturbance. The branches near the top of a tree on the far side shook violently. He looked closely for the reason, probably two young bears playing tag. The movement stopped as they decided to climb back down. Smiling, he waited to get a look at them.

His jaw dropped as the young Indian jumped out of the tree, dark hair flying. "Gotcha," Dufrey whispered. The Cajun hadn't seen the sack that the boy stooped to pick up. Lem had said the thief took the jerky, bag and all. This was the scoundrel he was looking for. The young man bent and started to pick things off the ground. Dufrey stepped away from the tree, and the squirrels overhead reacted anew. He felt a twinge of annoyance when the boy stood and looked directly at him. The Cajun pulled the hammer back as the long gun came to his shoulder. The front blade settled instantly into the "V" of the rear sight, and he lined both up with the top of the boy's head. His finger increased pressure on the trigger.

Pecans! For an instant, Dufrey's focus switched to the distinctive trees behind the Indian. He was picking up pecans! Even as the rifle erupted, spewing flame and death, he tried to pull the shot off target. He stepped to the side to see around the smoke, and felt sick when he couldn't see the boy standing. Dufrey cussed under his breath and started across the meadow.

Lem spotted Dufrey following the obvious trail that the mule's frequent trips to the river had left. He glanced at the sun overhead, and went back to work on the log in front of him. The saw made its final cut just as the Cajun puffed to a stop, leaned his rifle against a small tree, and sat in the shade.

"How can you work in the sun without a hat?" Dufrey asked and swiped at his sweating forehead.

"Seems a lot cooler to me if I don't." Lem put the saw down

and joined the Cajun, keen to hear how the hunt had gone. Lem let Dufrey enjoy the shade for a couple of minutes and then spoke. "I was about to stop and eat a bite. You hungry?"

"Found a few grapes but not enough. Whatcha offerin'?"

Lem opened his pack, and handed Dufrey some biscuits and a can of beans. "Ain't gonna be as good as what you're used to."

Dufrey grunted, and pulled his knife out of the sheath. With two deft pokes, he cut an "X" in the top of the can and folded the resulting triangles back. Lem did the same with his folding knife, and the two men silently ate their meal, alternating knife blades laden with cold beans and bites of the dry cracker.

A few minutes later, Dufrey threw his empty can into the undergrowth, and reached for the canvas water bag. He drank deeply, and then handed it to Lem who'd just finished his can. With a satisfied sigh, he leaned back against the tree.

Lem wiped his mouth with the back of his hand and belched. "Didn't find where he's living, did ya?"

"Nope. Learnt a lot about him, though."

"How so?"

"He's not very big. And he lives up a canyon, close to a spring, probably higher up in some rocks."

"How do you know that?"

"Footprints. The length of his steps. And he's well away from the river, couple of miles or so. Needs a waterin' hole."

"And how do you know he stays in the rocks?"

"That's a guess. There's lots of outcrops and crevices all through these hills. Natural places for a hunter to stay." Dufrey shrugged. "Like I say, jist a guess."

Lem couldn't keep a smile off his face.

"That make ya feel better? I couldn't catch 'im?"

"Oh, no. It's just . . . yeah," Lem chuckled: "I guess it does, a little."

"Enjoy yerself. It jist didn't happen today. It will." Dufrey let his hat drop over his eyes, and he folded his hands in his lap.

Lem watched him for a minute and then settled back himself. If the Cajun wanted a short nap, he'd do the same.

"My boy had hair the color of straw," Dufrey said softly just as Lem got settled.

"Light hair?" Lem replied, a little surprised.

"Yep. Hardly any color a'tall. Strange if ya look at mine. And my wife's hair was as black as a crow's wing." Dufrey pushed his hat up with one finger, looked at him for a moment, and then let it slip back down.

"My boy had dark hair. His ma let it get long." When Dufrey said nothing more, Lem continued: "They sneak into my head all the time. Yours too, I see."

"Yep. How big was that boy of yer'n? My Henry was gonna be short like his ma. Smart though."

"Mine was a beanpole." Lem smiled to himself. "Skinny, but tough as a hickory nut. Do you know, he knew more 'n me about roots and things like that. His ma taught him. The three of them would spend all morning in the woods gathering such."

Dufrey grunted under his hat. "Gittin' hotter as we sit here," he muttered, and let out a long sigh.

Lem let his thoughts dwell on his family for a few minutes, and then he put them back into the special place in his mind where they lived. His tired arms relaxed, and he drifted off to sleep.

They worked hard the rest of the afternoon, so the cool of the evening came as welcome relief. Lem sat on the ground, his back against the cabin wall, Dufrey, sideways on the bench, his short legs stretched out on the rough wood.

"What would make ya go back to yer old place, Lem?"

Lem looked sharply at the Cajun. "Told you. There's nothing

there for me."

Dufrey looked away and was silent for a while. "I visit m' family when I'm down there. I feel better fer it."

"You didn't cause their deaths, Dufrey."

"I've been thinking on that." He put out both hands as Lem sat up straight. "Now hear me out."

"I could have been there. I *should* have been there!" He scrambled to his feet. "Why do you want to make me remember that? What the hell are you doing?"

"Tryin' to help, Lem. That's all, jist help a little."

"Don't you see? If I'd have—"

"I talked to your friend Burt. There's no way you could have been there to protect them. No way."

"How—"

"You saw Barron and LeFarge about noon on a Friday. That means they were at your place Thursday night, or sometime the next morning. Even if you'd left Thursday like ya planned, you'd been too late to do anything."

"No. I could have hurried." Lem shook his head violently. "I would have rowed all night."

"Even if you'd known, Lem, ya wouldn't have made it. It's an awful thing, but it's not yer fault. Ya can't take the blame fer them two foul bastards."

The miles and the hours, the distance and the time, swirled around in Lem's head until he felt he was going to be sick. Was Dufrey right? He wanted to believe he was, but somehow he needed to feel guilty as well. Gone. His whole family snuffed like candles. And now Dufrey was telling him he wasn't to blame. He wanted to attack the swarthy man sitting on the bench. Beat him for making him think about it again. Weren't his dreams punishment enough?

As though reading his thoughts, Dufrey continued. "Yer dreams was what you was thinkin', Lem. They were makin' ya take the blame. I'm jist tellin' ya what has to be. Time and those miles of river ain't gonna change."

Lem leaned back against the cabin and sagged to the ground. He sat holding his head. After several minutes he looked up at Dufrey. "I see that you're right. And I should thank you for tellin' me, but—"

"I kin understand why ya don't, Lem. I fought the same demon. I thought I should have moved my family north when the fever started. I didn't know that they'd carry it with them. So, I know, Lem. That's why I wanted to help. Someone did it fer me." The Cajun got off the bench and laid his hand on Lem's shoulder for a second. "Think on it some."

Lem could not trust his eyes to look up as Dufrey walked into the cabin.

Lem lay in his bed and listened to Dufrey on the other side of the cabin gently snore away the last hour of early morning. During the dark hours, he'd played their conversation of the evening before over and over in his mind, and concluded that the Cajun was right. It was simply fate that put him far away from his family when they needed him most, and he just had to learn to live with it. Could he ever return to the cabin where he'd raised his children? Even though the desire was strong, he didn't think so. The wonderful memories might not be enough to force out the hideous ones that also lived in his mind.

It occurred to Lem that he'd spent another day and night without seeing his demon. Was it the same powerful force that had nearly drowned him, and then just as mysteriously disappeared? He had a strong sense that it had been Barron's condemned spirit, but as he himself needed it to be. And what of the light: mind-numbing, bright, white—so strong it overwhelmed the evil he had felt. Was it Rhoda? Lem again felt the power of her arms, strength beyond belief, yet ever so gentle.

Could she still have that effect even though she was gone? It was time to find out for sure.

Grimly, he brought the image of Barron's scarred face to life again, and stared as it hovered above his bed. Eyes that sparked with the fire of hell glared back, and the monster's blackened lips curled to expose rotten teeth. Slowly, Lem pushed his blankets off, and shifted one leg over the edge of the bed. A threatening scowl twisted the jagged wound on the ghoulish face, and Lem almost looked away. He forced himself not to blink, and as his heart beat faster, he swung his other leg over the edge of the bunk and sat up. The apparition retreated as Lem rose to his feet and stood in the faint light that now filled the room. Eye to eye, he faced Barron. Then, slowly, he advanced toward the door, stepping into the rank air left as the monster drifted back. Never taking his eyes off those of his tormentor, he continued moving as the apparition moved closer and closer to the wall. Breathing hard, Lem forced one foot ahead of the other. Two more steps, and the specter, now Barron in full form, reached the wall and stopped.

Lem took another step, his heart faltered, and then jolted alive again as Barron started to pass through the log wall. Taking one long stride, Lem grabbed at the dark form—a brilliant flash filled his head and he crashed backward onto the dirt floor. Shaking his head, he sat up and put both hands to his face, one to a bleeding lip, and the other to a knot rapidly forming on his eyebrow.

"I see you put him out."

Lem rolled to his hands and knees and scrambled for his bed at the sound of Dufrey's voice. He stood, shakily, and wiped his mouth. "I had help," he whispered, his voice weak.

"We usually do." Dufrey rose from his bedroll and went over to the fireplace. "I was hopin' you'd git to that real soon."

Lem sat on the edge of his bed. "I feel that it's gone. Where to, do ya think?"

"To hell, where it belongs."

"Why do you think it was here?"

Dufrey knelt to poke around with a stick. "I told ya. Spirits is jist like people. It was gettin' what it needed here. Ya fed it, give it a place to stay, even talked to it. Don't need much more than that, now do we?" He moved his hand slowly back and forth above the gray ashes, then picked up some splintered kindling and laid it in a small pile.

Lem found his handkerchief, spat blood into it, and then got up to go sit at the table. "But I didn't want it to be here."

The Cajun bent low and blew a steady, gentle stream of air under the wood. Almost immediately smoke started to curl up, followed by a lick of fire. "Are ya sure 'bout that?" Dufrey said it without turning around.

"Course I am!"

Dufrey gave one more little puff, then sat back on his haunches and faced Lem. "We have a strange way of pickin' our own punishment, Lem. It's like we think we'll feel better if we kin first make ourselves feel worse. I've thought on that some, and damned if it ain't true." He picked up some larger pieces of wood and propped them up on the small fire. "I saw the stack of wood they put on that steamer. No single man can cut that much without workin' till his guts ache. And that's jist the flesh part. Ya also took on this Barron fella to keep ya company when ya weren't breakin' yer back in the trees."

"You talk like you know a lot about this."

Dufrey closed one eye against an errant wisp of smoke. "Cuz I do, Lem."

"Well, what about Percy? You said he didn't have an enemy in the world."

"That puzzerlated me too. Till yesterday."

Lem's eyebrows arched and he winced. "Yesterday?"

"Yep. Found something else when I was looking for sign of that Indian. I'll go git a better look at it today."

"At what?"

"I s'pect a grave. Saw the toe of a boot stickin' out of the ground under a big serviceberry bush. I reckon I'll find a foot in it, if the critters haven't been at it too bad."

"Percy killed someone?"

"Maybe ol' Percy weren't as pure as I thought. We'll see." Dufrey turned his attention to the hearth. He filled the coffeepot, hung it on the kettle hook, and swung it over the growing fire.

Lem put his pants and shoes on, then grabbed the nearly empty bucket and went outside. For the first time in months, he strode confidently along the path to the spring, enjoying the smell of morning-damp woods, and the fresh, cool air of early fall. His lip had quit bleeding.

When he got back to the cabin, Dufrey was dressed, and the coffeepot was beginning to steam a little. Lem put the heavy wooden bucket on the hearth.

"I'm thinkin' I'll go get your tin pail back," Dufrey said from the table.

Lem shrugged his shoulders and smiled. "You said you couldn't find him."

"I said I didn't, not couldn't. I know where he is . . . near enough."

"Well, get my shirt back while you're at it."

"Yer shirt?"

"Yeah. I noticed he got my best long wool one."

"I kin do that. Factly, I'll git all yer stuff back, and maybe a bit more 'sides."

"More?"

"Maybe so, Lem . . . maybe so." Dufrey got up to dump coffee into the pot.

★ ★ ★ ★ ★

The heavy lead ball struck the tree even as the boy crouched and scrambled for the shelter of it, his toes digging into the dirt. Terror focused his mind on one thing, escape. Without so much as a backward glance, he shot around to the far side of the pecan, and with his head held low, broke into a run. Five long strides carried him to the edge of the brush, his eyes searching for the narrow break of a game trail. He spotted it, and dove headlong into the greenery, only to be brought up short when the bag he clutched in his right hand caught on a branch. It was only then that he realized he still held the sack of pecans. Jerking it free, he thought for an instant about leaving it, then clutched the round bundle to his chest, and slipped into the safety of the brush.

Sometime later, he cautiously stepped out of the streambed he'd been hurrying along, and onto the fallen tree that lay across it. Careful not to disturb the bark, he walked the length of it, looked till he saw firm ground, and then stepped off. Picking his way, he covered the last mile, satisfied that he'd left no sign of his passing, and ducked into the darkness of his cave.

He moved to the rear of his lair, and dropped the bag of nuts. He didn't doubt it was the same man he'd seen with the woodcutter. Had the man tracked him from the woodsman's cabin to the pecan grove? That didn't make sense. If he had, he'd have already been to the cave. And why had the man shot at him? For taking a few things? No, the man had been lucky to find him, and the shot, a warning. The chill he felt made him believe otherwise. The man in brown was a hunter, a good one, so how safe was it here? The boy sat on his bed and stared at the dim light to his left. Maybe it was time to leave. Could he find another place like this? Could he find it before the cold that he knew was coming got here? Did he dare continue foraging like he must? He looked around the cave and bit his lower lip.

The tear formed and slipped down his cheek before he could stop it. Angrily, he brushed it away and sniffed. Just when he thought that maybe he was being forgiven for abandoning his family, this happens. Was God punishing him for taking some food? He hadn't taken any more than he needed. What was he supposed to do, starve? The beast that tormented him before was back, only now it wore brown leather, and carried a long rifle. But he'd escaped both before, and he'd do it again. He wiped his nose on the back of his hand, and then went to the front of the cave to spread out his pecans.

CHAPTER 18

The boy dropped another branch on the shimmering bed of coals, and tapered tongues of yellow gently caressed the purple-gray bark. Hidden crevices in the cave wall yielded to the light as the hungry fire ate at the dry cherrywood. His feeling of contentment grew as the fire's glow pushed back the darkness. Lying on his side, his head propped up on one hand, he stared at the flames.

A smile crept over his lips as he thought about the hunter missing. For a few fleeting minutes after the sound of the shot, panic had controlled his body. Seeking the high ground, he'd charged blindly up the hill until his experience drew him up short. Running without thinking was dangerous. Crouching low, he'd moved to a patch of heavy brush with a good view of the meadow and the pecan trees. There, he'd watched as the man in buckskin made his way quickly across the open to the tree. Stooping down, the short man examined the ground for a moment, then stood and scanned the hillside, his hand shielding his eyes. Prepared to run again, he'd studied the hunter until the man put the butt of his rifle on the ground, and started to reload. Then, crouched low, he'd continued up the hillside, and put the meadow out of sight.

How far away had the man been when he'd shot? A hundred fifty yards? Maybe less. And he'd missed. He looked at the dwindling bag of jerky and even smaller piece of ham. If the woodsman still left to cut and the hunter went with him, why not go into the cabin and get more? He picked up his knife and tested the edge with his thumb; he needed a whetstone. There was a spring-born doe that came to the water twice a day, once early in the morning, and again late in the evening. For weeks he'd seen her walk the same path, stop in the same small patch of brush, and drink from the same spot. It would be easy to take her, but he had to be sure of his knife. One slash was all he'd get, and he had to be sure it cut deep. He pressed his forefinger against the blade edge; it would not do the job.

Chewing on a piece of jerky, he watched the fire slowly consume the wood. He'd done the very same thing when he'd been home—when he had a home. He shattered the growing image before it could take real form, stood and went outside. The sky was ablaze with stars and he found the dipper, located the two end points of light and lined them up with the North Star, just like his pa had shown him. How many times had he done that lately and then felt the same hollow feeling he had now? The way north meant nothing; he'd paid no attention when he'd run away. And even if he had, he could never face his father. Here he had to stay, south of whatever was north and east of what lay to the west. A long sigh escaped him.

He went to the fallen tree and gathered up an armload of branches before ducking into the cave. Settled again in the safety of the rear, he broke off several large pieces and laid them by the fire. He put a chunk on the glowing coals and as the fire took it, he looked around at his place. This wasn't so bad. The new shirt he'd taken was on his bed and he picked it up. With it on, he'd actually gotten too warm in the night. If he could get enough food he could stay here forever, and he knew where it was. Tomorrow, he'd go see what the men were doing, see if they left the cabin empty. The flickering light pulled his eyelids down and he yawned widely. Stretching out on his bed, he draped the wool shirt over his upper body and stared at the fire.

Soon his breathing became slow and deep and his skinny legs pulled up toward his chest.

He shifted in his sleep as his father's razor flashed back and forth across the broad leather strap. He marveled that his father never slipped and cut it in two. Sunday morning meant biscuits and ham gravy, and the boy's gaze flicked from his father to his mother at the hearth. She hummed one of the many songs she knew, while his little sister sat on a stool and took in everything.

He loved Sundays. No wood to cut, no weeds to hoe, no bulbs or berries to pick; just him and his family, safe and sound at home. His father put down the razor, dipped a brush in the pan of hot water in front of him, and then dribbled water into a shaving mug. After a few deft swirls with the bristles, the foamy soap was vigorously swabbed on cheeks and jaw, creating a thick lather. After a bit, his father put the shaving mug down, picked up the razor and dragged the blade from just under one ear to halfway down his neck.

The boy realized he was squinting in anticipation. "Ain't ya scared of getting your throat cut, Pa?"

His father snorted. "It's been known to happen, Martin." He swished his razor in the water.

"Does it hurt to cut 'em off?"

"Sometimes, when I don't pay attention." Naked skin appeared again as the razor scraped down the opposite side of his jaw.

"Why'd ya do it, then?"

"Your mother likes it. And for the same reason that you wash. Feels better." He cleaned his blade again.

"I don't."

His father looked down at him. "Don't what?"

"Feel better when I wash. Especially all over."

"Are we raising a heathen here, Rhoda?"

His mother stood up from the fireplace with a wooden platter heaped with biscuits she'd just lifted from the black iron kettle. She set them on the table, and then stood behind the boy with her warm palms on the sides of his face. "No. I don't think so." Then, she slipped her hands back. "But he needs to pay a little more attention to these." She tugged at both of his ears.

The boy rolled from one side to the other in his sleep and one hand found the spot on the back of his head that prickled. With his fingernails, he searched for the exact spot in the tangled hair. His scratching nearly woke him, but he soon satisfied the itch, and then drifted beyond the dream as a snore gently rattled the back of his throat.

When he woke the next morning the fire was completely out, and he cussed himself for not putting something a little heavier on it before sleeping. His matches weren't going to last forever. He suppressed his need to go out while he assembled a pile of small twigs and shagged bark, struck a match, and nursed the feeble flame into a healthy blaze. Then, he stacked some more wood on the growing flames, and hurried out of the cave.

As he stood by his chosen bush, he glanced at the morning sun. The height of it both surprised and irritated him. He'd intended to be at the water hole before the sun was up to watch for his deer. Maybe, if he hurried, he could still catch her; his morning meal could wait. He reached up with his free hand and dug at the back of his head. His hair was too long, and his knife would no longer cut it, even when he sawed at it. He needed the woodsman's stone. It had finally occurred to him where it was; the trunk by the door. It would be the first place he'd look when he went back. Today? Maybe. With the pressure relieved, he ducked back into the cave, glanced at the now roaring fire, grabbed his knife and went back out.

At the water hole, he put his face to the gently moving air and chose the side of the trail that would put him downwind of the deer. He'd learned the hard way that he stank, and the wild animals had no trouble finding him with their noses. He stepped into the brush and crouched down to practice something else he'd learned the hard way: patience.

Lem sloshed water on the two tin plates and propped them up on the bench to dry.

Dufrey came out of the cabin and stood in the early morning light, his rifle under his arm and his backpack slung over his shoulder. "Ever had a bug in yer face that ya can't see to swat?"

"Worst kind," Lem replied. "Ya got one?"

"Kinda do. Thought I could put it off fer a while, but I can't. I ain't gonna be worth a tinker's dam if I don't take care of it. Problem is, I give my word I'd help ya with the wood and—"

"If you have to be somewhere else, Dufrey, don't let that stop you. I owe ya more than I can pay now."

"Don't owe nothin'. 'Sides, the bug I got in mind can't stay out of sight for long."

"The grave?"

"Well, that first. More . . . that damned Indian. I might be gone two or three days." He shrugged the shoulder supporting his pack.

"I'll be up cutting. You do what you need to."

Dufrey nodded and headed across the clearing. Lem watched until he was halfway, then went back into the cabin to gather something for his noon meal.

Dufrey spotted the bright orange-red leaves of the serviceberry, and walked directly to it. Backing into the thick branches, he stepped around the half-buried boot and knelt. The fruity-sweet smell of long-rotted flesh reached his nose, and he scraped at the dirt with the butt of his rifle. Almost immediately, he uncovered the edge of some sort of wool fabric. A slight pull brought it partially out of the ground; enough to see it was the sleeve of a lightweight coat. Another tug exposed the front of a jacket with black buttons. He glanced at the half-hidden foot, only a few inches away, and let go of the fabric. "Don't need to see no more, stranger; shoes and buttons makes ya a white man. I hope yer soul's all in one piece, cuz yer mortal remains sure ain't." Dufrey stood and pushed his way into the clear. He blew a snort of air through his nostrils, got his bearing, and strode off purposely to the west.

As any experienced woodsman could, Dufrey moved rapidly across terrain he'd been over before, choosing the easiest grade and avoiding the more dense brush. Two hours later, the several dry ravines he'd crossed before were behind him. He stood overlooking the circular meadow where he'd seen the boy. Was it Lem's? Could that be possible? It certainly wasn't an Indian; no male Indian he'd ever seen would lower himself to gathering nuts. He'd had dark hair and appeared to be about the size he'd expect of a twelve-year-old. And damn, he'd almost killed him yesterday. He'd sensed that the boy had watched him as he'd looked around the pecan tree. He wouldn't be far away. Dufrey headed down the slope, moving easily and confidently.

Half an hour later, he leaned against the trunk of a tree, and let a wry smile cross his lips. Below, a narrow ribbon of water meandered along the bottom of the narrow rift. Less than a mile upstream, the ridges on either side intersected a rocky incline that rose steeply, almost vertical in places. Near the top of it, and clearly discernible against the gray rock and milky-blue sky, he saw what he'd smelled since he'd spotted the tiny creek . . . smoke. He grunted as he sat down. "White man's fire," Dufrey muttered. "Burnin' wood with the bark on."

With his back against the tree, he rummaged through his pack until he found a soft leather bag. Untying the top, he reached in with three fingers, took out an irregular shaped cake of pemmican, and bit off a piece of the red-brown mixture. His mouth filled with the flavor of red currants and dried beef, and he took a sip of water from his bag. Chewing slowly, he inspected the terrain, noting the heavier patches of brush, various stands of trees, and the steepness of the slopes. Slowly, he mapped out his approach to the boy's camp. He had the rest of the day to get into position to observe, and decide how best to get hold of the boy without hurting him.

The walk to the far end followed a wide detour that skirted the valley. Seeing a fire so late in the morning had made him that much more cautious. As he moved, the smoke had steadily diminished to the point where he hadn't seen a wisp for some time. Was the boy drying meat? Maybe boiling a big pot of stolen beans? He stopped again and sniffed the air for the tenth time in as many minutes. Something else wasn't making sense. All the sign pointed to the center of the steep slope. If the rocks there were the same as where he stood, the boy didn't have much cover. Dufrey shook his head and continued to creep through the crevices and around the weathered boulders.

He stopped, shook his head, and snorted derisively. "Greenhorn," he muttered and put his face to a narrow crack in the ground. The smell of smoke was so strong he could identify the wood as cherry. "Don't know why it never occurred to me. He's in a cave." He raised his head carefully above the rock that hid him from below and searched the red-orange landscape. He didn't want to go back the way he'd come, but he didn't want to get caught either. He couldn't be sure, but the stream appeared to come out of the hillside to the east. Choosing his path carefully, he inched his way down the slope with frequent stops to search for movement in the trees below.

It took him until nearly midmorning to reach the security of the trees, but he felt good about the route he'd taken. At the stream he topped off his water bag, and then found a place to hide. The oak he stood under gave him complete cover, the brown leather of his clothing blending perfectly with the fall colors. Directly uphill, he could see where the boy probably stayed, the low opening in the rock face directly below where he'd been two hours before. And for proof positive, a downed cherry tree lay not twenty feet away from the entrance. He couldn't suppress a smile as he settled down to wait for the boy to appear.

An ant found the boy's foot and made its way up the top of it to his ankle. He rolled his eyes and grimaced slightly. He'd endured this torture many times and knew if the ant stayed out of his nose and ears, he'd not have to grab it. Without pausing, the insect circled his shin twice as it spiraled to his knee. There it stopped and inspected a scab before continuing up his thigh. The boy gritted his teeth as it climbed past his balls to his belly button, and after a momentary pause to inspect that, continued up to his chest. As the bug started up his neck, the boy stuck his tongue out and thoroughly wet his upper lip. His six-legged tormentor stopped at the point of his jaw—the boy held his breath—and then hurried across his cheek to stop in the damp treasure it'd located. A pink tongue flicked out, front teeth crunched, the ant a slight acid taste in the boy's mouth. He smiled and continued to watch the trail.

His right knee began to throb as it stiffened up. Without moving his head, he glanced upward and frowned; past mid-morning and she hadn't appeared. Even as he decided to wait a while longer—once, he'd spotted her at nearly midday—he chastised himself for sleeping so late. His plan of attack played again in his head. Lunge out of the brush, throw an arm around her neck—as close behind her ears as he could—then draw the knife hard across her throat. He prayed the knife would make it through the deceivingly tough hair. Lunge, grab, slash.

Then, she was there. As if by magic, she stood not twenty feet away, sharp black hooves close together, her nostrils flaring with each breath as she turned her nose into the gently moving air. She dipped her head and sniffed the ground, then took ten steps down the trail, the boy counting each one. Another stop, more testing, and then she looked directly at him. The boy stared back without blinking an eye. Every muscle he could control froze, yet remained ready to respond instantly. He prayed that his right knee would not let him down, and willed her to continue toward him. She quietly snorted; turned to look behind, and then started for the water again. Only his eyes moved as she slowly approached; three more steps, lunge—two more, grab—one slash.

He attacked! His right arm shot over her neck, and he slammed his hip into her shoulder. When she instinctively straightened all four legs and hopped, he was ready; his arm reached around and he grabbed hold as tight as he could. She threw her head to one side, trying to shake him, and both of his feet left the ground for a moment. His weight overpowered her almost immediately, and he regained his balance. He bent her head back as far as his slender arm could manage, slipped the knife past her throat, and gritting his teeth, pulled the edge across the exposed neck with all his might.

Pain exploded in his foot as she stomped a sharp hoof into the top of it. He felt the skin tear between his toes. The deer dropped her head as a long quavering wail escaped her wide-open mouth. Her terrified protest blended with the boy's scream of pain and frustration, when, with a powerful thrust of her hind legs, she somersaulted and twisted from his grasp. The boy flew backwards and landed in a heap, his knife still clutched firmly in his left hand, while the terrified animal charged into the underbrush.

He lay there until the noise of her departure faded to silence, and then sat up. What he saw when he brought his right foot in close didn't surprise him. The slick, red blood covered the top of his foot but he knew where the cut was. Leaning over his knee, he spread his first and second toes apart and winced as the wound gaped. Fascinated, he studied the opening in his flesh, a hole he could have stuck his fingertip into. The blood flowed slowly but steadily, and he let his toes come back together again. He knew an open wound like his needed to be cleaned. His mother had done it for his father when he'd cut the palm of his hand on a bean can. He remembered the dark-brown bottle with the cork; she'd kept it in a covered box by her bed. The amber liquid she dribbled into the cut had a powerful smell, and his father's face had screwed tight with the pain of it. But, a week later, the bandage had come off, and though it still looked sore, she had not wrapped it up again. What had been in that bottle? Did the woodsman have something like it in the trunk?

Pushing himself off the ground, he went to the spring, and sat down to lower his foot into the water. The water blushed a faint pink as he wiggled his toes, and it stung. He swished his foot back and forth, frequently stopping to look at it. Each time he did, the red tendrils of blood that drifted away from the cut got smaller and smaller. Finally, it quit stinging, and he got up to try his weight on it. Surprised that it didn't hurt much at all, he picked up his knife, and favoring his right foot, started for his cave.

He was nearly there, when, out of the corner of his eye, something shifted in the shadows, something large. The hair on his neck tingled. Without slowing, he stepped off the trail and stopped next to a tree. Motionless, he let his gaze shift slowly back and forth several times as he scanned the trees and brush, and listened carefully. He didn't think it could be the young doe. Matter of fact, he doubted he'd ever see her again. The squirrel he'd heard as the deer fled downhill was silent, and in the distance, he heard two crows talking. Then, a single, late-leaving dove whirred overhead to land in a locust tree exactly where he'd been looking. He watched and waited for it to be flushed, and when it wasn't, he moved away from his hiding place to another tree a short distance away. There he stood for a few more minutes before stepping back onto the trail and hurrying the rest of the way to his cave. With one last look over his shoulder, he crouched and went inside.

He couldn't shake the sense of foreboding. It was as though the night stalker had come back, only in the daytime. It felt the same. He stood by the cave entrance and listened for a long time before moving back to the rear of the cavern. There, he added a few small twigs to the smoldering coals and waited till they started to burn. In the firelight, he tore a small strip of cloth from his nightshirt and bound his first two toes together. He thought about putting on a stocking. He'd worn a pair the day he'd stolen them and they made his feet itch. He shrugged. Finished, and satisfied the bandage would keep most of the sand out of the cut, he went to the front part of the cave and sat on the warm rock.

Staring at the dimly lit entrance, he played his deer ambush over and over in his mind, seeing what he'd done wrong, and thinking how he could have done it better. The strength he'd felt in her legs had taken him completely by surprise. Next time, he'd throw his entire weight on the deer, force it to the ground and then stab it. And next time, he'd keep his feet out of the way of her hooves. He gingerly wiggled his toes and felt the slickness between the first two. He didn't like the feeling and went back into the larger part of the cave, and his fire.

Dufrey sat in his hiding place; eyes open but unfocused, ears attuned to nothing while listening for anything, his mind left free to wander. He was in his small garden in New Orleans, carefully weeding his wife's herb garden. Sunday afternoons were lazy and relaxed, and the sound of his children's laughter felt soft in his ears. Chicken with rosemary, the scent unmistakable, wafted out the open back window, and his mouth flooded with anticipation. She was such as wonderful cook—affection for his gentle mate swelled his heart.

The full-throated bleat of a wounded deer snapped his eyes into focus, and his hand fell to his rifle. Following in the same heartbeat, a human cried out in pain, and then, off to his left, came the sound of trampled brush. In an instant, Dufrey was on his feet, his eyes in the direction of the sound. A flash of tawny brown flicked in and out of sight, and the sound of an animal in full flight moved rapidly down the hill. Except for the ubiquitous squirrel farther down the slope, silence returned to the woods in a matter of seconds.

Whatever had attacked the deer had been unsuccessful; that eliminated a large cat. From the color he glimpsed, it was a spring-born deer, and may simply have been startled by something like a badger or coon. Or—could it possibly be? He chuckled to himself. Wouldn't that be somethin'? He leaned back against the tree, and let his eyes slowly scan from side to side, knowing his peripheral vision was much more likely to see movement. His technique soon paid off; to his left he caught something in motion, and his gaze froze in place. The movement shifted into his direct vision, and a man's pride in his own skill made him smile.

The boy moved slowly, and seemed to favor his right leg. Dufrey was shocked by how slight he was. Even from fifty yards away, he could see prominent hips and ribs. The long knife he had in his left hand didn't seem awkward in the least; he carried it confidently, like he knew how to use it. The Cajun couldn't suppress another grin. Did that little rascal try to kill a deer with his bare hands and that knife? Dufrey's gaze shifted to an opening in the thick underbrush by the trail. As the boy approached it, he watched closely to get a good look at his right leg. The flash of blood red on the boy's foot gave the Cajun a start . . . he was wounded! Even as the thought formed, the boy crossed the short clear stretch, then stepped off the trail to stop behind a half-naked hackberry tree.

Dufrey stood stock-still and watched. Had he been spotted? A crow called in the distance and the minutes passed. He heard a dove wing by and still he stood. The boy moved into sight, quickstepped to another tree and stopped again. The Cajun marveled at the boy's trail sense. He'd obviously learned a lot in a few short months, providing he was Lem's lost son. Then, he was moving again, up through the woods to the steep rock, to stop at the black hole in the face. There, he glanced over his shoulder, and disappeared.

"Now I know where ya are. Problem is, how do I git m' hands on ya without one of us gittin' cut with that big knife?"

Dufrey imagined the darkness of the cave; the low entrance would be shaded in the morning. Should he try to go in now when it was fully lit? He didn't think he was going to be able to sneak up on the boy; all indications were he had good hearing and an incredible sense of his surroundings. He looked at the hole in the rock again. The boy had stooped to go in, so Dufrey would have to do the same. That made him vulnerable for a second or two—the vision of the butcher knife in the boy's firm grip appeared—too vulnerable. There were small bushes on both sides of the entrance where he could stand and wait. But maybe they were too small, and how long would he need to stand there? Dufrey made up his mind. He'd sit where he was until dark, just to make sure the boy stayed in the hole, and in the morning, he'd wait for the youngster to come out.

CHAPTER 19

The boy's foot hurt, and a long scratch on his back he'd received when he'd fallen the day before itched ferociously. With a groan, he sat up in his bed, and groped around for his matches. The sulfur caught on the first try, and he lowered the small flame to the tinder pile he'd built the night before. Soon, the interior of his sanctuary was lit, and his discomfort diminished with the growing fire. He stood, went to the very rear of the cave, and relieved himself in the sand. Returning to the fire, he sat down, turned the top of his foot to the light and undid the bandage he'd wrapped around his first two toes. The very top of the wound was a little red but not seriously so. He moved his big toe, then the next two. No pain. Leaning over his knee, he used both hands to gently spread them apart—the wound opened willingly, and he grimaced at the glistening white interior. He let go, and sat up straight. Was that going to be a problem? When his pa had cut himself, he'd heard his mother talk about not letting the septic in. And that he had to keep it clean. And something else. Poison blood? He wished he'd paid a little better attention. The brown bottle, that's what he needed. It had fixed his pa.

When the fire had burned down a little, he picked up the small pot with the beans he'd left to soak overnight and put it in the embers. He wiggled his toes again and then rewrapped them with the dirty strip of cloth. It would have to do until he got to the cabin. There, he'd grab some of the linen towels he'd seen last time. Maybe, he'd wear one sock just for the journey.

With his chin on his knees, he watched the pot simmer, adding more wood to the edges as the embers decayed to ash. His mind wandered back to his home and the big black kettle his mother used. How many times had he sat, mesmerized, as steam lifted from the pot, to be swept up the chimney and lost forever—like he was now. He was jolted from his wandering when he realized the bean pot was no longer throwing off lots of steam. He hurriedly cut the last piece of ham into bite-sized chunks, dumped them in and gave the beans a stir with his knife. With a satisfied grunt, he grabbed the bucket to cover the added ingredient. When he tipped it, all the water it contained went into the pot. He tilted the empty pail toward the light and looked inside, his eyebrows rose in surprise. He stood, and headed for the front of the cave. There was enough in the pot to finish the beans, but he'd need more. Just as well get it now as later. As he passed from the large to the small part of the cave, his bucket clanked on the naked rock, almost a cheerful sound, he thought. He'd learned from long experience what kind of day to expect by the quality of light that filtered into the cave. Outside he knew he'd find a crystal-clear blue sky and calm wind. He smiled to himself—perfect day to raid the woodsman's cabin. He almost hurried as he ducked and went out the opening.

The grip on his neck and head was so solid that at first he couldn't understand what had him. Then he saw the leather-sheathed foot. The hunter!

"Got ya! Little varmint."

The man's voice struck fear in his heart. It sounded familiar; like the voice he'd heard that night from his mother's bed. The sound of an outsider; the woodcutter and this man were outsiders. They had killed his mother and Mercy, and this man was one of them. With all his strength, he turned his head out a little, forced his mouth open, and bit down on the buckskin-covered arm.

"Arrrrgh! Damn, ya little weasel."

The muscles he'd bitten tensed, and then he was lifted off his feet as his attacker jerked forward. In one fluid movement the man hiked him shoulder high, and then stooped over. He knew what was coming next as the man's arm released his neck, but he could do nothing to break the fall. He slammed back-first to the ground, cracking his head and knocking the air out of him. Before he could inhale, a soft-soled boot stepped down on his neck, and blocked his throat.

"Lay still if ya wanna breathe."

The man towered over him and Martin kicked wildly at his crotch. The hunter deftly turned, and the boy's heel landed on a rump as hard as a ham. A smile parted the dark hair of the man's mustache and he leaned forward slightly, increasing the pressure with his foot. Panic started to rise. The boy grabbed the man's leg with both hands and kicked again, but now a shadow appeared to dim the light streaming past the man.

"Still!" The voice was gruff.

All the strength left his body, and he let go of the leather leggings. Heaving his chest made no difference; there was no air to be had. He willed his eyes to stay open, yet as he watched, the bright sky dimmed . . . and the shadow turned black.

He was back in the cave; he recognized the smell. He had as bad a headache as he could imagine and every beat of his heart was hammered out on an anvil deep inside his skull. When he tried to lift his hands to it, he discovered they were tied and both were fastened to his feet. He lay on his side in the sand. Opening his eyes, he saw the hunter sitting nearby, eating beans out of the pot using a short knife. There were four candles burning. The man looked back and smiled. Why would he smile?

"Feisty little critter, I'll warrant ya that."

The strange accent again. He twisted the leather thongs that held his hands and they drew tighter.

"I'll tell ya jist onct, young'n. The more ya fight them knots, the worser they's gonna git. I ain't gonna git cut, or bit, or anything else if'n I kin help it. Un'erstand?"

He looked up at the hair-covered face with the dark eyes, and quit struggling.

"At's good, ya do un'erstand." The man pointed at the pot with his knife. "Ain't andouille, but ya didn't do bad with the ham. We're gonna take a little trip so's you can talk to the man ya stole it from. Whatcha think 'bout that?"

The boy watched the man take another bite of beans, chew for a few seconds, and then swallow.

His captor wiped his mouth with the back of his hand. "Don't think nothin', huh? I know you kin un'erstand. Kin ya talk?"

He stared back at the intruder.

"Are ya hungry? Bet ya are. Had breakfast ready to eat." The man got to his knees, scooted over and knelt in front of him. One powerful hand reached around his neck and sat him up. "Ya want a bite 'r two of this? Beans is nice 'n tender." He loaded the flat of his blade and offered it. "Here, eat."

He turned his head.

"Suit yerself." The man snorted. "They ain't goin' ta waste."

The boy sat silent as the man ate the rest of the ham and beans. Finished, the pot went into the jerky sack, along with three of the candles the hunter snuffed with his thumb. When the man stood, the boy realized everything else he owned was in the bag too, except the long wool shirt.

"Now, we kin make a little deal. I'm gonna untie yer feet and put yer hands behind yer back. The strap is gonna go around yer neck and I'm gonna have hold t'other end. Ya go along nice and easy, and you kin git there standin' up. Else, I kin hog-tie ya agin, and you kin ride belly down on my shoulder. Thet ain't so comfortable. What ya say?"

In the dim light of the single candle, he glanced at the man's heavy, rounded shoulders and imagined how his head would react to being carried upside down half the morning. The thought made his stomach feel sick. He was trapped, and his frustration made it hard for him to think. He glanced at the wool shirt lying on the pile of moss and grass. What was the hunter going to do with it? Was his knife in the sack? Of course it was. He didn't see any way he could resist. Maybe, when they got to the cabin, he'd have a chance. It was clear to him that the woodcutter was going to get his justice. What punishment would they think fitting for his thievery? He thought about his wound. Would the bandage stay on? He didn't want the septic to get in it.

"Well?" the hunter interrupted his rambling thoughts.

He looked up at the man and nodded his head. His question about the shirt was answered when the hunter spread it out, laid the jerky sack on it, and formed a backpack with the sleeves making the shoulder straps. With that prepared, the man came over, untied his feet and hands, and then retied the soft leather thong around his neck. His head responded with a vicious flash of light and pain when the hunter gave the lead a firm tug. He couldn't stop the grunt that escaped nor control his jaws as they clamped tight.

"Yer noggin feel a little aggervated, does it?" With his thumb, the man massaged the buckskin on his left forearm. "This don't feel so good either. Now, git up, sling that shirt over yer shoulders, and turn yer back to me."

The hunter stood back a little as he got to his feet; the man was being very careful. He picked up the makeshift backpack, shrugged into it, and then turned around.

He felt the man move closer, and then a heavy hand gripped

him high on the arm. "Put yer hands back here where I kin see 'em."

He looked around at the cave—this might be his last chance—and felt his anger start to grow. In the unsteady light he searched for the long rifle. The instant he spotted it, leaning against the wall by the entrance, strong fingers clamped tighter.

"Rifle's temptin' ain't it? I know what yer thinkin' and maybe I oughta knock you in the head right now. Save me some grief later, eh?" The hunter jostled him. "Now, put yer hands back." The pain when a thumb dug into the back of his arm gave him no choice but to comply. Expertly, his wrists were crossed, bound tightly, and then the loose end of the strap went through a thong cinched around his neck. "There." The man pulled on the lead.

His arms lifted, and at the same time the thong around his throat cut off his air. He gagged.

The man chuckled. "See how that works?" He eased off on the strap. "You know where we're goin', and you know better'n me how to git there, so you walk ahead," the man ordered and pointed at the opening to the front part of the cave. "Remember what I said about walkin' 'r ridin'? Now let's git goin'."

The boy took another look at his cave, and headed for the opening. The man followed close behind.

Outside, the brightness of early afternoon intensified the sharp pain in his head, and he had a bit of trouble standing still. The view across the small valley seemed blurry and he blinked his eyes rapidly to clear them.

"What'cha waitin' on, then?" the hunter said from behind. "That little bump on yer head addle ya?" The man poked the backpack that rode high on his shoulders.

He turned right and started down the slope toward the water hole. As he moved, his mind mapped out the route he'd take to the woodcutter's cabin, selecting all the places where he might try to get free, and then rejecting them one at a time. He'd tried his hands once, and true to the hunter's words, the leather binding had gotten tighter. And with his hands bound, how could he fight? He could hear metal-on-metal in the pack. One source would be the knife. Maybe he could spin around and charge the man. And then? All he had were his teeth and feet. He'd tried both. Besides, the man behind him seemed to be able to read his mind. He glanced down at his bandaged toes. The piece of rag was gone. He stopped and looked back.

"What'n hell's the matter this time?" the hunter growled. He angled away to take a position off to the side, his rifle barrel slightly elevated.

The boy looked down at his foot.

The hunter's eyes followed. "I saw that. Had worse cuts on m' tongue and didn't stop talkin'." He nodded his head. "Git goin'."

The dizziness and nausea slowly dissipated as they walked the forest trails and climbed the ridges. By the time they'd reached the point where he'd first seen the river, an impending sense of defeat had stilled his mind. One step after another, he concentrated on keeping his right foot clear of the grasping weeds and brush, the area around his wound a glob of crusty red. It still didn't hurt, but he could imagine the bits of debris and dirt that must be stuck inside the cut. Surely, he'd get the septic.

"Hold up there, sprout," the hunter ordered and tugged on the lead.

He stopped, head down, and waited. Soon, he heard the hunter step closer, and then felt something cool and wet against his shoulder. He raised his head and looked at the man. He hadn't seen the hunter pick up a water bag, but then he hadn't seen the hunting pouch slung across his chest, either.

"Yer sweatin' like a field nigra. Drink this."

He looked at the uncorked spout aimed at his face. Desperately, he wanted to open his mouth, his throat so dry he couldn't make spit. But this man might be taking him to . . . he still hadn't decided what they might do. Maybe beat him and let him go? In that case, he'd need to be ready to run.

"I ain't one to make the offer twice." The man started to lower the bag.

He opened his mouth, and almost gagged at the first wonderful gulp. The hunter stopped pouring as his mouth filled up and allowed him to swallow, then did the same again several times before he lowered the bag. He watched the hunter's eyes, wary and suspicious, as the man reached into his pouch, and took out a leather sack. Without looking away, he untied the top, took out a small piece of something brown and offered it.

"Eat this."

His stomach had been complaining for the last hour or so, and the hunter's warning about offering once prompted him to open his mouth. The food tasted good, like meat, and then like berries, and then—he couldn't make out the other flavors that flooded his mouth, but he liked whatever it was. He chewed rapidly and swallowed.

"I see ya ain't stupid, either." The hunter gave him another piece, this time larger, and stepped back.

When he'd swallowed the last bit, the man lifted the water bag again, and he drank some more.

"Like it? Called pemmican. Indian grub." The hunter held out another big piece.

He nodded his head and took the offered food.

"Where'd ya come from, boy?"

The hunter was studying him carefully as he ate. Why did he want to know? Or did he already suspect and wanted to be sure?

"How long ya been out here? Ya can't be much older'n

fourteen 'r so."

He looked away, then down at his feet. The wound was seeping fresh blood through the grime. Septic was in it for sure. So what? It might not matter in the end. But then again . . .

"How'n tarnation did ya find a warm-spring cave?" the hunter asked, and then he chuckled. "Tell me, did ya tackle that little deer back there? Small doe, looked like. That how ya got cut? She git ya with her hoof?"

Then he'd been watching! How long had he been outside the cave? It wasn't possible for anyone to track in a creek bed, so how did he find it?

"Here, take a little more water and then git goin' agin. Can't be that far now." He dribbled another mouthful of water from the bag, put the cork back in, and stepped away.

They climbed up one more ridge, and the river with the rocky cliff on the far side came into view.

"You've a fair nose for the trail, boy. This was the spot I had in mind when we left. I know where we're at now."

Traveling without the use of his arms for balance had proved more strenuous than he'd thought. His legs were weary and his knee ached. Only an hour or so from his punishment, he had quit thinking about escape, and simply wanted to stop walking. His right foot ached now, and the flesh on top of it was red and puffy. He angled down the slope, picking his way carefully.

At last, the familiar circular clearing with the cabin to one side appeared. He heaved a sigh and stopped.

"Right to it, boy. Either ya been here lots, or yer a natch'ral woodsman. Which is it?" The hunter stepped up beside him. "Been here lots?"

No smoke rose from the chimney, and the angle prevented him from seeing the door. He looked at both paths that led away into the forest. The clearing had a sense of emptiness about it. A solitary squirrel darted from in front of the cabin and stopped. It sat on its haunches for a few seconds, tail flicking absently, and then sauntered away.

"This is where ya stood and watched, ain't it? Waited till he left and then sneaked down and had yer way. Can't say I'da done it any different. What I don't un'erstand is how ya don't know him. That's if what I'm thinkin' is true."

The hunter prodded his shoulder with his rifle barrel. He shot a glance at him and was met by a penetrating stare. Had the man asked him a question? He looked down at his feet.

"Yer gonna talk to him." The hunter pointed at the cabin with his rifle. "Jist as well set yer mind to it. Now, head on down."

For the first time since the hunter had grabbed him, the boy felt a real sense of doom.

CHAPTER 20

Lem finished the cut and leaned the saw against the log. It had been a long day, and it was only mid-afternoon. The sun felt good, but he was getting tired. It was not a matter of not sleeping well—that seemed to be past him—it was how he was eating, or more accurately, not eating; he missed the Cajun's food. As it had done hourly for the last two days, his mind went to Dufrey again. Had he found the thief? He didn't like the idea of someone sneaking around the cabin all the time. It would be good to be rid of the nuisance. His back ached and he arched it, his hands pressing into the tight muscles. His mule raised a sleepy head and fluttered its lips.

"Tell ya what Mr. Mule, I think we'll wait till tomorrow to drag these to the river. From the looks to the west, we're gonna have some clouds in here that'll take the edge off the sun."

The mule blinked slowly, and then lowered his head again.

"And that's all ya care for that?" Lem chuckled to himself, and picked up the saw again.

Two hours later, he strapped his tools to the back of the animal and headed for the cabin. Hopefully, Dufrey would be back. He'd said two or three days, so why not two? He was eager to talk to him about some things he'd run through his mind the last two days. It was nice having someone to talk to, and the ever-cheerful Cajun seemed to come up with answers that always made good sense. Maybe the hunter could stay the winter. Didn't he say he hunkered down till spring? Why not right here? He led the mule into the meadow, took off the towing harness, and put the hobbles on loosely. With a slap at the animal's sweating haunch, Lem turned up the trail to the cabin.

A smile wreathed his face at the sight of smoke. Dufrey. His lengthened stride soon brought him to the tree where he strung the harness well off the ground. At the big pine by the house, he swung the ax, firmly setting it in the trunk, and hung the saw on it. He could smell the strange spices his guest used, and his mouth responded with a gush. He hurried inside. Dufrey squatted at the hearth, the lid to the kettle in his hand.

Without turning his head, he spoke, "How do? Reckoned ya might be plumb sick of yer own cookin', so I rustled up something."

Lem glanced around the cabin and spotted his wool shirt and the tin bucket. When he looked back, the Cajun was looking at him.

"Brought ya that somethin' extra too. He's out there." Dufrey nodded at the door. "Let's go take a look." With a grunt, he stood, walked past Lem, and went outside. Lem followed.

"Round here. Put 'im in the sun." Dufrey turned left.

The Indian sat hunkered against the cabin wall with his back to them, his head slumped forward. Lem grimaced; the naked creature's hair was a tangled black mess, his skin grime-encrusted, and he could count the ribs. A wicked-looking scratch angled down his back. A strip of leather bound his hands, went up his back and through a noose around his neck and then tied off to the meat-drying rack. Lem felt a surge of pity. The filthy thing wasn't more than a boy. He looked at Dufrey who stood beside him, a strange smile on his face.

"He got banged up a bit. I didn't take no chances with him cuz he's scrappy as a pine marten." Dufrey absently rubbed his left arm. "He's got a sore hoof. Ya know, I think he tried to kill a deer this mornin' . . . with his bare hands." The Cajun looked proud as a rooster.

"Can he talk English?"

The Indian's back stiffened like he'd been stabbed.

Dufrey took hold of Lem's arm. "He's a little skinny, but I'd give 'im some room."

"You're not afraid of a boy, are ya?"

The Indian spun around, his eyes wide, his mouth formed to say something. Lem's breath went the wrong way, and as he tried to inhale, his knees gave way. He sank slowly to the ground, unable to see anything but the boy's eyes, now swimming with tears.

"Oh, my God, boy. It's you. Is it you? Martin?" The youngster disappeared as Lem's vision dissolved and he reached out to catch his son as the boy scrambled into his arms.

"Pa," the trembling youngster sobbed, the side of his head pressed to Lem's chest. "I couldn't stop 'em. I tried, but he was big. Pa, I was so scared."

Lem buried his face in the tangle of dark hair and weeds. "Not your fault, boy. Not your . . ." He could not trust his voice to finish. He tried to satisfy them both by holding his son tight while rocking gently back and forth on his knees. After a few minutes, the sobbing subsided and Dufrey stepped close to cut the bonds that held the boy. He felt the tenseness leave the slim body. Then, with his son's arms wrapped around his neck, Lem stood and the three of them went into the cabin.

The light outside had faded to dusk when Lem lifted the inflamed foot out of the warm water and dried it. Gently, he spread the toes apart and then looked up at Dufrey.

"Don't look too bad," the Cajun said. "Reckon he had the sense to clean it right after she got him."

"Does it hurt a lot?" Lem asked.

"Not much now, Pa. Did when she stepped on it. Hurt lots."

"This is gonna hurt some more." Lem showed the boy the bottle.

"I know. I saw Ma put that on your hand. You got tears."

"You saw?"

"I peeked in the door. That stuff made it better. So do it." The boy gritted his teeth and turned his head. "I'm ready."

As soon as the first drop fell into the open wound, Lem wished there was some other way. The boy's back arched and he cried out.

Dufrey grabbed the trembling shoulders and held fast. "You was named right, son, fer sure. Ya ain't feared a nothin'."

The boy whimpered.

"And you jist grabbed holt of thet deer?" Dufrey asked again. "I mean, wrapped yer arms round her neck, and held on?"

The child gasped again as several more drops fell, and the Cajun held on tightly. Lem looked at the stout man and tightened his lips in a grim smile of appreciation. He waited several seconds, and when the boy seemed to relax a little, let three more drops go, and put the stopper back in the bottle.

"There, that's all." He loosely wrapped the ball of the boy's foot in clean linen, and watched as his breathing returned to normal.

The Cajun shook his head, went over to the fireplace, and gave the kettle a stir. Then he dragged a chair over and sat facing the boy. "How long had ya watched thet deer?"

The boy's face became serious. "Two months . . . about. She grew a lot. But I'd had her if the knife wasn't dull."

"That reminds me." Lem swung the boy's foot over the bed and put it down. He then got up and went to the open trunk where he pawed around for a few seconds. He came back to the boy and handed him a sheathed knife. "This is yours. I saved it."

The boy took his gift and held it in his lap for a few seconds.

"I don't think I can, Pa."

Lem's heart ached as he watched tears build again. "I told ya, boy. You did more than anyone your size could've done. I know how big that fella was. I found 'em."

The boy looked up at him with brimming eyes. "Did ya, Pa? Ya sure?"

"I did. You marked the one real good. He couldn't hide it. They're both killed. By me."

"He followed me here," the boy said, his voice barely a whisper. "I heard him outside my hiding place."

"That was part of him, boy, a part that I couldn't kill."

Confusion showed on the boy's face.

"I'm not sure you're old enough to understand, but I wasn't good enough to do it all. The part that came here died when I was."

The look on the boy's face lasted for a few seconds and then changed to one of trust. "But you took care of things, didn't ya, Pa? Like ya always did?"

"I tried, boy, just like you did. And I'll keep trying, you can count on it."

"Thanks for the knife, Pa." He slipped the gleaming steel from the dark leather scabbard.

"You're welcome. Now sit there and rest your foot. Is there anything I can do for ya?"

The boy hesitated, his mouth opened for a second, and then shut again.

"I kin see yer wantin' to say somethin'," Dufrey said. "Spit 'er out. I ain't noticed ya had a bashful side." Dufrey chuckled.

"Could ya cut yer beard off, and some hair?"

"That's it!" the Cajun almost shouted as he got out of the chair. "All that fuzz ya got goin' there, Lem. Bet you was one of them odd ones what shaved ever' week."

The boy nodded his head. "Sundays. And Ma cut his hair regular."

"He didn't recognize ya, Lem, and ya wasn't friends enough to talk much, now was ya?"

"Is that true, boy?"

"You looked mean."

"He is . . . or was, till he quit eatin' his own cookin'."

Lem ran his fingers through his hair. "I'll cut it off tomorrow, first thing. And go back to shavin' every Sunday. How's that?"

"That'd be good."

"Anything else?"

"Will we go back home?"

The question was one that Lem had thought about while Dufrey went hunting the "Indian." He smiled to himself. He didn't want to go back. He'd done all he could there.

"You dead set on going downriver for the winter, Dufrey?"

"Pfft." The Cajun puffed his lips. "I ain't never dead set on nothin' no more. Why ya askin'?"

"With what I've stored up, and what I know you can shoot, we'd be fine for food if you'd like to stay here this winter."

"Ya askin' me, proper like, then?" Dufrey grinned.

"I'm invitin' ya, yes."

"I'm game. How 'bout you, Marteen?" Dufrey drew out the last syllable.

"I don't wanna go back there, Pa. Can't we just stay here?"

"I think we should, Martin. I've got some makin' up to do, and you need some fattenin'. This crazy Cajun will take care of that, and you and me can take care of each other, okay?" Lem wrapped his arms around his son's narrow shoulders and hugged him.

"Speakin' of which," Dufrey chortled, "supper's 'bout ready, Marteen. Ever eat boiled eyeballs? Uh-ummm gooood, I kin guarantee it."

"He's foolin' ya, son." Lem glanced at Dufrey. "Leastwise, I think he is."

ABOUT THE AUTHOR

Wallace J. Swenson was born and raised in a small rural town in southeast Idaho. From the very beginning he lived a life of hard work supported by a strong family, was taught by example the value of honesty and loyalty, and it was about such things that he wrote. His family numbered ten, and though poor in a material sense, he considered himself blessed beyond measure in the spiritual. He lived with his wife of fifty-plus years, Jacquelyn, near where both were born, and close to all their children and grandchildren, as dedicated to writing as he was to two successful careers in the US military and the Department of Energy.